Cutting Off A Whale's Head

K.C. Woodworth

Family is the American Dream!

From: K Woodworth

Aug. 24, 2014

PAGE PUBLISHING, INC.
New York, NY

First originally published by Page Publishing, Inc. 2013

ISBN 978-1-62838-183-2 (pbk)
ISBN 978-1-62838-184-9 (digital)

Printed in the United States of America

Chapter One

I had a large, silver meat cleaver, a foot-long knife, a heavy wooden mallet, 100 feet of nylon rope and a gauze dust mask, all resting on top of a blue bath towel and a change of clean clothing. It was all sitting in a large cardboard box, flaps open, on the bucket passenger seat beside me. I was in my extended Chevy cargo van, the travelling warehouse I had once used for my wholesale distribution business, murdered outright by the recession. I was on my way to San Francisco in a rush. Three days earlier the U.S. Coast Guard had spotted a dead killer whale floating on the ocean's surface, being carried by the tide toward the San Francisco Bay, where it subsequently crashed into the Golden Gate Bridge, and had been stuck there ever since at the base of the bridge's northern pylon. I had just heard of the event that Friday afternoon, on the radio, while driving to the post office to mail out some of my website orders.

There are not many times in the course of one's existence when an individual truly understands the significance of an event. We're all so busy with the minutia of life – working, shopping, going to the post office – a miracle could happen right in front of our eyes and we'd be oblivious to it due to the distraction of the mundane. But I understood the significance of this. It struck me instantaneously and hard! Like a bolt of lightening frying away the scales from my eyes!

I immediately drove home, gathered what I needed in the cardboard box, threw my inflatable yellow boat and two plastic oars in the back of my van, and called Dr. Gale Fischer, Dean of the marine biology department at the University of California Santa Cruz.

"Come on! Come on! Pick up!"

I heard her voice on the other end.

"This is Dr. Fischer."

"Gale, it's Cree!"

"Hi, Cree – Are you okay? You sound all hyped-up."

"You know about the dead killer whale, right?"

"The one stranded at the Golden Gate Bridge? Of course! It's all over the news."

"I'm on my way there right now! I'm going to cut off its head!"

There was silence, then obvious agitation.

"Look Cree, don't!"

"Hey! I'm desperate! So are you! I'm cutting that thing's head off. We're a quick trim of blubber, a cardboard box full of beetles and one month away from a beautiful skull! Now will you give me one hundred thousand dollars for it if I can pull it off?"

"No!"

We were both silent, breathing heavily as though gazing simultaneously at the signpost of a frightening crossroads.

I spoke first:

"You're about to lose your job. And do you think any other university is going to hire you after they learn about what you did?"

"It's not that simple, Cree!" Her voice was raised. "Orcas are protected by the Marine Mammal Act of 1972. You can't cut off their heads. It's illegal in the U.S. to traffic in any parts of their bodies. If you get caught, you'll be in a lot of trouble."

"Hold on a minute," I said. "You were going to give those guys in Canada one hundred fifty thousand dollars. I'm asking a third less."

"It's not illegal to possess marine mammal parts in Canada."

"But it's illegal to ship them to the U.S!"

"I was going to drive up there and bring the skull back to Santa Cruz in the trunk of my car in a suit case."

"What if they stopped you at customs and searched your car?"

"I was willing to take the chance!" she shouted. "I need a god damned killer whale skull!"

"Why didn't you do it?"

"They wanted two hundred fifty thousand dollars and I didn't have it!"

"Well, there's a killer whale skull right there at the base of the Golden Gate Bridge and I'm going to get it. If you were going to take a chance with the Canadian guys, why won't you take a chance with me? I'm your friend."

"God damn it, Cree!" she shouted. "Because they were traffickers! I don't give a damn what happens to them! I care about you!"

"You don't have to worry about it," I said. "I have a plan. It's all worked out. I'll do it fast, too! Now will you give me one hundred thousand dollars?"

"The money isn't the issue. You'd be putting yourself in peril. San Francisco's bay is inherently hazardous due to strong tidal forces, currents, and swells; not to mention the huge wakes created by cargo ships. A million things could go wrong out there and you could end up in the water, hypothermic or drowned. Have you considered this?"

"My only concern is to save my home and my marriage. Your only concern should be to save your job. Now are you in this with me or not?"

Hesitation.

"Come on, Gale," I urged.

"Why do you have to do it today?" she quipped. "It's Friday afternoon. It's sunny. There'll be a thousand tourists out there on that bridge and at the Marin County observation decks. They'll see you. Can't you wait a couple of days, do it early in the morning on Sunday?"

"No," I said. "There's a big lightning storm passing through San Francisco early tomorrow morning. It'll bring lots of rain and heavy swells to the bay. I heard it on the radio. I can't take a chance. The storm might wash the whale back out to sea. I have to do it now."

Hesitation again.

"Gale," I said enticingly.

"If you get caught, don't tell them my name, where I work, why you're trying to take the skull, nothing! Do you understand? Because if you do, I'll be arrested along with you and that'll be the end of my career forever. Understood?"

"Understood – will you give me the one hundred thousand dollars?"

"Yes."

Chapter Two

It was the middle of July, 2008, and hot. San Francisco was a two-hour drive away to the southwest. I had the van's windows rolled up and the air-conditioning on. I had just turned onto I-80, crossing over the elevated portion of the highway that spanned the dry, scrubby overflow basins on the outskirts of Sacramento; the city's sparse skyline was in my rearview mirror now, getting smaller as I drove away, but I could still see the top of the Wells Fargo building and the dome of the state capital.

Sacramento was where I lived with my wife, Lani, and our five-year-old son, Theo.

Two weeks earlier on a Saturday, Lani, Theo and I had visited our local branch of the First Sacramento Savings and Loan, our bank for the past ten years and the holder of our home's first mortgage. We met Mr. James Forbes there, the branch's General Manager. I had spoken to James many times. The years when my business was booming, he had treated me and my wife quite well, always smiling and shaking our hands with a firm grip, patting me on the back as though we had been great childhood friends, calling in the tellers to bring us in coffee or bottled water. Now that Lani and I were bankrupt, he didn't treat us as kindly as before, but he did say the bank was going to look for a way to refinance our mortgage at a lower interest rate, which would allow us to keep our home. So he was now our best friend.

"Good morning, Mr. and Mrs. Quinn," he said with a dour look. He then moved quickly to the thickly padded chair behind his large, ornate desk.

We stepped into his office and the glass door slowly closed behind us. We had left Theo in the main part of the bank where the tellers were. They had a room there set up for the kids with toys and books to read.

"Please have a seat," Mr. Forbes said, motioning to the two small, plastic chairs in front of his desk. He didn't even shake our hands, but that was okay. I just wanted to get this damn mortgage thing settled and get that heavy block of anxiety off of my back.

We sat down.

"Thank you for seeing us today, Mr. Forbes," Lani said. "I'm so happy the bank is going to help us."

She turned to me and we smiled at one another. She had a beautiful smile. With her long, curly black hair pulled back in a ponytail, her short, sleeveless dress, white with a navy blue belt wrapped tightly around her curvy waist, she looked very proper sitting there with her smooth, tan legs crossed and her folded hands resting gently in her lap.

"Yes, Mr. Forbes," I said, turning to him. "We're very grateful the bank is helping us."

Mr. Forbes placed his elbows on top of his paper-laden desk and touched the tips of his fingers together to form a tent just below his chin. He had a ruddy complexion, with sagging walrus cheeks and a sagging rooster neck. He had a lot of black hair for an older man, slicked back hard with a glowing gel. He was wearing half glasses, wire framed. His silky, amber-colored handkerchief was creased just right and tucked perfectly into the breast pocket of his royal sapphire suit coat. His shirt was light blue with white collar and cuffs. His cufflinks were shiny squares of gold with what appeared to be emerald inlays.

"Well," he said, looking back and forth between me and Lani, "let's get right down to it then. We here at the First Sacramento Savings and Loan understand what you're going through. It's not just you. This recession is deeply affecting the entire state and spreading quickly to the rest of the country. There are literally tens of thousands of people in California losing their jobs and having their homes threatened by repossession. They're not all going to be able to save their homes. A bank is a business. We have rules and regulations we must abide by. We were very sympathetic to your particular situation since you have had a relationship with this bank and this particular branch now for many years. Also, we were mindful of the fact that, in our discussions with your bankruptcy administrator a month back, we did say the bank would attempt to devise a refinancing plan for you, to include the six months payment you have already defaulted on now, at a much lower interest rate than you currently have, putting an end to the repossession process and allowing you to keep possession of your property. But, frankly, Mr. and Mrs. Quinn, I have to tell you --"

He shook his head, adjusted his glasses and continued:

"We ran an appraisal on your house and, to be quite honest with you, at this time, having studied your situation this past week and having gone over it with those in the refinancing department, and most of all taking the market value of your property into consideration, we simply see no way we can help you."

"What!" came our startled, simultaneous response. Lani and I looked at one another and then back at Mr. Forbes.

"You said you were going to help us, Mr. Forbes!" Lani said, her voice now raised and upset. "You've been telling us for a month now that the bank was going to refinance our home at a lower interest rate."

Mr. Forbes opened his eyes widely and peered at her over his half glasses.

"I said we would *try* to refinance your property," he said.

I sat forward in my chair.

"This is the only thing that's been keeping us hanging in there," I said. "We've lost everything else. We were hopeful – No! We were certain we were going to keep our home. Our bankruptcy lawyer told us you guys were going to find a way to refinance us."

He looked at me while adjusting his glasses.

"I'm sure your lawyer didn't tell you the bank was going to find a way," he said. "Since your lawyer is a professional and is, I'm sure of it, up-to-date on the law in these matters, I'm certain that your lawyer more than likely told you that the bank was going to **attempt** to find a way. That doesn't necessarily signify or guarantee success. And although the bank has looked into your particular situation quite thoroughly, since you have been very good customers with us for an extended period of time, we unfortunately find that we are unable to help you in this instance."

I sat back hard and folded my arms.

"And it's because of our home's market value?" Lani asked.

"Unfortunately, that is the case," Mr. Forbes said.

He raised a brown, official looking folder filled with papers from his desk, opened it, adjusted his glasses and began reading:

"This is your dossier. When you purchased your home three years ago in 2005, it was assessed at five hundred thousand dollars and you were able to put one hundred thousand dollars down on it. You originally had to borrow four hundred thousand dollars to acquire the property, which came in the form of a three hundred thousand dollar first mortgage with us and a one hundred thousand dollar equity line of credit with the Bank of Northern California, which constitutes a second lien. Now, with payments having been made for two and a half years but excluding these last six months where you've defaulted, you owe approximately three hundred eighty thousand dollars on the property, two hundred eighty thousand dollars to us and one hundred thousand dollars to BNC."

He lowered the dossier, looked back and forth between us over the top of his glasses, raised his eyebrows and asked:

"Why is your second lien with BNC still one hundred thousand dollars? That was your original loan amount. Have you not been making payments on it? Or have you continued borrowing off of that line of credit over these last three years?"

"We had to keep borrowing off of it," I said. "We spent all of our savings trying to keep my business afloat, and that included cashing out all of our retirement money and the small amount we had saved for our son's college fund. Then we charged up the credit cards to their limit. There was nothing left! We had no choice but to tap into it as a means for additional funds to help us pay our legal fees, get my website up and running so I could at least bring some money into the house, and other things; a lot of little things here and there that added up."

He gave me a curious look, tapping his chin with the opened dossier.

"So you have a website?" he asked.

"Yes," I said. "Even though the main and most lucrative part of my business was totally destroyed, which was driving to the retailers I serviced and filling their orders with inventory from the back of my van, I still have a lot of inventory left over. It fills our two-car garage from wall to wall, floor to the ceiling! I have a website now dedicated to the sale of that inventory, and it brings in a trickle of sales on a monthly basis."

"What do you mean by a trickle?" he asked.

"I guess I have a cash flow of about three thousand five hundred dollars per month now. And because my sales are actually going up a little bit every month, and with the tip money that Lani makes working part time on the weekends as a server at the *Gold Diggers Club* downtown, I know we can afford to keep our home if the bank would just refinance our loan at a lower interest rate. The first mortgage we have with you right now has already reset, and the interest rate is 9%! The interest rate on our equity line of credit with BNC is 13%! That's why we can't afford to make the payments. I saw on Channel 10 News just the other day, the federal government has begun loaning banks money at a very low federal funds rate so they can refinance people's homes at a lower rate. This bank has the money, Mr. Forbes."

He looked back down into the pages of the dossier.

"The problem isn't that simple," he said concertedly. "The value of your home has dropped by 30% since you purchased it back in 2005. Our own assessment came back at somewhere around three hundred fifty thousand dollars. The bank cannot possibly be expected to wrap up your first mortgage, your second mortgage with BNC, and the additional money you owe us for the past six months of defaulted payments, into a single first mortgage because that would mean we'd have to loan you approximately four hundred thousand dollars, which would include closing costs, for a house that has a three hundred fifty thousand dollar market value. We just can't do that. The federal regulators won't let us. There's no such a thing anymore as a 110% or 120%

loan-to-value mortgage. Those days are gone. They're dead!"

"You guys have the money!" I said loudly. "I saw it on Channel 10 News!"

"Only if it's the right fit," Mr. Forbes said. "Only if the numbers work and, unfortunately in your case, the numbers don't work."

"You guys aren't going to help us?" I said incredulously. I was really upset.

"I don't see how we can, Mr. Quinn. The numbers are too far off."

I looked at Lani, who sat motionless now, her folded hands pressed tightly against her breast.

"The bank said they would help us," she said softly. "Our lawyer told us that. The bank lied – You lied to us, Mr. Forbes."

Mr. Forbes exhaled, looked down at his desk and shook his head.

"Look," he said, turning from me to Lani, his expression one of half sympathy, half irritation. "We wanted to help you, but the numbers are too far off."

He closed the dossier and dropped it on his desk with a thud.

"Damn!" I said. "We've lost everything now! Everything! You're telling me there's no freaking way to save our home? Come on! There has to be a way!"

There was a momentary pause as he peered at me over the top of his glasses. He then said: "There is – but it's a long shot. If you can somehow pay off that one hundred thousand dollar second mortgage you have with BNC, then we'd only have to loan you around two hundred ninety thousand dollars because the bank would waive most of the fees in that case; and, since your house has a current market value of three hundred fifty thousand dollars, you'd still have close to 20% equity in it."

"How the hell can I do that?" I shouted. "How the hell can I come up with one hundred thousand dollars?"

"Please, Mr. Quinn, keep your voice down." He was tapping the dossier with his fingers. "Listen, sometimes people are unaware of the resources they have. For instance, people sometimes have old stock certificates or bond notes lying around in their draws at home, investments bequeathed to them by their parents or grandparents. Such securities can be quite valuable."

"We don't have any stock certificates or bond notes lying around in our draws at home!" I said. "If we did, I'd know about it. And I told you, we cashed everything out already! We're broke!"

"What about family members?" he asked.

"My father passed away from lung cancer 25 years ago," I said. "My mother died from the same thing 23 years ago. I have no siblings. I'm an only child."

"I'm sorry to hear that about your parents."

"Don't be! They were bastards!"

"What about you, Mrs. Quinn?"

Mr. Forbes and I both turned to her.

"My family owns a restaurant in Honolulu," she said. "My father, mother and seven brothers all work there. It's a family restaurant. They've been running it for many years now."

"Oh, that's wonderful!" Mr. Forbes said, placing his hands flat on his desk. "What kind of food do they serve?"

"It's a mix," Lani said. 'Italian dishes: antipastos, Chicken Cacciatore, Baked Shrimp Scampi, various pasta and meat-sauce specials."

"Is your father Italian?" Mr. Forbes asked.

"No, he's an American of Irish ancestry – he just loves Italian food. It's his favorite."

"Oh."

Lani continued:

"My mother's native to Hawaii. She cooks traditional dishes at the restaurant like Hawaiian bread, chicken and pork laulau, lomi lomi salmon on poi, tuna poke. They also serve lots of American food, too, like barbequed spareribs, meatloaf, hamburgers, open-faced turkey sandwiches, french-fries. Two of my brothers cook the American dishes. The other five wait tables, stock and do the cleaning."

"Sounds delicious," Mr. Forbes said. "Is it a successful restaurant?"

"They do okay," Lani said.

"Let me put it this way, are they in a position to help you and your husband out? You are their daughter, after all, and Cree here is their son-in-law."

"They don't have the money to give us," Lani said. "I just spoke to them a couple of weeks ago."

I sat up in my chair.

"You asked them for a loan?" I asked.

"No!" she exclaimed. "I haven't told them anything about what's happening to us, not the bankruptcy, our mortgage situation, nothing! I don't want them to know. I'm ashamed!"

"I understand," Mr. Forbes said. "But if you don't ask, how do you know?"

"They don't have the money!"

She was angry.

Then her face changed; and like that, she was sad.

"The economy in Hawaii is bad, too," she said. "They've lost a lot of business. They don't have the money and I wouldn't take it from them if they did. We're going to lose our home and there's nothing we can do about it. This bank lied to --"

Her voice cracked and a tear rolled down her right cheek. She wiped it away with her hand, exhaling.

Mr. Forbes pushed his chair back and rose to his feet. There was a box of tissues on one corner of his desk and I half expected him to reach for one and hand it to Lani; but he didn't. He just stood there behind his desk, looking back and forth between her and me.

I stood up, reached for a tissue and handed it to Lani. She took it without looking up and continued sitting there in her plastic chair, weeping softly, left hand over her eyes.

"I don't mean to sound callous," Mr. Forbes said. "Unfortunately, however, it seems our discussion has run its course. Now I'm sorry for your predicament but I'm busy and have to get to other matters. I wish both of you the best. Your foreclosure proceedings have been placed on hold these last three months pending first the outcome of your bankruptcy, which has been fully discharged now since last month and, secondly, pending the assessment of your property. Unfortunately, we have no choice but to continue with the foreclosure proceedings unless you can pay off that second lien with BNC. Again, I'm sorry. Have a good day."

He gestured to the door with his hand.

Lani stood up and we walked out of his office.

The glass door closed slowly behind us.

I held Lani's hand as she cried with the tissue up to her eyes, tellers and customers looking up at us, as we walked through the main part of the bank to get Theo.

Chapter Three

The van had a full tank of gas. The wiper fluid was full, too, and thankfully so. A menagerie of insects – wayward gnats, meandering moths, dive-bombing mosquitoes and reckless yellow jackets – obstinately chose suicide as their only option by flying headlong into my windshield, turning it into an abstract expressionist canvas of green and yellow guts. I turned the knob on the steering wheel, sending a stream of blue fluid onto the outside of the windshield and setting the wipers in motion, cleaning it all away.

I was passing the city of Davis now. The exit that led to the university was deserted due to it being the summer session but, in the fall and winter, that exit could be backed up for a mile with a flood of students heading for class. UC Davis was a part of the University of California statewide university system offering both undergraduate and postgraduate degrees in a plethora of disciplines, the more notable of their ivied edifices being UCLA and UC Berkeley.

There was another group of universities in California as well, known as the state system, which offered the same: these included universities like Chico State, San Diego State and San Francisco State. I had gone to the latter, San Francisco State, otherwise known as SFSU. I was a business major there, graduating Summa Cum Laude with a B.S.

in economics. I had studied economics because I believed it gave me a better chance at becoming rich.

I had grown up indigent and isolated in a rough, east coast industrial city called Lynn. It was in the state of Massachusetts, about 10 miles north of Boston along the eastern shoreline. I hated it there. Whore laden streets, bloody fist fights all the time, drugs, alcoholism and poverty cast a gloomy and oppressive cloud of despair over the entire city, so that one's life there was continuously cradled, raggedly, capriciously, in the chilling hands of fate.

I kept myself away from it all as best I could, alone most of the time in my bedroom, in the attic of my grandmother's colonial era house on Eastern Avenue, continuously engaged in my school studies. Upon graduating from high school, with top grades, nobody had any money to send me to college, but I had won a full scholarship to the University of Massachusetts at Amherst. I turned it down. I wanted to get the hell away from Lynn, as far as I possibly could. I had another, bigger reason for wanting to leave as well: I hated my mother and father.

So in the summer of 1979, at 18 years of age, I packed a scruffy green duffle bag with some clean clothes and nothing else. I didn't have anything else.

Penniless, I hitchhiked across the country to San Francisco. I had a mean-spirited, ulterior motive for going to San Francisco and for taking that particular duffle bag – it had belonged to my father and was the duffle bag he had used back in the late 1960's when he too, along with my mother, had gone to San Francisco to live the free-love, mind expanding, substance experimenting life of the free willed, abandoning me at my grandmother's house when I was only five years old.

Hitchhiking was easy back then and everybody was out on the road with their thumbs out. Not like in the 1980's when all that crazy stuff started happening, serial killers out on the highways looking to pick up unsuspecting thumbers, binding them with duct tape and torturing them in the woods until death.

I made it to San Francisco in six days, and was well fed, too. I got picked up mainly by lonely truckers working the interstate trade routes, who were happy to pay for my meals at the seedy hamburger, fried chicken and roast beef shacks populating the truck stops along the highways, in exchange for my company and some friendly conversation.

I wasn't much into friendly conversation or so-called small talk back then. I didn't really trust strangers -- I didn't trust **anyone** -- feeling they might turn on me at any second and give me a punch in the mouth, in the case of men, or start screaming at me and scolding me, in the case of women. I thought idle conversation to be fruitless, because one only engaged in it with people they didn't really know well – people who were going to be turning around and walking out of your life at any second, once their taxi arrived, or the elevator doors opened, or I stepped out of the truck drivers' trucks. Since these were people I'd never see again, why talk at all? Why not just sit there with my mouth shut and, at the end of the ride, give my obligatory *'thank you'* and be on my way?

But other people didn't see it that way. I had realized early on in life that this world was populated by individuals who base their entire existences – their very foundation of wellbeing – on the daily, insignificant utterances we peremptorily vomit to one another:

"Good morning!"
"Good afternoon!"
"See you later!"
"How's the coffee?"
"How's the wife?"
"How 'bout those Red Sox!"
"Have a nice day!"

This was the touch of the miniscule, the human interactions, minor as they were, we required each and every day of our lives to ensure we were being acknowledge, respected and loved as individuals, which bound us all together in a tightly wrapped, yet delicate tissue paper of humanity.

Disdainful of such liturgical trivialities, but aware, nonetheless, of the glaring reality that others not only expected small talk from one other, but would fly into a self-righteous, indignant rage at any individual not freely and fluidly engaging in it, I obliged these truck drivers with a hollow, fictitious narrative, made up on the spur of the moment on the passenger seat of the very first truck that picked me up. It was a narrative complete with feigned affectations – mirth, tenderness, laughter – and everything I felt they wanted to hear, since the conversation inevitable and unalterably began in this fashion:

"Where are you headed?"

"Where are you from?"

"How old are you?"

"You look a little too young to be out on the highway."

"Do your parents know you're out here in the middle of the night hitchhiking?"

And my response was an Oscar worthy performance, as I would relate to them how my parents did indeed know I was out on the road hitchhiking; it was a trek across the country intended to affect a rounding out of my already good character, so that I might have my oats sown prior to going to college that fall at Harvard University, where I was to study law as my father had before me, and my doting grandfather before him.

That always brought a smile to their faces and an approving nod, possibly due to a sense of goodwill they felt, seeing as how they were playing a part in my rounding out process; and if pressed for more details of my life, I would further relate how I had grown up in a mansion on Beacon Hill in Boston, with an absurdly wealthy family who showered me with gifts and cash on birthdays and holidays, and how the whole world, as I knew it, was just peachy keen to the max.

This entire narrative played very well with these truck drivers who, each and every one, seemed to be men of conscience, going on to tell me about their wives and children and how they were only out on the road, late at night, working hard, driving their trucks and delivering product, so their families could have a better life. And at the end of my ride with each of them, they all shook my hand, thanked me for both the company and the story of my life, and wished me the best of luck at Harvard that coming fall.

It tweaked my conscience a bit having lied like that, but there was no way I was going to tell them the truth. In the first place, who would believe it? Secondly, telling a *happy* story gave me a proper framework, a solid matrix, as to why exactly I *was* hitchhiking across the country, and it accelerated me into these peoples' good graces, instantly catapulting me from some wandering vagrant to a courageous soul; a good young man trying to make himself even better in the fires of a self-imposed adversity; someone they wanted to assist because it was for a good cause.

And without a doubt, the story was efficacious in helping me make it through those first difficult and exhausting three days, having been picked up by seven different truck drivers during that time, having to interact verbally with each one of them, then being dropped off on the side of the road again with my thumb flailing once more in the uncertain winds of chance. But don't get me wrong, either: I *was* genuinely grateful to those truck drivers, thanking them back as they had thanked me. I couldn't have made it two thirds of the way across the country, all the way to Cheyenne, Wyoming, without them, and I knew it.

A guy named Belial Abbot, black cowboy hat and wild grey beard, was the last trucker to pick me up. He ran the hay route from the southwestern part of the state of Wyoming all the way to California along I-80, then north to Eureka along I-5. There were flying-saucer-shaped bales of golden hay, double rowed and stacked, filling the back of his opened rig, all held in place with canvas coverings and a webbing of disorderly ropes; all livestock feed, he had told me. He had to drop off a roll here and a roll there at stops in Utah, Nevada and California.

That part of the trip seemed to take the longest, another 3 days, due to all the stops – the monotonous, lengthy time it took to untie the stack, remove the canvas coverings, use the fork trucks at the various stops to unload hay bales, then having to secure again the remaining frizzing, shedding, vegetable structure. And Belial was dogged about stopping for breakfast, lunch and dinner at the multitude of dark and dingy hideaways he knew along the road, him being propositioned by prostitutes at each and every one of them, and subsequently being MIA for at least an hour each day in a dilapidated motel room with a girl named Honeydew, Molasses or Lollipop, while I watched the truck and drank coffee on my own at greasy café counters with mean-faced, pink or green haired waitresses glaring at me the whole time.

He finally dropped me off in Sacramento, in a breakdown lane on the side of I-80, half a click before it intersected with I-5.

It was early morning, the yellow sun just rising over the Sierras, with a soothing wind – California freedom – brushing gently against my face. His cowboy hat and beard, left shoulder and arm, were hanging out of the opened driver's side window.

"Good luck, young-en'," he yelled over the top of his idling engine.

"Thank you, Belial," I yelled, reaching up to shake his gloved hand, my father's old duffle bag over my left shoulder.

Then, with a loud rumbling of diesel pistons and a blast of black smoke from the chrome exhaust pipe above his cab, he rolled forward, heading north.

I arrived in San Francisco latter on that morning, having been picked up on the side of the highway by a businessman in a black suit and a black tie, driving a Mercedes Benz.

We chatted the entire three-hour drive, which I hated to do, of course, but felt obligated. He told me he was an executive with Chevron, the company's liaison to the governor in Sacramento, but was headed to the company's west coast headquarters at the Chevron Building in San Francisco, where he was to participate in – as he himself described it to me – a hand-shaking, back-slapping, congratulatory puffing-up session on the company's surging profits due to the progressive rise in gasoline prices.

He dropped me off right on Market Street, right in the center of San Francisco's financial district, in front of the Embarcadero Center, its Picasso-like delineations lunging lustfully into the sky as did the entire city skyline. I was never so overwhelmed in my life – the beauty of the city's architecture, glass and steel, brick and mortar, old and new in a captivating mambo; the power of so much commerce in a frenzy all around me; thousands of people crowding the streets in a continuous, purposeful flow, shoulder to shoulder, but everyone intentionally avoiding eye contact with everyone else – I was in heaven!

It was Tuesday, June 12, 1979, the same day Bryan Allen, of California, flew his pedal-powered, single seated plane, the Gossamer Albatross, across the English Channel: two mavericks chasing a dream.

I walked down Market Street for a good ten or fifteen minutes, through the throng of people, the comingling of afternoon sun and cool wind on my face, a fluttering of light and shadow being cast by the passing street cars, and found multiple retailers with HELP WANTED signs in their windows.

Entering several stores in search of employment, excusing my appearance, telling them I had just arrived in the city after hitchhiking across the country – and you'd be surprised at how much respect that garnered me, comments like *"You got guts!"* and *"Hey, I did that ten years ago myself!"* – I quickly found myself a job at a place called **The San Andreas Fault Videos**, where they sold adult videos and all sorts of adult entertainment products.

It was kind of weird at first being in the store because I had only been in a place like that one other time in my life, when I was 14 years old, and had taken a bus to Boston with a friend of mine, Patrick Bradley, whose nickname was **Badley.**

Badley was three years older than me – I always got along better with kids who were older than me, and older kids always seemed to gravitate to me as well. I think it was because of my height: at 14, I was 6ft tall. It made me look older than I really was.

Anyway, Badley was familiar with this section of Boston called the Combat Zone, where all the strip clubs, XXX theaters and prostitutes converged. He took me there and we walked around for about a half an hour, passing all the dark theatres, eyeballing cautiously the menacing men hanging around in the street. We repeated and then laughed at the names of the strip clubs – **THE NAKED BIRD, THE FOXES DEN, SHEWOLF'S** – and we gazed lustfully, transfixedly, at the many women in miniskirts and unbuttoned, breast-revealing blouses, doing their swinging, hip-swooning strolls along the wide and dirty sidewalks.

Badley finally brought me to this place called **Naughty's** which sold videotapes and all sorts of strange looking and suggestive gadgets I had never seen before. I almost laughed at the oddity of it all. We were only in there for a moment, until some mean looking bastard smoking a cigar, big and hairy as a bear, dressed in a black shirt, white slacks and tight vest with a row of gold buttons, started moving toward us, yelling for us to get out because we were too young.

We flew out of there, ran half a block down the street and, turning back to see no one following us, looked at each other and began laughing hysterically, slapping our knees, and then started walking toward Haymarket Station to catch the bus home.

Now here I was, four years later, in *The San Andreas Fault Videos* in San Francisco. Truth was, I needed that job, and it paid $6.00 an hour, which was more than two times the minimum wage back then. It paid that much because the hours were 3pm to midnight on the weekdays, 5pm to two o'clock in the morning on the weekends, with two alternating weekdays off per week, and every third weekend off.

"Sure?" Whelan asked me from behind the cash register. He asked it loudly, too.

Whelan Kearney was the owner of *The San Andreas Fault Videos* and my new boss. He was a big guy, 47 years old, 6ft 4in tall, flattened nose with odd twists to it as though it had been broken on more than one occasion. He had a big upper body and muscles that popped out of his lagoon-green, polyester shirt, and wore his light brown hair short and neat. He looked like a boxer standing there, his big forearms sticking out of his short sleeves as he picked up a box filled with videos, a delivery that had just arrived on a truck, wheeled through the front door by a man pushing a two wheeler.

"'Cause I don't like problems!" he continued, carrying the box to the rear of the store and placing it on the floor behind the counter.

I was on the opposite side of the counter from him, the customer side, and I followed him to the back of the store.

"I hired lots of guys in the past, just like you, who told me the hours weren't a problem. They work three weeks, maybe a month, then *BANG!* After two paychecks I never see 'em again! Understand? You got me?"

He was giving me a stern look, his burning green eyes staring dead into mine.

"I'm sure!" I said. "Like I told you earlier, I just got here this morning, six days hitchhike – I'm exhausted, I'm dirty. The last time I bathed I was on the East Coast. I feel like crap."

He laughed, then got all-serious again and shook his large index finger at me.

"I know you just got here. That's why I'm hiring you. Number one, it takes guts to do what you did. Number two --"

He turned to the delivery guy who was thin, with a pale face, scruffy whiskers, wearing denim overalls and black work boots, standing at the front end of the counter, tapping the glass with a pen, waiting for a signature.

"I'll be right there!" Whelan said loudly. Everything he said, he said loudly.

He turned back to me.

"Okay, where was I? Yeah! Number two – You say you know no one here in this city?"

"No one," I said. "I don't even have a place to sleep tonight."

"Don't worry about that," he said. "Upstairs I have a kitchen with a gas stove, refrigerator, sink, a bathroom with a shower and a bed. I used to live up there before getting married. You can stay there until you're on your feet. There's even a TV up there that gets more channels than that piece of crap Zenith I have at my home in Sausalito because it's here in the city. My wife is going to be happy I hired you. She's been on my ass about never comin' home. She's drivin' me freakin' crazy. But what can I do? I have a business to run here!"

"Perfect!" I said. "And thanks. I won't let you down. But I am here to go to college ultimately. I told you, right?"

"Yeah, you told me," he said, pulling a ten-dollar bill out of his pants' pocket. "Don't worry about that. You can go to college during the day and work here nights. Here --"

He passed me the ten-dollar bill:

"Go next door to **Happy Dragon** and get yourself some Chinese food. You must be starvin'. Let me go sign this guy's paperwork."

"Thanks," I said. "Want me to bring you something back?"

"No, no," he said, waving his giant hand and walking toward the delivery guy at the front end of the counter. "My wife is chicken shake n' bake tonight!"

"You mean your wife is making chicken shake 'n bake tonight," I said.

"No," Whelan said, a gigantic grin on his face. "I mean my wife *is* my chicken shake 'n bake tonight!"

26

Chapter Four

Working at ***The San Andreas Fault Videos*** was a great experience for me in many ways. First, it helped me to overcome my aversion to small talk. There were people walking in and out of that place all shift long, especially at night and on the weekends, and I had no choice but to interact with them; it was my job. Local men came in mainly to ask if we had any new videos available, especially from Sweden or Japan, the two biggest sellers or they'd go behind the lite blue curtain in the private room to check out the video selections on their own.

Lots of tourists came in – Asian men in dark suits or Europeans in Hawaiian shirts, shorts and sandals – usually in groups of five to ten, to check out the paraphernalia on the shelves at the front of the store: dildos, blowup dolls, ticklers, handcuffs, chains, whips, lotions, lubricants, condoms, penis pumps. They would hold the items in their hands, turning them over and over again, looking at one another and laughing, but most of them just usually bought a girlie magazine from our extensive, colorful rack.

The women who occasionally walked into the store were always embarrassed, red faces peering at the green linoleum floor as they brought their purchases to the counter – usually dildos or flavored condoms – giggling nervously as they explained, without variation each and every time, how they were not purchasing the item for themselves, but as a joke gift for a friend's birthday.

We had a lot of regulars, as well, with whom I became acquainted, one becoming my best friend, Taggart Riese, or Rye, which was his stage name when he did open-mic nights at the local comedy clubs. He was a tall, wiry, energetic guy who lived in the extensive, multistoried apartment complex across the street. He came in every other Friday afternoon, after cashing his paycheck. He worked as a sandwich maker at this place called **Bay Gourmet Sandwiches**, just two blocks down the road on Market Street, and he always bought one of our new videos. He said they gave him lots of good material to work with for his act. He always dressed the same, too: Yankees baseball cap, tie-die tee shirt, blue jeans, a pair of converse sneakers and his wireframe glasses.

"I have some new material for my act," he said one Friday afternoon, leaning on the glass counter top at the front of the store.

I was on the other side of the counter from him, sitting on a padded stool behind the cash register.

"Go ahead," I said. "Lay it on me."

"A guy walks into a bar with a blowup doll under his arm. The bartender says, 'That jackass isn't allowed in here anymore.' The guy says, 'That's no jackass, that's a blowup doll.' Bartender says, 'I was talking to the blowup doll.'"

"That's a remake on an old one," I said, swooshing the words away with the back of my hand.

"Okay, how about this one," he began. "The Church and the Temple, in order to promote interfaith relations, decided to have a football game. 'Okay, father', the rabbi says, 'gather up 12 Christians to be skins and I'll gather up 12 Jews to be shirts.' An hour later they meet on the field. The rabbi has 12 scrapping Jews in blue shirts behind him. The priest is alone. 'Where is your team, father?' the rabbi asks. 'I'm sorry rabbi,' the priest says. 'I could only find four skins.'"

"Better," I said.

He went on:

"What's a female porno stars favorite holiday song?"

I shrugged.

"O come all ye faithful – Why was Moses stuck in Sinai without a ride? Someone kicked his ass – You and your father have a fortuneteller visit you at your house. 'Your father will die mysteriously today,' the fortuneteller says. 'Oh, no!' you say, cupping your father's hand on the table. Outside on the front porch, the mailman, struck by a sudden heart attack, keels over, dead."

I tried to laugh but all I could muster was a wry smile.

"I don't know," I said.

"Come on! This is the best shit I have."

I always lied to him and told him he was funny, and he *was* sometimes; but the real truth was, he had been doing standup for five years now – two years in Los Angeles, leaving there, as he had told me, because there was too much backstabbing, and now three years in San Francisco – and there was a reason he had never been offered a paying gig.

"Yeah, it sounded pretty good," I finally said. "It was funny."

He smiled.

"Open-mic tomorrow at the *Funny Bone* in the Richmond?" he said. "This is your weekend off, right?"

I nodded.

"Coming to see me?"

"I'll be there," I said.

"Bring that blond girl I saw you with three weeks ago. What was her name?"

"Claudia."

"She was pretty hot. Does she have a sister?"

"No. And I'm not with her anymore."

"How come? You guys looked perfect together!"

I shrugged.

"You go through girlfriends like I go through tubes of toothpaste," he said. "How come you never stay with anyone very long?"

"I'm *trying* to have a permanent relationship," I said. "But it's this job! I'm always working nights, with only one weekend off every month. Girls don't like that. If you're their boyfriend, they expect you to go out with them every weekend, and I can't. They don't like me working here, either. They think this is a bad job."

"Who said that?"

"Claudia said it, and Juanita, too."

"Which one was Juanita?"

"That girl I dated for about three months last year, remember? She was just a pinch portly but angular, long black hair, always wore tight jeans."

"Oh, yeah, I remember her now. You brought her to the **Rib Tickler Cafe** in the Mission District that one time to see me perform. She was a little cutie, too."

He looked down, tapped the glass counter for a few seconds with both hands, and looked up at me again.

"Why don't you quit this job and find a new one?"

"No way," I said, shaking my head. "I've been here for three years now."

"Aren't you getting sick and tired of living in that tiny little studio apartment upstairs?"

"Aren't you getting sick and tired of living in your studio apartment across the street?" I said back.

"Hey! That's a four bedroom apartment!"

"Yeah, but you got three other roommates living there. Your one bedroom is really the only room you have over there, and you have to share the kitchen. It was a rat hole that one time I helped you carry your new stereo up there. Half-filled cereal bowls, egg-cemented plates, greasy frying pans, dirty coffee mugs, glasses and utensils all piled up like Mount McKinley in the sink. It stunk like a sulfur marsh."

"I know!" Rye laughed, holding his stomach. "My roommates are pigs! But what can I do? This city's so expensive. Can't afford my own place."

I looked at him, pointed upward to the ceiling and said: "Besides, Whelan lets me live up there for free."

"Yeah, to save his marriage!" he exclaimed.

"Big deal," I said. "I'm still up there for free. You know how much it costs to live in this city?"

"Of course!" he said, throwing his hands in the air. "I live here! I can't save a dime."

I looked at him for a long time, trying to decide whether or not I should confide something to him.

"You look like you have something to say," he said. "What is it?"

"You know how much I've been able to save these past three years because of living rent free upstairs?"

"How much?" he asked.

"Fifteen thousand dollars," I said.

"You're shitting me," he said, his jaw wide open, peering at me in disbelief over the top of his glasses.

"And look at this," I said, reaching for a white magazine on the counter and sliding it beneath his eyes.

"What's that?" he asked.

"San Francisco State University's bulletin for the coming fall semester," I said.

I picked it up with both hands and held it out so he could read the large, black lettering across the front which read: *SFSU 1982 to 1983.*

I flipped it open to a page I had earmarked earlier by folding down the corner, and I slapped the open pages down on the counter in front of him.

"Look at how much it would cost me to go to school there," I said, pointing to the middle of the right page.

"Five hundred dollars a semester," he read. "That's dirt cheap! It cost my parents eighty grand to put me through NYU for four years."

"What'd you get your degree in?" I asked.

"English," he said. "I was a creative writing major. I thought it'd help me with my jokes."

"How long have you dreamed of becoming a comedian?"

"Ever since I was a kid," he said. "Guys like Woody Allen, George Carlin and Jackie Gleason really influenced me."

He looked down to the bulletin and moved his eyes back and forth across the pages, silently reading it.

He then looked back up at me.

"What are you going to major in?" he asked.

"Economics," I said.

He gave me a funny look.

"Why economics?"

I smiled.

31

"Because I want to be rich."

So that's the other big thing that working at *The San Andreas Fault Videos* had done for me: it gave me the chance to go to college, and that's exactly what I did that fall semester beginning in 1982.

It was difficult at first balancing the long work nights with the morning classes, but eventually I learned that I could only do two or three classes a semester if I was going to keep working fulltime, which is what I wanted to do, since making money was a top priority for me.

I went to Powell Street Station on the mornings I had classes and rode the grimy, clicking, swaying subway cars all the way to SFSU. I was always punctual and enjoyed sitting in on the lectures, no matter what type of class it was: whether it be a core course required by my particular major, such as financial accounting and calculus, or an elective such as history or psychology. I found all subjects equally fascinating and eventually decided that only taking the courses required to fulfill my economics degree was not good enough for me. There were many subjects I was curious about.

So one semester, I decided to take a geology class, and I enjoyed it very much. On subsequent semesters, I took a biology class, a chemistry class, an archeology class, and an American literature class. That one was tough because of the length of the papers that had to be written. I even came to enjoy the little bull sessions after class with the professors or a few of my classmates.

In late afternoon, I'd ride the subway downtown again and go to work. And right there on the glass counter top in the store, sitting on that padded stool by the cash register, I would study my texts, write my papers, complete all assignments that were due, all the while helping out the store's customers and ringing up the sales on the register in the interstices.

I lived my life in the interstices.

I occasionally saw how other students did not take their studies as seriously as I did, missing classes, not turning in papers, half-comatose or asleep at their desks on a Monday morning. I don't know if it was my desire to overcome my impoverished past or the absence of a sense of entitlement, since I was paying for my own education with cash;

but, whatever it was, it caused me to perceive my studies as a sacred trust. I was honored by this education I was receiving and would do nothing to dishonor it, and even though my studious eyes often drew the form of my female classmates, always aching for the companionship of a woman during the slightest aperture of my schedule, I always put my studies ahead of my personal life.

I was always upfront with women in college as well, sometimes to my own disappointment, whenever it chanced I was having a conversation with a female friend in the student union café while sipping coffee together, or in a hallway talking after class, always letting them know, prior to asking them out on a date if they were friendly and had a good personality, what my situation was, where I worked, what type of job it was, that I didn't have much time to spend with them due to my long evening work schedule, and the high value I placed on my studies, but if they could be flexible with me, I would be just as flexible with them.

My suffering as a child had made me a tuning fork to others' singing feelings. So I tried my best never to be responsible for another person's emotional distress; although that is quite difficult to accomplish a lot of the times because emotions, by their very nature being so fluid and whimsical, can be hurt with something as simple as a 'hello.'

So I did date during the interstices, trying to keep a steady relationship with one woman as long as possible because I hated breaking up – the pain was almost unbearable at times and I'd sometimes cry over the event if I had been seeing the woman for some time. But I wouldn't let anybody see me cry. I did it secretly in my studio above the store. It was embarrassing. It was also frightening how much pain a woman could cause me: the hands of an emotional correlative, a breakup, shoving me off the cliff into the raging river of my childhood memories.

But breakups in college occurred to me all the time due to my job and its alienating hours. I didn't know what to do about it, either. I needed that job because it paid double what all the other jobs I was qualified to do paid, which was minimum wage. I wouldn't have been able to pay my tuition, buy my textbooks or go out on dates if it wasn't for that job. It was a dilemma! People always say they're in a dilemma but most of times it's not true. They're just having a hard time trying

to decide between two equally tempting scenarios, or they're a bit con-
fused about which direction in life they should go. Mine, however,
was an honest to god dilemma. I needed the job in order to have a
girlfriend; I couldn't keep a steady girlfriend because of the job.

As painful as the trough of breakups were to me, I enjoyed ex-
quisitely the peak of having a relationship, especially in the beginning,
which was always so romantic, lustful and explosive! Lunches together at the various ethnic restaurants along Taraval Street; walking with
arms around each other's waist along Sunset Beach; on my evenings
off, dining together at the fresh seafood and trendy steak houses downtown, clinking our wine glasses in a just-for-us toast and smiling at one
another across the table; seeing a play or a movie at one of the city's
many theatres, hands folded warmly together on the arm rest; hiring a
limousine to go see a rock concert together at the Arco Arena in Sacramento; going to clubs and moving sexily together on the dance floor;
staying in fine hotels on my weekends off, naked together on the plush,
king-sized bed, beneath a pile of fluffy blankets, feeling the enamoring
warmth of one another's flesh, the electrifying anticipation of sex, only
getting out of the bed and putting on a robe to let in the room service
cart and to tip the orderly, then off with the robe again and back into
the bed, conjoining breathlessly in the sweet, wet slurry of love!

So that was college for me, an endless, oscillating sine wave of
pain and pleasure, relationships and breakups, all the way up to the
time of my graduation. And I did finally graduate – but not in four
years. Because I was forced to limit my course load due to my difficult
work schedule, and because of all those extracurricular classes which,
believe me, I was glad I had taken, I didn't graduate until the spring
of 1990. That's right! It took me eight long years to get my bachelor's
degree in economics. I was 29 years old by that time and had been
working for Whelan for eleven straight years.

In that time, I had become very close to Whelan and his wife,
Becca. Not so close that I considered them to be surrogate parents, because the appellation *parent* carried negative connotations for me; but
I liked them very much and felt comfortable around them. I actually
trusted them. They were always there for me, even that time the store
was robbed and the robber shot me in the arm with a handgun because

he didn't think I was passing him the cash fast enough. Whelan didn't blame me for that one bit, even though it was me who hadn't locked the door at 2am that Sunday morning, and was counting out the cash right there at the register by the front door, when the store policy was, and always had been, to immediately lock the door at closing and carry the cash tray to the back room to count out.

Becca slept on a pullout bed in my room at Saint Francis Hospital the entire four days I was there, fast by my side and even helping to feed me because the bullet went straight through my right bicep – a clean wound, the doctors said – making it difficult for me, for two days after the surgery, to manipulate forks and spoons: my whole arm just didn't work right, and I had to relearn how to use it. And, *boy!* was I glad they had caught that robber. He was a crack addict, which was hitting the city hard by the mid 80's. There wasn't a trial, either. He had died in his holding cell, tearing his tee shirt to shreds and swallowing it, causing him to vomit internally and asphyxiate. Becca had read that in the Chronicle two days after the robbery, telling me about it as I lay in my bed, hooked up to wires and IVs, bandages heavy around my arm, shaking in a cold sweat.

Yes, without a doubt, Whelan and Becca were quite fond of me, giving me gifts on my birthday every year, Becca always hugging me when she was at the store, bringing me new bedding and groceries all the time as though I might freeze or starve to death in my little studio which, if truth be told, was actually quite comfortable, and I did get better TV reception and more channels than they did, until they got cable in 1985, which was the same year Whelan changed the name of the store, dropping the word video and changing it to CD, making us now *The San Andreas Fault CDs.*

They were always inviting me over to their house in Sausalito, too, for the holidays, invitations I occasionally accepted but to a larger degree did not. Not that I had anywhere else to go on the holidays. Rye always went back to New York on the holidays to be with his family and I didn't really have any other close friends, just a few acquaintances.

It was difficult for me to make friends and, truthfully, all I really had in the whole world were Whelan, Becca and Rye. And I, *too*, was all that Whelan and Becca had. They had no children. I had asked

35

Whelan once why, and he told me his business came first and had never had any time for kids. In fact, they had no relatives or friends at all as far as I knew. There was never anybody over at their house on the times I had visited. Neither one of them ever spoke to me about anyone else being in their lives. It was a paradox prevalent to not only San Francisco but, from everything I had ever heard or read, to all big cities: so many people, yet so many all alone.

But my time with Whelan and Becca, unfortunately – at least with regards to working at the store – was coming to an end. I had my degree now and I wanted to find a real job: become a stockbroker or a banker with one of the large financial institutions in the city. This was where the money was, I believed, on the top floors of those skyscrapers downtown. So that's where I wanted to be.

Chapter Five

I was thinking about Gale.

I was glad she was onboard with me, offering me that one hundred thousand dollars in return for the killer whale's skull.

I felt badly for her, also, having had one skull, her flower, so rudely plucked away from her like that and finding herself in the nerve-racking position of requiring another one.

It was karma, I guess, or fate. Which ever it was, they both came down hard on you when it was your turn, just like the boiling sun at that very moment, like a hammer, was coming down hard on my head.

I reached down to the dashboard and turned up the air-conditioner.

The rush of cool air on my hands and face refreshed me.

It was not only hot that day, it was bone dry. There hadn't been a cloud in the bright, cobalt sky for weeks.

The cardboard box on the bucket passenger seat rattled as I drove the van straight over some large clumps of dirt that had somehow been deposited on the highway.

I could see the Vacaville Outlets coming up in the distance, surrounded by golden foothills and dry, grassy fields, all kindling now due to the lack of moisture. I-80 seemed to wind into the shimmering, mirage-like distance like a long line of gunpowder; one careless match, one negligently discarded cigarette butt, and the entire state would erupt into a blazing bonfire, like it did every summer in California.

I was driving too fast: 85 mph.

I slowed down.

Not that I had any problems with driving fast. In the wholesale distribution business, when you're running routes, you must be out on that road early in the morning, and I mean by 4am sometimes, drive like a bat out of hell to get to the six or seven locations in that territory you're visiting that day, and make sure service is delivered to all of those businesses on that very same day, because there's no sense in driving a long distance and missing one or two of your stops; you just have to go back the following day to finish up. Your customers expect it; but going back to the same location two days in a row is a tiresome, costly and inefficient way of running a route business.

So I was used to driving fast; also, having had seventeen years on the road with a territory encompassing 500 square miles – from Reading in the North, Santa Cruz in the South, all the way East to Reno and other towns in the western part of the state of Nevada – it had developed in me an unusually keen honing sense, a cop car radar: relentlessly scanning the distance with my eyes in order to catch the partially obscured curves and U-turn connectors where the various law enforcement vehicles, like rouge wolves, loved to hide and then pounce on their unsuspecting, speeding prey. I knew when to speed up. I knew when to slow down. I was slowing down now because Vacaville had a lot of traffic due to all the auto dealerships, retail stores and restaurants there. Then Fairfield would be next, and their city police vehicles were like locusts on the highway, swarming and devouring speeders like a biblical plague.

As I drove, my stomach began cramping up – *painfully!*

Mainly it was due to hunger. I hadn't been eating lately. But also it was due to the anxiety I was feeling over what I was planning on doing. I kept visualizing the scene on the movie screen in my mind: me standing there on my yellow inflatable boat, out on the ocean beneath the Golden Gate Bridge, hacking away with the meat cleaver at the killer whale's flesh until I got down to the skull.

I'd have to do a lot of hacking; and not only did I have to de-flesh the skull, I'd also have to expose the first one or two neck vertebra. Then I'd maneuver my boat directly beneath the skull, use my wooden mallet to pound the meat cleaver through the gelatin disc between two of the vertebra, separating the skull from the rest of the body and *plop!* The skull would drop straight down, right into the bottom of the boat.

But what if I got caught? What were they going to do to me? I mean, come on – I heard what Gale had said: it violated the Marine Mammal whatever Act. But seriously, that sounded like a bunch of nonsense to me. The beast was dead, for crying out loud! It no longer required the use of its head. But that head, and in particular that skull, meant everything to me. *Everything!*

I was tense. There was no doubt about it. I could feel the pressure in my head, throbbing temples and eyes ready to pop out of their sockets.

I began squeezing the steering wheel to help relieve some of the anxiety.

I guess I was squeezing too hard, because a thin stream of blood began pouring out of one of the two holes I had on the fleshy, chopping part of my left hand.

The blood rolled in a thin line, down the back of my hand to my wrist. It surprised the hell out of me, too! That wound was five days old now. It should have been healed by now.

The Saturday last, I had vigorously searched the Internet all day and night, looking for any way I could to make fast money. There were lots of suggestions online too, but they were all either impractical, nonsense or outright scams.

One website suggested I write a letter to everyone I knew, requesting each one of them send me a dollar; then all of those people would write letters to every one they knew requesting a dollar be sent to not only them, but to me as well, and so on; and that way, if everyone kept the cycle going and there were infinite numbers of letters being written and mailed off, I potentially could have infinite numbers of dollar bills coming to me. I could see me opening my letters, one by one, taking out the single dollar bill and bringing it to the local BNC branch where we opened that equity line of credit:

"Only $99,992 dollars to go before we have this thing paid off!" I'd shout out merrily to the teller.

Other online suggestions seemed both whacky and plausible at the same time: I could raise sea horses and sell them to tropical fish stores; I could rear butterflies and sell them to schools for dissection; I could herd ostriches because the lean meat was in high demand, the leg leather was soft and durable, one of their eggs could make an omelet for twenty.

Some suggestions made perfect sense: there were thousands of people out there giving away their furniture for free on Craig's List, just because the stuff was junk to them and they wanted it hauled away. I could get that furniture and, with a few nails, glue, a splash of paint and varnish, sell it out of my garage, to the neighbors, or at the flea market. But I was losing my home now! How long did it take to rehab an old sofa, table, and chest of draws? How long would it take me to make one hundred thousand dollars that way?

I needed money right now! I needed an idea, a pristinely unique concept. I needed to do something where, in one fell swoop, I would have that one hundred thousand dollars in my hand, and I needed an above average chance of being able to pull it off, even if it was only quasi-legal.

Lani and I had already been through a living hell with me losing my business, the gradual attrition and then utter loss of our savings, then the credit card debt, the months and months of harassing phone calls by debt collectors, the bankruptcy, and now the impending loss of our home. I didn't want anything else bad happening to us. I didn't want to end up in jail. So any thoughts of armed robbery in the middle of the night with a stocking cap over my head were completely squashed as soon as such ideas came upon me; and, quite honestly, fleeting images of such events – me at some retail store, pharmacy or cigar shop, pistol in hand, tearing through the cash register for all that was inside – did flash upon the movie screen in my mind. I think it's natural when one is drowning in a sea of debt and swimming desperately for the shore of solution. It's not the thinking of an action that's wrong, however; it's the action itself which defines the betrayal of a social more; the crossing of a line that should not be crossed.

After countless frustrating hours of scanning the Internet and finding nothing topical in the way of soothing my financial paradox, my depressed, head throbbing, spiritually numbed form collapsed onto the living room sofa, and I began the time honored, efficacious healing process of distraction, practiced by Americans everywhere. I began watching TV.

The History Channel was on. They were talking about the last Ice Age and the melting of the glaciers and the fauna prevalent back then: mammoths, mastodons, the Irish Elk, wooly rhinos and saber-toothed tigers, and wouldn't you know it, they claimed that saber-toothed tigers had roamed all over the post-glacial California landscape back then, their fossilized bones sometimes found in ancient mud deposits, which were now upturned, flaking rock outcrops.

Bingo! That was it! My problem solved right there in those old fossil bones! All I had to do was find some fossilized saber-toothed tiger bones and I knew they would sell on E-Bay for at least one hundred grand, if not more!

So the following day, Sunday, I told Lani I was going up to Reading, a three hour drive to the North, to attempt to collect a debt that one of my past customers owed me up there.

"No, honey, don't go," she said softly, pleadingly. She was standing in the kitchen in a short, sleeveless, aqua nightgown, frizzy trim on the bottom with small, green sea turtles made of felt all around the frizzy trim.

Theo was in the family room watching the Sunday kids' shows on the wide screen, platform TV that was angled in the corner by the fireplace. I could see the back of his small head as he knelt on the thick, creamy carpeting beside the coffee table, clapping his little hands and singing along with the long line of colorful cartoon cats who were marching in a band on the TV screen. His hair was wild, sticking out in all directions as though he had just woken up. It was wavy and black, just like his mother's hair, although Lani always got her hair permed, so it was always curly. Other than the curls, Theo looked just like her. But he acted just like me, according to Lani. The perfectly proportioned progeny of a doting mom and distracted dad. But I believed he had way more of his mother in him than me, and of that I was glad. Lani was nothing but beautiful, both inside and out. So was he.

"We need to go looking at apartments today," Lani said. She took a sip from her coffee mug.

The kitchen curtains were wide open and, with the flood of morning sun light streaming in, I could see the curves of her shapely body right through the sheer material of her nightgown.

"I have to go," I said. "This guy owes me five hundred dollars."

"But what about me and Theo?" she asked, setting her coffee mug down next to the sink on the gold-speckled, black marble countertop.

"Do you want to come with me?" I asked.

I was hoping she'd say no because I didn't want her to know I was going to the woods that day to search for saber-toothed tiger fossils. She didn't care for stuff like that. She thought it impractical. She thought I acted like a child sometimes and she told me that all the time.

"We need to go look for an apartment today," she insisted. "We're not going to be in this house for much longer. The bank is repossessing it."

"I'm still trying to find a solution," I said.

"Give it up, honey," she said. "You're dreaming. Did you eat breakfast? You look terrible!"

I had barely eaten all week, the evidence of my malnourished condition seen quite vividly in the reflection of the stainless steel refrigerator – concave cheeks, narrowing face, paling complexion; as, too, did the lack of conceptual foodstuffs to feed our financial dearth affect an equal and parallel malnourishing of my soul.

It had been the incident at the bank with Mr. Forbes, the scene replaying in my mind over and over again, with Lani sobbing hopelessly at the end. The image of her crying troubled me greatly. The thing was – I was afraid. We both had been through so much already, and while we were going through it all, the emotional pain had caused me to occasionally have flashbacks to when I was a child in Lynn.

Before he and my mother abandoned me, my father was a biker in a motorcycle gang, and my mother was an alcoholic. They were both heavy drug users. I didn't know any of this back then because I was just a kid, but looking back on it now as an adult, remembering the empty beer bottles, vodka bottles, whiskey bottles, and a plethora of variously colored pills and plastic bags filled with marijuana, all over the table in our kitchen each and every day, seven days a week, I knew now what they had been.

My memories of them way back then are fleeting, but I remember them arguing and fighting constantly, yelling and screaming as they went after each other with hurled objects, clenched fists, sometimes knives. My mother had been hospitalized more than once with broken bones and bloodied, black-and-blue facial wounds, and this was the 1960's. Nobody gave a shit back then. So my father was never arrested or spent time in jail like he would have if he pulled that kind of crap today.

He was bare-chested once, in the kitchen. They were arguing over money and my mother threw a pot of boiling water on him. The neck to waist scar it left was horrifying: the flesh all peeling off his chest, dissolving his right nipple, and nothing but a webby lattice of veiny scar tissue remaining, but they never broke up: two coequal nightmares feeding off of one another's rage.

It all culminated with the big event which changed my life unalterably forever: them abandoning me when I was five years old, left in the Spartan dining room of my grandmother's house, sitting at the table by myself with a cookie in my hand, while they slipped down the back staircase, telling me they were just running across the street to the store to buy some cigarettes. And I waited for them, and I waited for them, kicking my legs beneath the table; after a long while had passed, a terrible feeling overcame my small heart, bringing physical discomfort to my stomach and chest, as I turned my head, pulled the curtain back, and began looking out the window to the store across the street, waiting for them to step outside and begin making their way back – but they never did come back.

My mother was 21 years old at the time; my father was 22.

And my grandmother – unaware that the abandonment was going to occur, but not surprised by it nonetheless – was now my guardian.

She was an ancient, white-haired, wrinkled faced witch who hated boys because, as she so often stated, *"they were vessels of Satan and therefore incorrigible."*

She never attempted to instruct me in any way, neither for the good nor the bad; she never read to me, hardly spoke to me other than to demand a chore be done like taking out the trash or washing the driveway down with the garden hose. She never laid a hand on me either, neither to harm or embrace. We stayed away from one another for the most part, me going to school in the morning, playing with my few friends outside in the afternoon and early evening for as long as the sunlight would allow, and then alone in my attic bedroom in the haunting black night. Two good things the years of isolation had done for me: first, it nurtured my appreciation for rock and roll music which was my escape at night, and I would play my radio loudly for hours before going to bed: The Rolling Stones, Aerosmith, ELO, The Doors; second, it turned me into a half decent chef. My grandmother refused to prepare meals for me when I turned seven.

Ten years after the abandonment, when I was 15 years old, both my parents showed up together on my grandmother's doorstep in Lynn. They had spent the past decade in San Francisco, the mid 60's through the mid 70's, trying to *find themselves* through the use of illegal yet easy to obtain substances, and copious liters of alcohol. They were only in their early thirties by that time – my mother had given birth to me when she was sixteen years old – but the drugs and alcohol had aged them to the point where they both looked like they were knocking on death's door as opposed to my grandmother's door. I didn't even recognize them, they were so scrawny and short, and my father's hair was turning grey, for god's sake, at 32 years old! My grandmother had to tell me it was them. When they had left ten years earlier, they both seemed like giants to me. Now, ten years later, they looked like nobodies.

They were very apologetic, though; told me they had seen some terrible things in their decade long journey: beatings, suicides, murders and drug overdoses; even a self-immolation once. They had tried to clean and sober up several times by going to spirituals and counselors, but nothing seemed to work; until one day, both of them bleeding and vomiting in an alleyway after being beaten and robbed of their drugs by some gang members – both of them violently raped, both anally and orally – they simultaneously came to the transcendental understanding that their rightful path lay with their son.

So they were there to ask me for forgiveness and beg that I let them back into my life, and I did, to a limited degree. I had, for a very long time, suffered from a type of post-traumatic stress disorder caused by their abandonment. I didn't know that back then, but in retrospect, remembering my juvenile reactions, for instance, if one of my friends couldn't play with me because his parents wouldn't let him out of the house, or if one decided to leave me to go play with another friend, and I wasn't invited, how I would lock myself into my attic bedroom and cry hysterically for hours while simultaneously throwing a fit, banging away at the walls with my baseball bat. Oh! How many holes did I leave in those old, plaster bedroom walls? Too many to count! And my grandmother never tried to stop me or calm me; saying nothing after the fact except: *"See, tools of the devil."*

So, in a way, my parents returning had a healing effect, at least somewhat, because I had always blamed myself for their abandonment, but they made it perfectly clear to me that I was the victim, and the fault was entirely theirs; but even though we did spend some time to- gether after that as a family, with us all living together in my grand- mother's house, I never truly forgave them, and was verbally caustic to them as often as my conscience would allow it, screaming at them for the most minor infractions, frequently bombarding them with a flurry of insults, letting them know how insignificant they were in my life and how I was going to leave them as soon as I could.

My grandmother died about a year after their return. Memories of her wrinkled, age spotted flesh, that old-fashioned Quaker dress she wore, light green with horn-of-plenty pattern, blanketing her from neck to ankles as she lay stiff in her casket, still haunt my dreams to this day. In particular, for several years after her death, I would on a nightly basis almost, have the most vivid, recurring dream where I had to make my way slowly up the steep, creaking, circular staircase of her two story house, then walk slowly to the bedroom in the back of the house where she had passed away on her bed, and I'd see her face on the static-y screen of her old black and white TV; she'd be calling out my name, sorrowfully, trying to whisper something to me but the words never came out clearly. I was never so happy to see someone put into the ground. After she was gone, my parents then owned the house, a fitting legacy for my grandmother to leave behind: her ghostly, dilapidated house bequeathed to two with equally ghostly, dilapidated souls.

Two years after my grandmother's death, when I turned eighteen, having graduated from high school with very good grades – sinking myself into my studies was the very best way I had found to isolate myself from this world's myriad, capricious pains – I left them and did to them what they had done to me: I moved to San Francisco to spite them, just as they had done to me, but unlike them, I never returned, not even when I got the news of my father's lung cancer, nor a few years later when my mother was afflicted with the same disease. My father died with only my mother at his side. My mother died alone, and I didn't give a rat's ass.

But this thing with Lani and our home – this I cared deeply about, and it frightened me more than anything ever had in my life.

I had heard stories through forgotten snippets of media – news reports, magazine articles, variety shows of the Hollywood elite – where a loss of money and subsequent social standing had caused the blackened, withering death of not a few great hearts, spouses abandoning one another on the cold and lonely slab of despair due to financial hardship.

How much more could Lani take? Was this going to be the straw that broke the camel's back? With most of our financial buoys – savings account, checking account, stocks, cash flow – now sunken into the abysmal sea of financial ruin, the belief that we were at least going to be able to keep our home, our finest possession, that one life preserver thrown to us, was what had kept us out of the abyss of despair. If we lost it now, if we had to go through that very painful process of packing up all of our belongings into boxes and stretch wrap – sofas, loveseats, chairs, beds, tables, pots, pans, utensils, ironing board, clothing, TV's, microwave, pictures, refrigerator magnets, keepsakes, all of those personal things that go toward making a loving home – was she going stay with me and take that torture? Or would she be on a plane to Honolulu with Theo, me never seeing either one of them ever again?

The thought of it was too much for me to bear, and I secretly cried, hidden in a bathroom with the door shut and the faucet running, whenever I thought of it. And I couldn't get it out of my head that she might leave me. I had to somehow find a way to save our home, even if it meant doing something crazy; something dangerous.

"Are you going to answer me?" Lani asked.

Her voice had shaken me out of my reverie.

"Yes, darling," I said. "What was it again that you asked?"

"Have you eaten? You look terrible."

"Yes."

It was a lie.

"Then let's go take a shower and go looking for apartments today."

"Let's go later," I said. "I won't go to Reading, okay? That's too far of a drive. But Mike Sack at the *Sacramento Adult Depot* downtown owes me two hundred dollars. I'll go try and collect that this morning and I'll be back in a few hours, I promise, and we can go out then."

"We're going out to look at *apartments* later, right?" she said, slightly tilting her head in a questioning glance.

I hesitated.

"Say it!" she insisted. "You have to get out of your fantasy world. We're losing this house. It's no longer our home."

"We haven't lost it yet!"

She placed her hands on my cheeks, stood on her toes and gently kissed my mouth with her soft, full lips. Then, stepping back and smiling, she whispered:

"Okay, dreamer – keep dreaming."

Chapter Six

I was going to look for saber-toothed tiger fossils that morning. So I got into my van and drove the one-and-a-half hours north to the Sacramento National Wildlife Refuge. It was still early when I arrived there, only 9:30am. I parked on the expansive, graveled parking lot outside the **Nisenan Gift Shop** and the **Acorn Restaurant and Cafe**. Two workers, both teenagers, were outside on the wooden steps that led to the back of the restaurant, chatting and smoking. They were both wearing blue caps and blue kitchen aprons. The young man was leaning closer and closer to the young lady, as though he wanted to give her a kiss. They ignored me as I passed them.

Lani and I had visited the refuge several times in the past. The last time we went, about two years back, I carried Theo around on my chest in one of those baby harnesses. There were hiking trails through the woods going in all directions, leading to reedy marshes all a-buzz with crickets and frogs, duck filled ponds and fish laden lakes. If you kept your eyes opened, you'd see animals off of the trails – woodchucks, squirrels, deer, beavers – and thousands upon thousands of birds, all different colors and sizes, filling the sky.

I walked a good twenty minutes into the dense forest along the main trail at first, then a side trail, until I reached a large clearing.

The bright morning sun lit up the green canopy of the dish-shaped valley like a kiss from God.

Down in the valley, I could see large, greyish-black outcrops of flaking rock. I left the trail and headed downward, surrounded by a vast kingdom of tree trunks now, the giant umbrella of greenery way above my head blocking out most of the sun. The thick carpeting of dead leaves and twigs on the ground crunched with each step.

The first outcrop of rock I reached popped out of the ground like a giant blackhead. It was about fifteen feet high, forty feet wide, ashy-grey with round, teal mosses growing all over it. It was only partially exposed, with both stony sides slanting gradually back into the earth and the entire top of the structure was covered with decaying leaf litter and twigs. The portion of rock that was exposed was irregular, tilting, scaly, and littering the ground beneath it with small and large flakes of itself.

I began inspecting the flakes on the ground, picking up the smaller ones and turning them over and over in my hand, looking for the outlines of fossils. The larger pieces I kept on the ground, using both of my hands to turn them over so I could inspect their undersides. After about a half hour of that, having inspected every single flake on the ground and finding no trace of a single fossil, but determined not to give up, I decided to make some new flakes. I had brought a hammer with me and was going to use the claw to pry pieces of rock off of the main outcrop. The smaller scales were at the top of the structure. So, with the hammer snug in the large side pocket of my shorts, I began climbing up the slanted face of the outcrop, using the scales as stairs. I could have just walked around to one of the sides where it slanted back into the ground, and could easily have walked up to the top of the outcrop, but I liked rock climbing. It was fun.

The stone was cool to the touch and rough on my fingers as I climbed. The many scales made it easy, although my right sneaker did slip on a moss at one point, but I was so close to the ground and the leaf litter was so thick, I don't think a fall would have hurt me.

At about eight feet up, standing on a mid-sized, oval shaped scale at the center of the structure, I reached my left hand up to the top of the outcrop and brushed away the leaf litter, feeling around for some rocky niche or stony rung to grab, so I could help pull myself up. And then it happened.

"Shit!" I yelled, pulling my hand back fast. It stung painfully, and burned, as though I had been stabbed. I shook it and then looked at it. There were two puncture wounds in the fleshy, chopping part. The wounds were bleeding and two lines of blood rolled down the back of my hand and onto the back of my forearm.

"What the hell!" I yelled and, pulling myself higher, just to the point where I could see where my hand had been, I saw a rattlesnake at the top of the outcrop. About four feet long, cream colored with a bronze pattern down its back and sides, dark brown stripe around its nose. Its midsection was bulging as though it had swallowed a softball, and it was curled and ready to strike.

I let go of the scales I was holding and dropped to the ground in a thudding crackle of leaf litter, falling backwards onto my ass. I then jumped to my feet and moved away from the outcrop in case the rattlesnake decided to slither off the top and land on my head. I checked myself up and down. I wasn't hurt, except for the bite.

"Shit!" I exclaimed. "I'm bit!"

I turned and began running up the valley through the trees. Once on the side trail, I ran toward the main trail, looking around for others that might help me.

I kept looking at the puncture wounds on my left hand.

"When's it going to happen?" I kept saying frantically in my mind. I was waiting for a feeling to overcome me, nausea or dizziness, whatever that feeling was that eventually overtook poisonous snakebite victims.

On the main trail, I ran like crazy, hoping to get to the gift shop and restaurant in time for them to call an ambulance. I didn't want to die out there in the woods, all-alone. It's what I feared the most in the whole damned, rotten world: being alone.

At the restaurant, I ran up the side stairs where the two teenagers had been and pushed open the rear door.

"Huh?"

An old man turned to me. He was wearing brown slacks, a yellow t-shirt, a blue apron around his neck, washing pots and pans in a large metal sink. He was Native American.

I was holding my bloodied left hand in the air.

"What happened?" the old man quipped loudly, moving toward me and drying his hands on the front of the apron.

"Rattlesnake!" I shouted. "Call an ambulance! Please!"

The two teenagers came running into the kitchen.

"What happened?" they queried simultaneously.

"Rattlesnake bite," the old man said calmly. "Call Barry, tell him about this. Tell him I'll be there soon so he better have some anti-venom ready."

"Okay!" the girl said, disappearing into the front of restaurant.

"Come on," the old man said, heading for the rear door.

"Who's Barry?"

"He's the medic at the Miwok Ranger Station about a mile from here. That's where we're headed. Come on."

We climbed into his pickup truck, him on the driver's side, me on the passenger side, and the old man stepped on the gas. I could hear gravel hitting trees.

At the ranger station, a man with a neatly trimmed moustache, dressed in a tan shirt and a tan tie, dark green pants with a brown stripe running down both sides, was standing in the dirt parking lot waiting for us. He was wearing latex gloves and had a stethoscope around his neck.

"Good to see you, Barry," the old man said, climbing out of the truck.

"You too, Vidur," Barry said, putting one arm around my waist as I stepped out of the passenger side.

"It's a good thing this happened today. Last Sunday I missed work for my niece's wedding. "

Barry opened one of the two glass doors and we moved together into the station's main office, which had two cluttered but unoccupied desks, and then into a small, back room containing a hospital bed and multiple cabinets on the wall. The glass doors of the cabinets revealed all sorts of medical accoutrements within: medicine bottles, rolls of gauze, hypodermic needles, cotton balls, rubbing alcohol, bandages, splints, tongue depressors.

"How long ago did this happen?" Barry asked.

"About half an hour ago," I said, sitting on the bed. I could feel the hammer. It was still in the large side pocket of my shorts.

Vidur came into the room and sat on a round, metal stool in the corner. He was still wearing his blue apron.

"Let me see it," Barry said.

I held up the bloody hand.

Barry held it in his gloved hands and examined it.

"No swelling, no bruising, no discoloration, nothing," he said. "And this occurred half an hour ago, you say?"

"At least, maybe longer," I said.

He then shone a small light into my eyes.

"Are you nauseous?" he asked.

"No," I said.

"Dizzy?"

"No."

"Do you have a funny taste in your mouth, metallic, rubbery, minty?"

"No."

He turned off the small light.

"Other than the pain you're feeling from the bite, do you feel out of the ordinary or strange in anyway other way?"

"No."

He turned to Vidur and said: "A dry bite."

"A dry bite," Vidur repeated, nodding.

"What's that?" I asked.

"Did you see the snake?" Barry asked.

"Yes."

"Did it look like he had just eaten? Did it have a big bulge in its stomach?"

"Yes."

"Well, Mr. --"

"Cree Quinn," I said.

"Well, Mr. Quinn, a dry bite means the snake had no venom to inject into you, because it had used up all its venom killing its meal. It takes a rattlesnake some time to make more venom after a kill. You got lucky. But why don't we give you some anti-venom anyway, just to be sure, and let's clean up this wound."

I exhaled hard while looking down at the white floor tiles, and shook my head. I was still shaking a bit, but was terribly relieved. I had been frantic for a while there. I could hardly believe it, if you wanted to know the truth. A dry bite. I had never before in my life heard of such a thing, and now I was lucky enough to have experienced one, if you want to call being bitten by a rattlesnake lucky.

Barry cleaned my wound in the sink with warm water and a bar of soap, sterilized it with antiseptic and then bandaged it up. He then gave me the anti-venom via a needle in my left arm, and put a band aide on that.

"I have to write up an incident report now," he said. "Just ten or fifteen minutes more and you'll be on your way."

The phone rang in the main office.

"I'll be right back," Barry said, exiting through the door.

I looked at Vidur.

He was still sitting on the stool in the corner, but he had taken the top of his apron off and it was lying flat and blue across the top of his legs. He had been very quiet for a long time. I looked at him from where I was now sitting on the hospital bed. He had long, grey hair, pulled back tightly in a ponytail and the bottom of that ponytail was resting on the right shoulder of his yellow shirt. He had strong facial features: a protruding, powerful chin, high cheekbones, deep creases in his high, dark forehead. He sat there calmly, looking over at me.

"I want to thank you for helping me today, Vidur," I said. "If it had not been a dry bite, you would have saved my life today by taking me here."

He acknowledged the comment with a nod.

"I'm also sorry I've kept you from work for so long," I said.

"It's no matter," he said. "Snake bites are not to be taken lightly, even dry ones. They can become infected if not treated properly."

"Just the same," I said, "when you take me back, I'll talk to the restaurant's owner."

"You *are* talking to the owner," he said. "I've owned and operated the Acorn for over twenty years now. Those teenagers you saw – the girl

53

is my granddaughter. The boy is her boyfriend. They help out on the weekends so they can make some spending money. They know how to run the whole place by themselves."

I smiled at him and said, "That's great. They look like very nice young people."

"Do you have children?" he asked.

"Yes. A five year old son named Theo."

"And a wife?"

"Yes, her name is Lani."

"Why are they not here with you today? It's a beautiful Sunday."

I looked down at the white floor tiles for a few seconds and then turned back to him.

"I needed to go into the woods on my own today," I said.

He gazed at me intently. His black, inset eyes seemed to reach inside of me, searching.

"Where were you when the rattlesnake bit you?" he asked.

"In the valley," I said.

"Were you on a trail?"

"No, I had left the trail."

"Why did you leave the trail? It's dangerous in the woods when you're alone, as you found out today."

"I was looking for something."

"Looking for what?"

I lowered my head again, exhaling an unsettling laugh.

"It's kind of embarrassing," I said, looking back up at him.

"It shouldn't be embarrassing," he said. "Lots of people at certain times in their lives find they need to go into the woods on their own to search for something."

"It's not as metaphorical as you think," I said. "I was actually looking for something physical."

"Then what is it? Maybe I can help you find it."

I looked at him but said nothing.

"Cree," he said slowly, "you have a good name. I think you're probably a fine young man. But your words say one thing and your actions say another."

"I was looking for saber-toothed tiger fossils," I said.

54

"Why?"

"I believe they can help me."

"They cannot help you and you will not find them here."

"Why?" I asked. "The show on TV I saw last night said the fossils were all over California. Other people have found them. Why not me?"

"Because you're not really looking for saber-toothed tiger fossils."

"I'm not?"

"No."

I shrugged my shoulders.

"Then what am I looking for?" I asked.

He sat up in his chair, looked me straight in the eyes and said:

"Nobody knows what you're looking for, not even you. That's the thing about discovery – you'll only know what it is after you find it."

Barry came back into the room and asked me multiple questions – name, address, and phone number etcetera – so he could write up his incident report. He then photocopied the report and gave the copy to me. I shook his hand, thanked him, and Vidur drove me back to the **Acorn Restaurant and Cafe**. On the gravel parking lot, I shook his hand, thanked him again, and then drove away in my van, him watching me the whole time from the rear steps of the restaurant, his blue apron, from the waist down to his knees, getting smaller and smaller in my rearview mirror as I drove down the narrow road that led to the exit of the refuge. As I turned onto the highway, he disappeared.

When I got home, I had no choice but to tell Lani what had happened, seeing as my hand was all bandaged up. She was shocked at first, holding her hands to her mouth in disbelief as I relayed the morning's narrative. Shock turned to affection, with her hugging me and kissing me on the mouth, telling me over and over again how happy she was I was alive, calling Theo away from the TV so we could all have a group hug so they could let daddy know how much everybody loved him. Affection turned to anger, with her crying and screaming at me, berating me for almost getting myself killed, which would have left her and Theo all alone in the world with no one. Finally she stopped talking to me, storming into our bedroom and locking the door behind her.

We did not go out looking for apartments that day.

That night, I slept on the sofa.

Chapter Seven

I stopped squeezing the steering wheel because I didn't want to tear open that other puncture wound and have that one bleeding also. I had a bottle of water in one of the van's cup holders. I opened it, poured some of the water onto a napkin and used it to clean the blood off of the back of my hand and wrist. I then drove with only my left hand, using my right and the napkin to apply pressure to the snakebite wound. I guess I had taken the bandages off too soon.

I was up to Vallejo now. Up ahead to my right, a state trooper had pulled someone over. I could see the brightly spinning blue lights on the side of the highway.

There were two adult stores in Vallejo. I had serviced both of them prior to going out of business. One of those places, **Big Mario's**, still owed me money. The owner, who I thought had become a good friend of mine over the years, Marinos Azarola – everyone called him Big Mario – didn't pay me for six months one time. This was about a year back. So I had to stop going there. I called Big Mario all the time on the phone and mailed him invoices but he never responded, until finally, one day I called him, and the phone was disconnected.

A month later I went to Vallejo to service my other store there and, after driving by Mario's place, found out he had gone out of business: the front doors were locked up with a bike chain and pad lock, with a big FOR LEASE sign in one of the windows, and the large, red letters that spelled out *BIG MARIO'S* had been taken down from the rectangular signage box above the doors.

It wasn't just **Big Mario's**, either. A lot of these places were going out of business or paring down their purchases to the bare minimum. It was the Internet – the ready availability of free adult entertainment on the World Wide Web. The entire adult industry was under threat by it, and there was nothing anybody could do about it.

So as my customer's sales plummeted, so did mine, but my sales plummeted even more because I didn't carry any of the big sellers of the adult industry, what one would call the staple items: movies, CDs, magazines, erotic toys. These were the items that would always be in high demand at adult stores. I had once carried those items exclusively my first ten years in business, from 1990 through the end of 2000, but the few big drop shippers out there – *Bam-Bam, Lickety Split and Long Gun* – began a price war in 1996 which lasted for four years, and it almost put me out of business. So I switched product.

Starting in January of 2001, I had completely re-tooled my business and began making a niche market for myself in what I termed *novelty* adult items, things like key chains in the form of the male and female genitalia, racy blackjack sets, bawdy playing cards, amorous shot glasses and the sultry talking box: a plastic box with steamy pictures on it, and a voice box in the middle that, when you shook it, said all kinds of sexy things to you in either a male or a female voice, depending on which way you flipped the little switch on the side.

There were various, hard to obtain lotions and lubricants from China that I carried due to my connection with Mr. Lee, and certain pharmaceuticals, non-prescription, 10 orange or 10 yellow pills to a package, made from the concentrated extracts of certain sea organisms and Chinese herbs, imported from the Xinjiang Province and, according to Mr. Lee, carrying aphrodisiac-like qualities. I was even the only distributor out there who carried a certain line of sexy lingerie: these were Gale's items.

So, since I did have a very unique niche in the industry now with my novelty items, products that the big wholesalers just didn't carry because my items were viewed as small potatoes to them, this was what had made me so successful for those five years between 2001 to 2006. And let me tell you, those five years were amazing. I had a cash flow of between twenty thousand and twenty-five thousand dollars per month, and Lani, Theo and I lived the high life: we ate filet minion, Alaskan king crab legs, ahi tuna steaks and lobster every night at home during the week, and we dined at the finest restaurants with all of our Sacramento friends on the weekends, ordering whatever we wanted. It didn't matter if the bill was a thousand dollars or two thousand dollars, I paid it; I didn't give a damn.

On the spur of the moment I'd fly my family and Sacramento friends on a Friday afternoon out to Las Vegas. We always stayed at the Venetian, renting out two adjacent suites; one for Lani, Theo and I, the other for our friends. The men would begin the evening dining at one of the Venetian's steak and ale establishments. We'd do multiple shots of either Irish Whiskey or Kentucky Bourbon. After a glow, we'd all get the most expensive cigars we could find at one of the tobacconist shops in the lobby and smoke them while cruising along the Grand Canal in one of the gondolas. Finally, off to the roulette wheels and blackjack tables, gambling, smoking, drinking and hooting it up all night long, before staggering back to our respective suites around 2am or 3am, me sometimes ten thousand dollars or once twenty thousand dollars lighter. Lani didn't like the way I acted when I was in Las Vegas, but she shielded herself and Theo from my madness by shopping all day long with her female friends in the expensive clothing and jewelry stores lining the promenades of the Venetian, going together to see the high wire acts and animal shows at Circus Circus, and dining in the most opulent restaurants they could find out on the strip.

But only on the weekends did I ever let lose, never during the week, and other than our occasional weekend excursions to Las Vegas, never had we gone on a real vacation during those five years. I couldn't. I had 24 routes representing 160 retail stores that had to be serviced on a regular and consistent basis. The schedule couldn't deviate. Other business people would have hired an employee with so many stores and such a vast territory to cover. Not me. I had it down to a science: when to wake each morning, how much time I had for toast and coffee before needing to be on the road, the amount of gasoline required, which roads and highways were necessitated for that particular day's route, the inventory required which was always – but always! – loaded up in the van the night before, and I always finished my routes on the same day, except for one time, and that one time only.

Finishing a route on the same day was important to me, even if it meant me not getting home until one o'clock in the morning. I had on more than one occasion used my cell phone to call the manager or owner of one of my stops, requesting them to stay late if I was running late myself, and they always did – except for that one time – because that's what good business people did: they accommodated one another. That was why they bought from me. I had unique items that were moneymakers and I was consistent in the supplying of those items. Not one of my items made a whole hell of a lot of money. I had things that I wholesaled for $2.00, $3.00, maybe $4.00. The retailers in turn would mark them up 100% and sell them for $3.99, $5.99, $7.99. My most expensive items were Gale's lingerie collections – a panty/ bra combination might wholesale for ten dollars. The stores would retail that for $19.99. Of the ten dollars that was made on the wholesale side of that deal, I only got half, and Gale got the other half. But it was the selling of these not so expensive items in such large quantities to so many retailers that made it so lucrative for me. That's why I had so much money; that sweet, sultry, sexy and seductive business transaction known as *"Bulk Sales!"*

Pampering ourselves with spur of the moment weekends in Las Vegas was not our most extravagant expenditure, however. I could never have fulfilled my hunger for excess with merely that. Oh, no – I required excess on a daily basis, crammed down my throat through a funnel if necessary. So with half a million dollars just sitting in my business account at the First Sacramento Savings and Loan, at an insultingly low interest rate I might add, what we did in July of 2005 was – and I should say what I did, because Lani wanted nothing to do with it at first – we bought five new construction homes in the newest and trendiest section of Sacramento, North Natomas, close to Arco Arena, the Sacramento Kings' home stadium. I thought it would be a good investment for the future, for Theo, who was two years old at the time, and that's exactly how I got Lani to sign all those contracts.

I put a one hundred thousand dollar deposit down on each one, bought them all from different builders, which meant different lenders, each having no idea about the other. Somehow I felt profligate buying houses in bulk, the way my retailers bought product off of me, and felt a certain amount of secrecy was in order.

Getting the loans was easy. Banks were *giving* money away back then, no income verification at all. They just asked you from across the table with a wink and a nod, *"Can you afford this mortgage?"* And, of course, my answer was always, *"Yes,"* because that was a fact back then. I then hired a property management company who found tenants for four of the houses, and we moved into the fifth one, 212 Ostentatious Drive: one acre of emerald lawn and small gardens right there in the city, surrounded by a lighted stone wall, a pool, fruit trees, a fashionably long driveway, a two car garage on one side and a one car garage on the other, gabled Spanish roof, copious large windows, stone façade covering the entire front of the house, and 3,500 square feet of heaven inside: Spanish tiled hallways, Berber carpeting in all the rooms, granite counter tops in the kitchen and stainless steel appliances, four bedrooms and four full bathrooms, wooden-shuttered windows, built-in wine cellar in the finished basement, spiraled ballroom staircase. It might not sound like much to some, but it being the very first home in which we ever lived, to us it was like a dream come true; and we dubbed the place *The Quinn Estate*.

So now we had not only route money coming in, but rental income as well. Although, truth be told, the rental income didn't fully pay the mortgages on our four investment houses. We had a negative cash flow there of around four thousand per month; but I didn't care. My business made more than enough money to cover the deficit; and I hadn't bought those houses to hold on to them for very long. In just three or four years, I planned on flipping them. Yes, they weren't our primary place of residence so we'd have to pay the government their share of the profit, but what the hell. Money was money.

We lived like kings and queens. Everything was going great! I had even bought into another large investment just a year-and-a-half after purchasing the houses. I found it on the Internet. I was always searching the Internet for potential investments because, the way I felt, there was no sense leaving a pile of cash in the bank where it made very little in interest.

Anyway, this investment I found was perfect, because it was a clean, alternative energy source, something everybody needed: natural gas. This guy in Dallas named Geier Campbell owned a company called T-Rex Fuels. Through T-Rex, Geier would go around buying up land and drilling rights from the big oil companies – Exxon/Mobil, Shell, BP – in the states of Texas and Colorado. He'd then find investors with a lot of cash, form LLC's with them, and drill new wells adjacent to older, capped wells that weren't producing oil anymore. He'd then frac those new wells, releasing the natural gas that the big oil companies had left behind in the porous sandstone.

Natural gas had risen substantially in price all throughout 2005, and even though prices had been declining in 2006, Geier told me not to worry about it, that it was just a natural fluctuation in the market. He told me the only thing I needed to concern myself with was the fact that we'd probably average $9.00/MMbtu. I had no idea what that meant. All I knew is Geier had marketing literature predicting, if everything went as planned, a 6:1 return on my investment. So I told him to send me the contract.

It was like pulling teeth to get Lani to sign that contract, and when I took out a two hundred thousand dollar cashier's check from the First Sacramento Savings and Loan to send to Geier along with that contract, she became livid! She demanded every day for a whole week that I deposit that money back into my business checking account. But I couldn't do that. I had to have that investment. Our money was just sitting in the bank collecting dust. It made no sense to me. Rich people took chances. They searched for, investigated and thoroughly weighed alternative forms of wealth creation. That's how they became richer. That's how I would make us richer.

She finally broke down and signed the contract. She had no choice. I wasn't giving in, and every investment I made was always in both of our names; a joint tenancy. The stress of my business caused me agony on a daily basis in the form of incessant heartburn, chest pains, high blood pressure, throbbing headaches, and because of having to sit and drive for each and every day for unusually long periods of time, I had un-ebbing back aches that felt like someone was ponding a rail road tie into my spine! I survived on a cocktail of Prilosec, aspirins, prescription sleeping pills, high blood pressure medication and a sedative, all taken down in one big fistful with a glass of water each evening prior to going to bed. It was my nightly ritual. I had an uncanny feeling that every day might be my last, and didn't want Lani having any legal problems collecting the money that was rightfully due her on our investments, after my demise.

It was January of 2007 when I sent that contract and the two hundred thousand dollar cashier's check off to Geier. Our investment had bought us a substantial percentage in the up-and-coming T-Rex *4-Corners Project*, which would be a series of four wells drilled individually in two month intervals, in an area of Texas, along the Gulf Coast, that had once been well known for its oil reserves. The ground breaking on the first well wasn't slated until January 2008. The project couldn't be started any earlier because Geier wouldn't be done drilling the holes of his current projects until then and there were only so many rigs to go around. But that was fine by me. The entire T-Rex *4-Corners Project* wasn't slated for completion until July of 2008.

So everything was in place now. The route money was pouring in, rental money too, and soon the natural gas money would complete the triathlon of *The Mighty Quinn Wealth Creating Conglomerate*, which is how I saw myself and Lani – we were a business, and we were on our way to becoming multimillionaires. Lani would never have to work a day in her life ever again if she wished it. Theo would go to the finest private schools, have private tutoring at home, and end up in the best colleges and universities money could buy. We'd move into an even bigger house! Hire servants! I even had thoughts of one day owning my own yacht and a private jet. Nothing could stop us -- And then the housing market collapsed.

Chapter Eight

No one could see it coming – Until after the fact, that is. And then everyone was a sage.

"I saw it coming!" I'd hear people say.

"I knew it was going to happen!"

Bullshit! No one saw this one coming because no one ever thinks they're going to be a part of that generation who would endure the greatest collapse in the housing market in the history of the world! That was the kind of thing that happened in the past, to our ancestors; things we read about in history books. Things like that didn't happen to this modern generation. No way! We're too smart.

The problem was, the moving parts of this collapse were obscured from the general public, in the high-rise offices of bankers, investment firms and lawyers, dreaming up those usury interest rates tied to specious indexes, giving a mortgage to anyone alive enough to crawl into a bank with no income verification whatsoever, and all those bogus loans wrapped up into a fiendish investment peddled by Wall Street like a circus pitchman peddling tickets to a freak show!

No. Nobody saw this one coming. We were all sunbathers on the same beach, making sandcastles, watching the low waves softly striking the sandy shore. Except one of those low waves was a tsunami, the bulk of its howling maelstrom hidden beneath the water, turning into a 100ft high, 200mph wall of death upon striking the shore.

The only real sign preceding the disaster was the fact that new construction sales had been dropping steadily in both California and Nevada since early 2006. But everywhere I inquired for answers – shop owners, realtors, the Sacramento Business Journal – all chalked it up to a natural dip in the market, and assured me the cycle would uptick again real soon, in six months, maybe a year, and then housing prices would do a turnaround as they always had, and begin once more their steady climb, ad infinitum!

What was it that everyone told you when you were a kid? You want to get rich? Put your money into real estate! Wasn't that both the white collar and blue collar, *"common sense"* perception on the world and how it worked and how the rich kept the rest of us down because the rich owned land? They owned real estate! And there in that rock, dirt, clay was the power to control one's own destiny!

The third quarter of 2006 was when I started to see a slight drop in sales. Not so much that it worried me. It's just that I did notice it. And it was all coinciding with two events: first was the dip in new home sales in California and Nevada, which literally meant a dip in all sales, because if people weren't out there buying new homes, then they weren't at the home improvement stores buying lawn seed, garden hoses, lawn movers and emergency generators. That meant they weren't at the furniture stores buying new sofas and love seats, end tables and coffee tables, new bedroom sets and tabletop lamps. That meant they weren't at the large retailers in the malls buying new curtains and curtain rods, sheets and blankets, pillows and pillowcases. They weren't at the paint stores buying cans of paint, calling the security companies to have new security systems installed, or visiting the auto malls to find that car that looks just right in their new driveway. Just about every single big-ticket sale in America was driven by new home sales, and they were dropping now.

Second was the resetting interest rate on all those millions upon millions of bogus, indexed loans – those Frankenstein's monsters all popping to life now with the electric bolt of rising interest rates – created by some Wall Street hustler with a penchant for high larceny, and a small cold stone bereft of morality perched in the vacuous cavity where his heart once beat. With property values tanking now, nobody had any equity in their homes anymore. Those with interest rates adjusting upward had to literally borrow off of their own equity lines of credit in order to pay their now outrageously high mortgages, and that was that – hardly a single soul in California or Nevada had any disposable income anymore, and it sent the adult industry, which was already cracking under the stress caused by the World Wide Web, into a slow, barely noticeable, but definite downward death spiral.

It didn't happen overnight but it did happen relatively quickly, over the course of about a year and a half. It all began in Fresno. I had completed that route one day in early 2006, and made only five hundred dollars. I found that quite odd and it troubled me the entire time I was driving home, because that route had always been one of my better ones and it had consistently, over the course of five years, yielded me at least two thousand five hundred dollars and sometimes three thousand dollars each visit. One might say, okay, it wasn't as much as usual but at least five hundred dollars was something. Well, here's the problem with that: Fresno was a four-hour drive from Sacramento. So whenever I went to Fresno, I'd have to fill the van's gas tank up the night before, which was one hundred dollars because the price of gasoline was through the roof. I'd have to leave the house at 4am so I could get there at 8am when my first stop opened, then ten more hours of driving around so I could hit everyone on that route, which was seven retail stores, and then I'd have to fill the tank up again before leaving Fresno which was another hundred dollars.

So, taking into consideration my cost for the goods – I kept about 65% of what I grossed due to the high markup one receives on novelty items – but then turning around and spending two hundred dollars of that on gas, that means out of that five hundred dollars I made that day, I really only kept one hundred twenty-five dollars, and that's for an 18 hour day! Do the math: that's $6.94 an hour. Why would I put in a punishing, 18-hour day like that only to make less than minimum wage? It didn't make any sense. And worst yet, two months later when I went back to Fresno, I came home with zero! That's right! Not a single sale made that day because all the stuff I had sold them four months back, even six months back, was still sitting on their shelves.

None of my stuff was moving because I only carried novelty items and when people are hurting for cash, they can't stop buying the staples – milk, bread, toilet paper, triple-X CDs – so they stop making impulse buys, which is what my novelty items were, like the Hollywood magazines and foot-long candy bars by the cash registers in the grocery stores.

So it was novelty items that had **made me** those first five years after re-tooling my business; it was novelty items that would **destroy me** in my last two. I couldn't afford to gamble on going to Fresno any longer, risking making no sales and losing two hundred dollars in gasoline purchases on top of that; not to mention losing an entire day of sales that might have been made elsewhere. So the entire Fresno route was abandoned, torn out of the pages of my financial dossier, and soon after went the Modesto route; then the Vallejo route, and so on and so forth, until out of the 24 routes I had built up over those first eight years in business, by December of 2007, only nine remained. Having once supplied, at my peak, 160 retailers, I was now down to 60 stores. I had lost 63% of my accounts, but a whopping 80% of my business, because even the accounts I retained had no choice but to pare down on their purchases in order to compensate for their sagging sales.

By January of 2008, my cash flow was down to four thousand dollars per month. Lani had to take that job as a server on the weekends at the **Gold Diggers Club** downtown. The negative cash flow on our investment houses became much worse, because the interest rate on all of our mortgages had just adjusted upwards. The first well in our T-Rex **4-Corners Project** had been drilled. It was dry and had to be capped, and because I had sent that two hundred thousand dollars to Geier Campbell at the beginning of 2007, we had no cash on hand. I couldn't afford to pay our mortgages, not even the mortgage on our primary residence. Not if we were going to buy food and pay our utility bills and make our auto loans.

So I contacted a realtor and put all four of our investment houses up for sale. If we could sell them off, hoping only to break even with home prices falling so precipitously at that time, it would be a large weight off of our backs. But by that time, it was too late. People weren't buying homes in Sacramento at that time. They were abandoning them! And it wasn't unusual at all to see, between late 2007 and early 2008, *for sale* signs in front of every single home, on either side of the street, for blocks and blocks, in the North Natomas section of the city.

I was being suffocated, the air crushed out of my very lungs as if some titanic weight were bearing down on my chest and breadbasket – *hard!* And I had no one to go to for help. So we borrowed up to the limit on our credit cards and exhausted our equity lines of credit and cashed out the small savings we had in the bank set aside for retirement and Theo's college fund, until nothing remained – no more dining at fine restaurants, no more weekends in Las Vegas. Nothing! And Lani and I were abandoned by all of our so-called Sacramento friends like orphans in a flood.

The stress of catastrophic financial collapse, the gasping and thrashing about for air as one is drowning in a sea of debt, is difficult, almost impossible to bear. At times I thought I might not live through it, searching frantically for a solution, feeling as though I were walking through a fog, my head in a vice; at all times I felt certain a stroke or a heart attack was about to end my life any second. But I didn't want that to happen because of Lani and Theo – they needed me. I had only felt such utter oppressiveness, such devastating helplessness and loss, one other time in my life.

It was shortly after the 4th of July, 1990. I hadn't seen Whelan or Becca for two straight months, not since my graduation ceremony in May at SFSU, which they had both attended. Whelan kept the store closed that entire day which was the first time that had ever occurred in the entire 25 years of him owning the place, with the exception, of course, of holidays. He did it for two reasons: first, it was a Friday, and he didn't want me working after the ceremony because, instead, he wanted me to celebrate with Rye, who had made plans for us to rent a limousine and cruise the city that evening looking for women and drinking wildly from the limo's wet bar, which is what we indeed ended up doing, even though I had to pay for it all because Rye didn't have two nickels to rub together. Second, because he himself wasn't feeling well and said he needed to go home to rest after the ceremony. I had asked him if he was going to be alright, and he smiled and said yes, that it was nothing, just an upset stomach.

It was more than just an upset stomach, though. Whelan had missed each of his scheduled shifts for the following two months after that – I was the one who did the schedule now – and I was stuck at the store seven days a week running the place by myself. I was fine with that because, seeing how Whelan was so ill – a cold that had turned into pneumonia, Becca had told me – I wanted to do everything I could to help the both of them out. I called Becca on the phone often to see if Whelan was getting better and to ask if I should come over in the mornings when the store was closed to help out in any way, but she always said no, don't bother, Whelan was going to be alright, he just needed some more rest.

So when I was invited by Becca the week earlier to come over to their house that 4th of July and celebrate with them, I was happy to do so. I was hoping, since she said we'd be celebrating, that it meant Whelan was better now and I was eager to see him in good health and spirits. I also needed an opportunity to let them know, in a subtle and gradual way, of course, not just springing it on them, that I didn't want to work at the store anymore. I wanted a job in finance.

I took a taxi to Sausalito by way of the Golden Gate Bridge. I paid the driver the fare and gave him an additional $20.00 for a tip, it being the holiday.

The neighborhood was a familiar one to me. I had been there many times before. It was quaint and quiet, speckled by colorful stucco homes here and there, low picket fences and green shrubbery. Whelan and Becca lived in a small, single-storied cottage, scuffed-up white with black shutters, tan brick fireplace running up one side, the slanted, ce-dar-shake roof blanched to the color of driftwood over the years by the buffeting gales coming off of the bay. One could see the red tops of the bridge's pylons from their backyard.

I opened the green picket gate and moved toward the house along the familiar, uneven path, lines of smooth moss, rising from between the red bricks of the walkway, softening each step. It was cool out that day, the wind from the bay blowing hard against my back. I could see their black front door was already opened for me, with just the screen-door closed. I opened it and stepped inside into the small living room. It was well lit but there was nobody there, just their old-fashioned, 1950's style furniture – red sofa and chair, two end tables sporting beaded lamps like the 1920's and a heavy, walnut coffee table. The cuckoo clock bird on the wall tweeted 12 noon!

"I heard the screen door," Becca said, moving quickly around the corner from the kitchen. She had on red lipstick, black eyeliner, her dirty blond hair pinned up in an orderly bun. She was wearing a matching brown top and pants, a sweater-like material that fit loosely around her ample body.

"How are you today, sweetheart," she said, reaching up to hug me.

I hugged her back.

"Happy 4th of July," I said.

"Happy 4th of July to you."

We stopped hugging.

"How's Whelan?" I asked.

"Ask him yourself. He's in the back yard relaxing. There's beer out there. Help yourself. The grill's out there too, so make yourself some hamburgers and hot dogs. It's all out there. I'm baking homemade pecan pie. Your favorite."

I hated pecan pie, always had, but she loved making it, so I never had the heart to tell her, and always forced myself to scoff down two or three slices to make her happy.

I smiled at her.

She smiled back and then moved quickly into the kitchen.

I walked through the living room, down the yellow hallway past the two bedrooms in the back of the house, opened the back screen-door and stepped into the back yard.

It was windy and cool outside, but bright. I was glad I had on my jacket. Whelan was sitting on a Cape Cod style chair, white with wide-spaced wooden slats. I could only see the back of his head, but could tell right away that something was wrong.

I approached him slowly along the dry grass, rounding the chair so I could see his face.

"There you are!" he tried to shout, but what came out was weak and hoarse.

He looked two inches from death – unnaturally thin, grey complexion, concave cheeks and elongated, gangly form, nothing like the figure of a boxer he had once cut, and much of his light brown hair was gone, replaced by frizzy, stunted patches of white.

I was in shock, mouth wide open, staring down at him as he sat there in oversized blue pajamas.

"I know!" he shouted, waving his hand then taking a green stocking cap out of his big pajama pocket and using it to cover his head.

I shook my head in disbelief.

"We've been hiding it from you!" he said.

"What's wrong with you?" I asked.

"Prostate cancer," he said. "Got off the meds two weeks ago. Forget about it. I feel great today, though." He slapped his leg and let out a feeble laugh.

"Should have seen me last week," he grinned. "Thanks for taking care of things at the shop."

"All this happened to you in just two months?"

"No – I've been sick for longer than that," he said. "But two months ago, that Monday after your graduation, I started the chemo. I was holding off – didn't want to miss your graduation ceremony."

"How long have you known about the cancer?"

"Six months."

"I wish you had told me."

"Why? Could you do something about it? No! – I didn't want to upset your studies or graduation celebration."

"You shouldn't have held up your chemotherapy for me."

"Why?"

"What if it doesn't work because you held it off for too long?"

"Are you afraid of death, Cree?"

I thought about it for a while then said: "I don't know. I guess I just never think about death."

He folded his blue pajama arms together, his gnarled fingers holding his sagging biceps.

"We all think of death," he said. "The very second you saw me today there was nothing on your mind except death – **my** death! I could see it in your eyes. Don't be afraid of me dying, Cree. It's going to happen, one way or another."

I continued standing there in the golden grass, motionless, staring down at him.

"Stop staring at me like that!" he quipped. "I'm not a zombie. It's still me. Sit down. Have a beer or something."

I sat down slowly on the Cape Cod chair across from him, resting my forearms on the white wooden arms. The sun was in my face and a cool breeze as well, resulting in a sum of nothing: neither warmth nor cold. I put my hand over my eyes to block out the sun and scooted my chair to the right a bit.

"Have a beer," Whelan said, smiling at me.

"I don't feel like it," I said.

"Come on, I want this to be a happy day for us."

"How can it be a happy day when I see you like this and know you put off your chemotherapy for me?"

"You know, I feel great today!" he extolled, extending both hands over his head in a salute to the day. His lose pajama arms slid down exposing his boney arms. He put his arms down and adjusted the pajama sleeves, hiding his arms again.

"Is the chemo going to work?" I asked.

"All we can do is wait and live our lives in the interim," he said. "Now let it go."

"I can't," I said.

He nodded and said: "I'm going to die – maybe not today or next week or next year, but –"

"What happens to the store if you go?" I asked. "Becca never worked a day in there."

"I know," he said, laughing, slapping the arms of his chair. "She hates that place."

He thought silently for a few seconds.

"You can have it when I go if you like," he said. "Besides me, you're the only one who knows how to run the place, deal with the customers, the vendors, make the deposits, stock the shelves."

"I don't want it." I said. "I've graduated. One of these days –" I hesitated.

"Go on," he said, "one of these days what?"

"Well," I began slowly, "I've been meaning to tell you and Becca this and, ah-h-h —"

"What? That you want to do something more meaningful with your life than work at an adult store?"

"I mean, not in those words," I said, "but yeah! I have my B.S. in economics now. I'd like to get into finance. Maybe be a stockbroker or a banker."

He nodded approvingly.

"Becca and I always knew this about you, Cree. We knew you were headed for something bigger. The store is my life! I love that store. It's never made me a whole hell of a lot of money but it has given me and Becca a nice life, a good home and all the comfortable things life has to offer. But just because the store has been *my* life, doesn't mean it has to be yours. We want you to succeed. You can go look for a job in finance any time you like. It will be difficult to find someone to replace you because, as you and I both know well, the hours are a bitch! But Rye is looking for a better job, isn't he?"

"Yes. He's been bouncing around from job to job for years now. He worked at *Bay Gourmet Sandwiches* once as a sandwich maker, at *Woolworth's* as a stocker, *Sully's Diner* as a short order cook. He's working at that big music store on the corner of Powell and Market now, as a sales clerk. All he ever makes is minimum wage. He's broke, too, always bumming money off of me. I don't care, though. He's my friend."

"You start looking for a job in finance, mornings and early afternoons when the store is closed, and talk to Rye next time you see him and ask him if he'd like to work for me once you're gone."

"Great!"

I was smiling now at the thought of it: finally being able to leave that store and find a better job with more accommodating hours, and maybe find a steady girlfriend as well, which I eagerly wanted to do. But my elation quickly turned to deflation again as I continued staring up and down at Whelan's gangly, weakened form, sores all over his hands, face and patchy white head.

"Stop with those horrified looks!" Whelan gripped. "Come on! Don't start up again about me dying. We're in a good place now. You didn't act like this when your mother sent you those letters."

"You mean when my father was dying of lung cancer?"

"That's right," he said, nodding, "And then the one a few years later when she was dying from the same thing."

"Because they didn't mean anything to me," I said.

"Oh, really?" he said, turning his head askew and gazing at me in disbelief. His green eyes looked unnaturally large in his gaunt head, like alien eyes.

"I know your father meant nothing to you, but what about your mother?"

"I hated her," I said.

"What about the postcards?" he asked.

I looked at him, motionless, then folded my hands, resting them in my lap, all the while saying nothing.

"Ah ha!" he sneered. "You thought I had forgotten! It's been so long."

He nodded steadily, staring me straight in the eyes for several seconds.

"I remember, Cree," he began. "It started right when you first began working for me. You told me your parents were dead but you'd go to **Woolworth's** and buy postcards and write messages on them, right there on the counter in the store, and then you'd put a stamp on them and go put them in the mail box outside the store. I said nothing about it for a long time because it was none of my business, but you told me you had no one in your life so I was always curious about who you were sending those darned postcards to. Remember?"

I nodded.

"I remember asking you one day, after you had been with me for about a year, 'Who do you mail them postcards too?' Remember?"

"I remember," I said.

"You didn't want to lie to me anymore because we had grown close, so you told me you were mailing them to your mother, which shocked the hell out of me. I thought she was dead! Remember?"

I nodded.

"But then you told me about your childhood and how your parents had abandoned you and how you couldn't find it in your heart to forgive them, which is why you had told me they were dead, and I understood all that. You didn't want to have to talk about them."

He bit his lower lip, rubbed his left temple with two fingers and squinted at me in a questioning manner.

I looked at him, wondering what he was going to say next.

"Here's my question to you, Cree – You could never find it in your heart to forgive them, but why did you mail them postcards off to your mother all those years?"

I sat there silently, not really knowing where to begin. The matrix of those postcards was complex. So articulating an answer wasn't going to be easy. I knew why I had sent them all those years, stopping only after receiving my mother's letter detailing her lung cancer, failing chemotherapy sessions, asking if I could find it in my heart to fly back to Lynn one last time to see her before it was too late. But I never did. And shortly thereafter, her letters stopped coming.

"The postcards," Whelan said, knocking me out of my reverie.

I looked at him, his alien eyes gazing fixedly at me; inquisitively.

I said nothing.

"Why?" motioned his thin, grey lips.

So I blurted it out.

"At *first* – to be mean," I said, looking straight at him. I then lowered my head and peered at the golden grass because I was ashamed of my answer.

"To be mean?" he said incredulously, shaking his green stocking head. "How is *that* being mean? You're sending postcards! Communicating with her! Telling her where you were! That you were safe and doing well! I don't know about you, but that would make my heart glow if I were your parent and in that situation!"

"That's the traditional view of postcards," I said. "Someone takes a vacation to Hawaii and is happy, wants to transport a packet of that happiness to someone else, so buys a postcard, jots down ' Having a grand time here!' then mails it off to a friend. The friend gets it two, three days later and reverberates with joy, 'Oh! How wonderful! Jane's having a grand time in Hawaii!' It's the linear view."

"Any other way of looking at it other than the linear?" he asked.

"Yes," I said, "the sine wave point of view. The peak of the sine wave brings happiness; the trough brings sorrow. After abandoning me, my mother would periodically for the next ten years send postcards to my grandmother, glossy snippets of San Francisco's skyline, Sunset Beach, the street cars, Fisherman's Wharf, and messages on the reverse in blue ink, my mother's flowing cursive, letting my grandmother know where they were, what they were doing, how much fun they were having in California. They brought a half-smile to my grandmother's face, if that witch could even muster one – my mother was her daughter after all. But never once, not a single time in any of those postcards, did my mother ever ask about me – 'How's Cree?' 'Is he doing well?' 'Will you tell him we say hello?'"

I lowered my head. The memory of it saddened me terribly. But I looked back up at him and went on. I could see that he was sad for me too.

"Not once in ten years did my mother ever ask about me in those postcards. My grandmother would slide them under my bedroom door when I got older. I don't know why she did it – to be cruel, or maybe she genuinely thought I had a right to know about the goings on of my parents; but just seeing those postcards there on the floor of my bedroom would cause the pain of the abandonment to come rushing back into my heart, something I was desperately trying to forget; and then reading them and seeing how she never once inquired as to my health or wellbeing – it just made the sorrow of it that much more difficult to bear. That's why I sent the postcards. I was sending them, hopefully, on the trough of sine wave: hoping in their careful crafting – writing only of *my* good tidings but never once inquiring as to *her* health or wellbeing – that they would affect a similar pain, over my absence, within her heart."

He looked at me in a fatherly fashion, nodding that he understood, and reached over in his chair to touch my shoulder. He could barely reach, so I scooted my chair closer to his so he could accomplish the act.

"I know you live your life on the sine wave," he said comfortingly, patting my shoulder. "You always have, ever since I've know you. You never see things the way other people do. You're unique. I've always liked that about you. It drives most people crazy. Rye can put up with you but that's because you two are exactly alike."

I tried to smile.

Whelan sat back in his chair, adjusted his pajama sleeves down and went on talking:

"Now you said that it was only at *first* that you had sent those postcards for revenge. Did that motive change one day?"

"Yes," I said.

"Why?" he asked.

"I don't know," I said. "It just did. I was in San Francisco, a city I loved, working for you, making money, which made me happy, meeting new people at the store, Rye, you, Becca. And suddenly one day, two or three years into my employment with you, I was jotting down a message on the back of one of my postcards and I didn't feel that hate or anger anymore I had always felt toward my mother. Fact is, I had no feelings for her at *all!* And I almost stopped writing the message and was going to throw the postcard into the trash and be done with it, but I didn't for some reason. I had become accustomed to sending out a postcard to her every three or four months. So I kept writing them and mailing them. And now that I'm thinking about it, I don't even understand why."

"You weren't ready to give up the connection," he said, "just like you're not ready to give up the connection with me."

"I guess so," I said, shrugging.

His thin fingers scratched his concave cheek as he gazed at me thoughtfully.

"You believe you have no feelings for your mother," he continued, "but that's not so. It's just like that geology class you once took in college years ago."

"Geology?"

"Yeah! You took a geology class once, remember?"

"I remember the geology class," I said, "but how does geology help explain my situation with my mother? I would think my psychology text might hold some answers."

I had kept every college textbook I had ever owned. There were a hundred of them, all lining a bookshelf I had in my studio above the store.

"Now who's being linear?" Whelan said. "Just hear me out. You were very excited about that geology class, remember?"

I nodded.

"You'd come to work and tell me all about your professor's lectures, remember?"

"I remember," I said, smiling at the memory.

"What'd you tell me one time about the continents being created, destroyed and created again?"

"The Theory of Plate Tectonics," I said. "The edges of some continents are submerged by the weight of subducting continents into the hot mantle, until the whole continent is melted away. But up comes that melted material again to the surface of the earth at the separating plates, and new layers are created, layer upon layer, until new continents form, in a never ending cycle of creation and destruction."

"Human interactions," he said, "which create memories, are like those layers. They keep building up and up until suddenly a new person forms! That's really why you sent those postcards – you wanted your mother to see the new person you had become, and that's also why you didn't go visit her when she was dying from cancer. You didn't want to take the chance of being submerged and melted again."

"Here are the pies!" Becca sang, stepping into the backyard in her brown sweater-clothing, a pecan pie in each hand. She set them down on the wooden picnic bench beneath the old cork tree, the only tree in their small backyard. I looked over at the picnic bench and at her, standing in the short, golden grass, the thin branches of the dark leafed cork tree overhead. It was all a familiar sight to me, and comforting somehow. Comforting still to see the other items on top of that picnic bench – the old, round grill, red with three aluminum legs, a bag of charcoal, a can of lighter fluid, a plate filed with raw hamburgers and a package of hot dogs.

"Did you two have your talk?" she asked, turning to us.

"Yes," we said simultaneously.

She came rushing toward me so I stood up, and she hugged me.

I hugged her back.

"Sorry," she said. "We had to keep it from you. Didn't want to upset your studies. We've been in denial, too, these past two months.

But things are looking brighter. He's getting better! I've noticed it!"

She was smiling, broadly, her red lipstick and black eyeliner accentuated by the sunlight. She then went back to the picnic bench and began laying out paper plates and plastic utensils. Whelan and I followed her.

I poured coals into the bottom of the grill, sprayed smelly lighter fluid and started a fire. I then got to cooking, placing several raw hamburgers and hot dogs onto the now glowing hot grill. I was standing beside that old cork tree, poking at it every once in a while because the texture felt so unusual. I always poked at that tree when I was in their backyard.

"Stop poking at that tree!" Whelan called out jokingly.

"I have a surprise for you, Cree," Becca said. "I have a third pecan pie in the kitchen all wrapped up for you to bring home latter."

"Thank you," I said, smiling at her.

We forked juicy hamburgers and sizzling hot dogs into soft buns and rolls, topped them with mouthwatering tidbits – shredded lettuce, sliced tomatoes, ketchup, mustard, pickles and diced onions – and eagerly ate, all the while regaling one another with recollections of our past experiences together, laughing and smiling and nodding agreeably. Whelan and I drank imported beers from chilled steins he had retrieved from his freezer, and I forced down three slices of pecan pie, rubbing my stomach and making yummy noises the whole time as Becca looked on approvingly.

It was a bright, sunny, heartwarming – albeit windy – 4th of July: a true celebration of our eleven years together. When late evening arrived, we turned our eyes in the direction of the Golden Gate Bridge, the tops of its two pylons still visible in the clear, night sky because of the bridge's safety lights, and we all marveled at the glorious fireworks extravaganza exploding cacophonously above, all three of us clapping vigorously at the larger, more colorful explosions.

Whelan died a month later. The chemotherapy had not worked and he felt too ill and too exhausted to give radiation treatment a chance. He was buried three days after his death, hastily and unceremoniously, beside some California Pines in a Marin City graveyard, a service attended by only Becca, the priest and myself.

A week after his burial, in the same brown sweater-clothing she had worn that day, Becca, in bare feet, walked from her home in Sausalito to the pedestrian sidewalk of the Golden Gate Bridge, the Marin County side, and jumped to her death.

Chapter Nine

I was up to the city of Pinole now, about three quarters of the way to San Francisco. I could see the Pinole Plaza on my left, with all the retail, fast food and gas station signs sticking way up in the air. Further up the highway on the left, I saw the expansive wooden sound wall on the hill protecting the thousands of homes on the other side from the highway noise. On my right, along San Pablo Bay, were the giant silos that held oil and natural gas, round and white and clunky, all webbed together by a maze of tar covered pipes, meters and giant valves.

The traffic was beginning to bunch up because we were getting closer to the city, but we still moved at 55mph. There was a brown Mercedes Benz ahead of me. The woman driving it had a long, blond ponytail sticking several inches out of the back of her head which dropped straight down, hidden by the neck rest and driver's seat, except for when she would look this way and that, sending the ponytail flinging about.

I leaned sideways, toward the bucket passenger seat, eyes still on the road and, pushing away the closet flap, I reached into the cardboard box with my right hand and pulled out the meat cleaver. It was heavy, about two feet long, all stainless steel including the handle.

I placed the tip of the cleaver on the meaty part of my left hand which still clutched the steering wheel as I drove, and gently pulled. It sliced a thin, now bleeding line between the two rattlesnake puncture wounds, connecting them like a giant letter "I." I was just checking out the sharpness of the instrument. Without a doubt, it was more than capable of getting the job done. It was just going to take some patience and some time.

I carefully placed the cleaver back into the cardboard box and began playing out the scene again on the movie screen in my mind, trying to figure out if I had missed any nuances, any new ways of approaching the problem, of cutting off that whale's head. There I was, out there in the middle of the ocean on a tiny, inflatable boat, right up next to that whale, hacking away like a madman, chunks of black and white skin and blubber, bloody red muscle tissue, veins and tendons, flying everywhere. What if too much tissue filled the boat? It might cause me to overturn into the water. I'd have to be very careful not to let that happen. I'd have to be very careful with that meat cleaver, also, not allowing it to slip, not even once. My hands were sure to be slippery with the dead whale's blood, and if that meat cleaver slipped, it would surely puncture my boat, sending me sinking *fast*!

Also, there were going to be people on the bridge and on the observation platforms on the Marin County side. Most of them would be tourists. I wanted as few of them as possible to notice me. So I had conceived of a plan to distract them. I was going to go to **La Castor Velu**, one of the many adult retailers I had serviced in San Francisco when I still had my business. The owner there, Pelage Trappeur – everyone called him Pelli – was my friend. **La Castor Velu** was the first account I ever had. I was going to ask Pelli if he would give me two female blowup dolls. I would then inflate the dolls using the hand pump I always carried around with me in the van – for inflatable items I had occasionally wholesaled – and then use the nylon rope I had in the cardboard box to hang them from either side of the bridge on the San Francisco side. This would create an odd and amusing distraction for those tourists, drawing at first those closest to the San Francisco side of the span, but the ones further away on the Marin County side, noticing a crowd gathering at the opposite end of the bridge, would soon move closer themselves to see what the hubbub was all about.

This should keep it down to a bare minimum the number of eyeballs on me as I engaged in my fileting endeavor.

Even though it was a good plan, I was still nervous about the impending undertaking because I knew a million things could go wrong, like Gale had said.

I reached down and turned on the radio to take my mind off of things. It was a little past 3pm now and the *Mike and Ike Show* would be on. Mike and Ike were my favorites. They were funny as hell. I was hoping they'd be talking about the whale. That's what everyone else was talking about.

The van had good speakers: the sound came through not crackly at all, but clear.

After several boring commercials, I finally heard Ike's voice.

"Okay! Welcome to the Mike and Ike show. If you're just tuning in, we're talking about that dead killer whale that washed up against the Golden Gate Bridge three days ago, last Tuesday morning."

"That is right, Ike!" exclaimed Mike. "And we have right now in the studio with us on this fabulous Friday afternoon, and it is fabulous out there – have you seen the sun just bursting like a firecracker in that audaciously clear sky out there this afternoon?"

"I have, Mike."

"I'm telling you, Ike," Mike continued, "there's no place better on Earth to live than this oasis called San Francisco. Especially on gorgeous days like this one. But, even here in the beautiful Bay Area, we still have our complications and somewhat unique problems such as this whale and, as I was saying, we have here in the studio with us this afternoon Lieutenant Ajax Papadopoulos of the United States Coast Guard who is going to talk with us about this situation. I'm sure he will most assuredly give us a chronology of what has occurred thus far regarding the conversations between the various private and governmental agencies that are presumably responsible for taking care of this mess, and I'm sure he will share with us the Coast Guard's perspective on why no authority as of yet – and I mean no one! – will take responsibility for the removal of this animal's carcass, a rather gigantic and grotesque carcass which is decaying out there quite vividly before everyone's eyes, especially in this unusually hot weather. I have been told, and by no means do I know this as a fact, but we have had some callers yesterday inform us that if you are walking up there on one of the pedestrian walkways of the bridge on the Marin County side, that the smell, that decaying, rancid, morbid, putrefying omega three fatty acid odor is detectable by the old olfactory sense and is shocking in its offensiveness."

"Yeah, Mike," chimed in Ike, "and I've read some accounts in the Chronicle this morning that aren't too positive with regards to the removal of the carcass happening anytime soon."

"I hear you on that one, Ike. This is a mess. So we'll hear from Lieutenant Papadopoulos a little later in the show. But for right now, we also have in the studio with us today Dr. Waverly Seymour with the California Academy of Sciences here in San Francisco, and she is going to begin our discussion."

"Good afternoon, Dr. Seymour," Mike and Ike said in unison.

"Good afternoon, gentlemen."

"Dr. Seymour," Mike said, "Let's start off with the obvious question, shall we. How is it that this whale, although quite large – how large is it by the way?"

"Approximately 28 feet long, weighing 9 U.S. tons," Dr. Seymour said.

"And was it a male or a female?"

"Male."

"Okay, how is it that this killer whale – although quite large as animals go but still tiny compared to the entire Pacific Basin – how did this particular animal end up getting stuck at the base of one of the Golden Gate Bridge's pylons? I mean, why didn't it just sink unobtrusively, away from the detection of human eyes, into the briny and immeasurable vastness of the open sea? Isn't that what happens to whales and other sea creatures on a daily basis?"

"That's correct," Dr. Seymour said, "but not in this particular scenario. When cetaceans die --"

"Cetaceans?" Ike said questioningly.

"Whales," Mike answered.

"That's correct," Dr. Seymour said. "When whales die, the abundant oils in their blubber sometimes cause them to float for some period of time on the surface of the ocean, until such time as nature's giant predators eat away enough of the blubber to cause the animal to sink. This particular type of Orcinus orca, being a Transient, most definitely died close to shore because it predates the abundant pinnipeds indigenous to California's shoreline."

"Predates pinnipeds?" Ike asked curiously. "What exactly does that mean?"

"Pinniped means fin or flipper-footed," Dr. Seymour said. "They eat the various seals and sea lions that inhabit the beaches all up and down California's coast. Not to mention porpoises and the young of other whale species."

"Oh, got cha!" Ike said. "That's why it died close to shore: the beach is its food plate."

"Indeed," Dr. Seymour said. "It died close to shore and then was picked up by the tidal currents, carried toward the bay and ultimately hit the Golden Gate Bridge where it rests today."

"Is it stuck there permanently?" Mike asked. "I mean, that behemoth carcass has been stranded out there at the base of that pylon for three stinking days now, quivering in the ebb and flow of the high and low tides like a monstrous bowl of black and white gelatin! If the tide can capriciously cause a carcass stranding, can it not also just as capriciously one day carry the sea gull bedeviled leviathan back out into the open sea where it belongs?"

"That's always possible," Dr. Seymour said, "but it hasn't happened now for three days and when I was out there, Dr. Bhattacharya with the U.S. Geological Survey --"

"Wait a second, Dr.," Mike interrupted. "You mean to say you have actually been out there on a boat to visit the animal?"

"That's correct. I was one of three researchers last Tuesday afternoon out on the motor patrol boat *Marine Mammal Watch*. Dr. Hamasaki with the Marine Mammal Center and I were out there to retrieve blood and tissue samples from the carcass, and to examine wear patterns on the cetacean's tooth enamel so we could determine the specimen's approximate age at death. Dr. Bhattacharya was out there to take photographs of the Marin Headland sea cliffs to compare them to past photos of the same areas, attempting to gauge the severity of sedimentary deposition around the edges of the bay caused by transformational shifts."

"Sedimentary deposition," Mike repeated. "You mean he was out there to look at how badly the cliffs are falling apart and filling in the bay due to seismic activity along the San Andreas Fault?"

"That's correct."

"And as a geologist," Mike continued, "what was Dr. Bhattacharya's association with the whale?"

"Dr. Bhattacharya was interested in the orca only as a curiosity. His function that day was separate from ours, acting as surveyor for the U.S. Geological Service. Their west coast offices being in the same building as ours in San Francisco, he saw joining our expedition as an opportunity for him to do his work as well."

"How is the whale actually stuck out there?" Ike asked. "It seems to me that the high tide should have just washed it away by now."

"Dr. Hamasaki and I were asking ourselves the same question on Tuesday because, thoroughly examining the large specimen from the boat, from its broad flukes which were the only part of the specimen fanning back and forth with the tide, and then down the smooth tail to the massive bulge of its saddle patch or upper back, where the dorsal fin lay floating in the water, all the way past its blowhole and down again to its ocular and head region, we could not see any attachment point whatsoever.

Interestingly enough, it was Dr. Bhattacharya who provided us with an answer. He reminded us of the recent seismic activity which had been occurring along the San Andreas Fault, and then pointed out, along the face of the cliff adjacent to the bridge, rather extensive patches of crumbling rock and dirt, devoid of vegetation, and informed us that a loss of vegetation like that could only have been caused by recent avalanches. He then took some depth measurements around the carcass, which confirmed his belief, that those avalanches have created a new and rather heavy sedimentary layer of soil and rocks, the water being only two feet high in some areas around the northern pylon. That's when we realized that our very boat was in danger of going aground if we moved too closely to the head section of the specimen. So we stayed out by the tail. But to answer your question, 'how is the Orcinus stuck out there?' It is grounded out there on that debris; at least the upper half of its body is, resting immobile on its left side, head toward the cliffs, tail in the waterway, its white underbelly being pressed ever harder by the tide against the cement base of the pylon."

"That's incredible!" Mike piped. "So we have geology and biology and seismic activity all paying a role in this poor creature's fate."

"Indeed."

"And the upper half of its body is just stuck out there on the sediments?" Ike asked.

"The entire body is stuck out there," Dr. Seymour said. "The tail, although floating, is still attached to the upper body."

"How deep is the water where the tail floats?" Mike asked.

"Relatively deep," Dr. Seymour said. "The pylon itself rests on the edge of a shelf that drops precipitously down into the deep channel of the inner bay."

"So the creature is not going anywhere anytime soon?"

"That's correct."

"Well," Ike said, "there's going to be a big lightning storm coming through San Francisco early tomorrow morning. They've been forecasting that for two or three days now. If that storm creates large enough swells in the bay, I believe it's possible the whale could be freed that way."

"Yes," Dr. Seymour said. "It is very possible. But it is not necessarily the case that the storm will wash the cetacean's carcass out to sea. It is just as likely it will be beached somewhere along Marin County's shoreline, in the vicinity of the bridge no less, and we will still have our problem of decaying flesh offending those on the bridge's pedestrian walkways."

"What do you think needs to be done about this problem?" Ike asked.

"In my opinion," Dr. Seymour began, "one of the many agencies in the Bay Area responsible for marine safety needs to take a ship out there, not too close so it doesn't get grounded, but send a skiff or a motor boat over to the specimen dragging a towline from the ship, tie a big knot around the orca's tail and tow it out to sea, *way* out so it doesn't get carried back into the bay by another tidal current. This would allow the giant predators, the Great White sharks, to eat away enough of the blubber to cause this Orcinus to sink, allowing seabed organisms, flatfish, crabs, sea worms and others, to do their job of recycling this carcass."

"Aren't these waters filled with Great White sharks, Dr.?" Ike asked.

"Indeed. When we were out on the boat on Tuesday, all three of us, Dr. Hamasaki, Dr. Bhattacharya and I, actually watched as a 15ft Great White bit a chunk of flesh out of the specimen's tail."

"That's amazing!" Ike exclaimed. "That must have been so cool! To actually see that happening in real life."

"Indeed. It was fascinating."

"Why can't the Great Whites just devour the carcass right there where it's stuck?" Ike asked.

"They can get to the tail portion of the specimen only. They have no access to the grounded upper portion of the Orcinus."

"Hey, I have a suggestion," Mike said. "I realize the beast has passed on to a better place now, at peace with the great god of the whales and in whale heaven by now, but we've been calling this misfortunate creature by all kinds of stodgy scientific terms – Orcinus, Transient, specimen, cetacean – so I say we give him a real name now. How about we call him Moby Dick?"

"I'm for that," Ike said. "But let's make it more personal. Moby Dick is too strict."

"Okay," Mike said. "We can call him by merely one of those nomenclatures: either Moby or Dick."

"Let's make it Dick," Ike said.

"Dick it is," Mike agreed.

Dr. Seymour laughed.

"Dr.," Mike began, "if the coming storm's swells do not dislodge Dick off of that sedimentary layer tomorrow, how long do you think it will take before the sea gulls peck that wave wobbling carcass into nothing but a simmering pile of gull turd?"

"Quite long," Dr. Seymour said, "because they only have access to those sections of the tail that the sharks have already ripped open for them. But you must admire them; they continue to work at it diligently."

87

Mike laughed: "Holy cow! On the news last night, it looked like a giant ball of feathers out there around that tail!"

"Let me ask you this, Dr.," Ike began, "I should already know this but, are Killer Whales an endangered species?"

"Some types are. Not this particular specimen."

"No, no, no, Dr.," Mike chided jokingly. "We're calling him Dick, remember."

She laughed. "Okay! Okay! Dick is not endangered but is still protected – as are all whales – by the MMPA, the Marine Mammal Protection Act of 1972."

"But you say some other types are endangered?" Ike asked.

"That's correct."

"What are some of the other types of killer whales out there in the ocean?"

"Well," Dr. Seymour began, "orcas were for a long time considered to be monotypic, or belonging to only one species. However, due to recent genetic studies and morphological evidence, cetacean biologists are now postulating the existence of multiple species or subspecies. For instance, the dwarf forms in Antarctic waters that subsist mainly on squid are distinctly different, both behaviorally and morphologically, from all other orca groups. Here in the eastern Northern Pacific, there are three distinct types or groups: the Resident population, which *are* endangered according to the ESA or Endangered Species Act. They swim around Puget Sound and off of the coasts of both Washington and Oregon, subsisting mainly on salmon. Then there are the Off-shores which reside in deeper water and subsist mainly on fish, but have been seen eating sharks. And we've already discussed the Transient population, Dick's kind, the marine mammal eaters."

"What killed Dick?" Ike asked.

"Pneumonia, our tests conclude. We believe brought on by a weakened immune system due to old age. The wear pattern on Dick's teeth revealed he was approximately 40 years old!"

"Is that old for a whale?" Ike asked

"It varies from individual to individual, sex makes a difference of course, but the typical male orca lives for approximately 30 years, but have been known to live for as long as 50 or 60 years. The average female orca lives to be around 50, but can live for as long as 80 or 90 years."

"So Dick lived to a ripe old age," Mike said.

"That's correct."

"Can we talk about beachings?"

"Yeah," Ike said. "What is it with all these beachings? Why would a whale do that to itself?"

"Indeed," Dr. Seymour said. "More case studies need to be done, of course, but cetacean biologists theorize that when whales are under extreme stress, possibly due to illness, injuries caused by sharks or boat collisions, or are having their biological sonar affected by the artificial sonar of naval ships, this causes them to attempt to alleviate that painful distress by leaving the water. So they beach themselves, maybe believing they can somehow wiggle their way back into the water at a later time; but what ends up happening, outside of the water environment which counteracts to a large extent the force of gravity, their own weight crushes their internal organs and they die."

"That's not a nice visual," Mike said, "crushing your own organs."

"Indeed!"

"Well thank you, Dr. Seymour," Ike said. "It was a pleasure having you on the show. We learned a lot about killer whales today."

"We did!" Mike said. "And next we'll be talking to Lieutenant Ajax Papadopoulos of the United States Coast Guard and find out why, as of yet, no private or governmental agency has offered to tow Dick's dead body out to sea?"

Chapter Ten

I turned down the volume on the radio so the commercials didn't bother me. I was passing through the city of Richmond now, on that section of I-80 that spread out into ten lanes, all five east heading lanes congested in long lines of traffic, like a swarm of ants neatly arrayed within the perforated white highway lines. That geometric community of high-rise apartment buildings – a collage of tan, red and steely-blue bricks – was on my left, rising to various, rectangular heights upon the rusty cliffs above the cement sound wall, now covered in a shaggy coat of emerald ivy.

I passed the San Pablo Dam road exit first, the Hilltop Mall and Auto Plaza exit next. Soon, I could see the familiar Cutting Blvd exit up ahead. Richmond had been one of my best routes when I was still in business and things were going well. There had once been eight adult retailers there and I had serviced all of them. By January 2008, however, only three of those retailers remained, and of those three, none of them would work with me. Ning Lee had personally seen to that.

Ning Lee was Mr. Lee's son. They both lived and worked together in Richmond with their large families. I had never personally seen their estate, only photos on the cork board in their office which Ning loved to point to, showing-off the multiple interconnections of their expansive white mansion, its arched windows, castle doors, the lake-sized swimming pool in the back yard and the savanna of well-kept lawn surrounding it. The office was inside one of their two long warehouses, right by the port on Harbors Way South, just behind the terminal where the giant cargo cranes loaded and unloaded the ships coming in from the western Pacific – China, Japan, Taiwan, Australia, New Zealand.

I remember vividly the first time I had ever met them. It was 18 years earlier, in September of 1990, a few weeks after Becca had taken her own life. It was a series of three interrelated events which caused me to seek a meeting with Mr. Lee. If only I had the foresight back then, those tomorrow gleaning binoculars that are rare, but hanging around the necks of the few business survivors who adapt to change before everyone else does. That way I could have seen the future collision between me and Ning, a collision which unavoidably, like Titanic and the iceberg, would doom one of us to sink.

The first event was Whelan's death. He had left the store and all its contents, including the van, to me in his will. I didn't want the store. But someone had to take care of the loose ends of closing up the shop and getting rid of all the stock, both in the store and in Whelan's large storage unit, which was on 7th Street in San Francisco, right next to the county jail. So I had to hold off my plans of looking for a job in finance until all of that was taken care of.

The second event was a meeting I had with old Mr. Richardson, the owner of the high-rise masonry building on Market Street where *The San Andreas Fault CDs* was located. I hadn't seen him for a long time. He had occasionally dropped by the store to say hello and shoot the breeze with Whelan. But then he stopped doing that about a year, year and a half back. I had phoned him the week prior, asking him to stop by the store so we could discuss my plans to close down the place and a tentative timeline as to how long that might take. I wasn't keeping the store opened any longer either. The door was locked and had an orange CLOSED sign in the window. Rye begged me to keep the place open and to hire him at double the minimum wage so we could work together all day long and have fun. But I didn't want to have fun. I had serious plans for myself. I did come up with an idea, though, seeing as Rye was my best friend and I did want to help him out if I could. I told him that if he could borrow the money from his father in New York, who was a physician with plenty of cash according to Rye, then I'd sell him the place and stay on for several months to train him. But after that I was getting the hell out of there! I told him I felt the store was holding me back

The thing is, I would have just *given* him the place if I could have, but I was going to have to find my own apartment now, an expensive proposition in San Francisco, because there was no way I was going to live in some dive. I had been living in that small studio apartment above the store for eleven years now. It was time for me to move up, to find a place commensurate with the new vocation in finance I imagined for myself. I was going to get myself someplace nice, in a high rise building smack-dab in the middle of the financial district, and it was going to cost! My eight years in college had seriously cut into my savings, and I wasn't even working now. I calculated it was going to take me at least a month to drive around in that van, searching out other adult retailers in the Bay Area who I could approach to see if they wanted to buy the large amount of stock that I had inherited. After that, I calculated it would take me another two or three months to find the job I really wanted, because I wasn't just going to settle for anything. I knew what I wanted. I wanted to be rich! Like Mr. Richardson!

So in order for me to get an apartment, put a deposit down, first month's and last month's rent up front, and then be able to live for the next three or four months without a paycheck, I was either going to need the money that selling the stock was going to provide, or Rye was going to have to buy me out for twenty thousand dollars, which is what we had agreed on. But his father wouldn't loan him the money. Rye wouldn't tell me why. So he asked me if I would let him have the store on just monthly payments. I told him I needed a lump sum of cash if I was going to survive for the next several months without a paycheck. He asked me to please think about it and I said okay. But we both knew what the outcome had to be, and finally, a few days later, it was Rye himself who told me to forget about it, that he had given it a lot of thought and decided he really didn't want the store because he knew the long evening hours, especially on the weekends, would totally put an end to his open-mic night appearances and, although he did for a little while consider giving up his dream of becoming a paid comedian so he could take over the store, he decided he loved comedy too much and had put so many years already into accomplishing his comedic goals, that he was going to stay on the comedy track. I told him he had made a good choice.

I met Mr. Richardson on a Wednesday, August 22, 1990. I waited for him on the sidewalk outside the store at 10am, which was when we had agreed to meet. It was foggy and freezing outside. San Francisco, being a peninsular and surrounded on three sides by unusually deep ocean waters, was plagued by the continuous comingling of both warm and cold tidal currents, casing a Fall-like pall in the spring and summer and an African savanna heat in November and December. The city was a puzzling yet pretty paradox.

There was an old man approaching me along the sidewalk, hunched over and walking with a cane.

"Is that him?" I was thinking to myself. I couldn't tell because he had really aged since the last time I had seen him; his white hair was long, sticking wildly out of the sides of his flannel hat. He was wearing a pair of gray slacks that went way above his ankles. I could clearly see his black socks, old sneakers and a patch of pale leg in between where the pants ended and the socks began. The pants were being held up by suspenders, tight against his white tee shirt, which I could see through his unzipped, pea green army jacket. I almost suspected he was a street person.

"Cree, my boy!" he said excitedly. He still had that deep, authoritative voice I always remembered him having.

He tapped my sneaker with the bottom of his came and chuckled.

"Good to see you again, buck!" He was smiling, with glowing white teeth, tilting his head upwards so he could see my face. He then frowned.

"Sorry about Whelan and let's not discuss the other," he said, shaking his head. "Too sad is all. Fought in both wars. Twenty years old in 1918 at Armistice in France. Seen and heard of some vicious stuff. Doughboys dead, blood and guts splattered all over the place. But to go phut like that and now pushin' up daisies."

He shook his head and continued.

"She was a pretty young thing. Any who-o-o --"

He tapped my sneaker again with the bottom of the cane, somewhat harder this time, and chuckled.

"Let's go inside and talk."

He pointed toward the door.

I unlocked the door and we went inside.

He sat on a black plastic-chair in the rear of the store near the private CD room, the light blue curtain hanging over the door-less entrance.

I carried the padded stool from the front of the store to the back, and sat down a few feet away from him.

"I'm glad you're givin' up the store," he said. "This neighborhood's gentrifying. A better class of people is movin' in so I want to turn this space into a coffee shop or café with seating outdoors."

Mr. Richardson had those tomorrow gleaning binoculars around *his* neck.

"That's a good idea," I said, nodding.

"But I don't like the other things you told me over the phone."

"What's that?" I asked.

"You goin' into stock brokerage or banking."

"Why's that? I have my degree in economics now."

He brushed the air with his hand and turned his head with a disappointed grunt. His pants were really high now because of the slump in the chair, and I could see the lower portion of both his calves, skinny and white.

"Because they're crooks!" he grunted. "Half the stiff shirts you see walkin' down the streets these days are in banking or stock brokerage in this crooked town. They don't last long. There's no money in it. Nothin' in their god damned brief cases except their lunches."

"How do you know?"

He gave me a funny look with his face all wrinkled up. He then adjusted the flannel hat on his head.

"I'm 92 years old," he began. "Been in business for 45 straight years. Ran a used car lot for my brother-in-law after the war in 1945, bought it off of him then sold it at a profit. Used the money to buy some land here in the city back in 1955 then sold that many years later for a leprechaun's pot of gold. Had so much cash, I bought a multi-storied apartment building at the top of the hill on Bush Street. Ran that for many years and got to know and like my tenants, but it didn't matter. When the market was up it was time to sell so I sold. Used the money to buy this high-rise building we're sittin' in. I know how to make money. You told me over the phone last week you wanted to be rich like me. Okay. That's a worthy goal. But I'll tell you this – you ain't ever goin' to be rich workin' for someone else, especially those big companies you're talkin' about, the banks and brokerage firms. Yeah, some of 'em get lucky, but it takes thirty or forty years of bustin' your hump every day of your life with no time left over for family. Family's important, lest your little lesson last week didn't teach you that. You want to wait that long to get rich?"

I shook my head.

"Then you need to start your own business," he said.

I thought about that statement for a while as we looked at one another. Besides putting your money into real estate, that's the other thing that people always told you while you were growing up – *If you want to be rich you have to own your own business.*

"Doing what?" I finally asked.

He shrugged, laying his cane across his lap.

"I have no money," I said.

"You plan on sellin' all this crap, right?" He looked around at all the never used items on the store's shelves.

"Yes," I said. "There's also a 15ft by 15ft storage unit on 7th Street filled from the floor to the ceiling with boxes of brand new items. It all needs to be sold. But I won't sell them retail. I refuse to keep this shop opened any longer, it's holding me back. I want to get rid of it all in one fell swoop! Find one, two, maybe three adult retailers around the city who will buy all of this stuff off of me at wholesale prices. Hell, I'll even sell it below wholesale just to get rid of it!"

"Those are the ones who make the real money!" he chortled, wiping his mouth with the sleeve of his army jacket.

I looked at him curiously and asked: "Who are the ones making the real money?"

"The wholesales!" he snapped. "They buy the crap for pennies off of the importers, mark it up big, and sell it in bulk to all the little retailers who hardly make anything off of the crap."

"Whelan made money," I said. "We always doubled the price we paid the wholesalers."

He laughed at me mockingly as though I were a child, then reached over playfully with his cane and hit the bottom of my sneaker with it.

"Here's the difference, buck," he began, "retailers have all the expenses: monthly rent, CAM, alarm service, employee payroll, maintenance like garbage disposal and window washings, repairs to the plumbing and electrical systems, marketing expenses, insurance coverage in case some damned jackass comes in and decide to slip on the floor. Wholesalers have nothin' but a stinkin' old warehouse they drop ship the crap out of, and maybe not even that because most of 'em just work from home, using their garages as storage units, and they get to deduct that from their god damned taxes every year!"

"It's my dream to get a job in finance," I said.

"Then change your dream!" he snapped. "Your dream stinks!"

He smiled at me with his sparkling white teeth.

I liked Mr. Richardson. He was giving me the straight scoop as he saw it. I liked people who did that. Like Rye. Just say what you have to say and don't keep me guessing.

"I see you have good tooth brushing habits," I said, smiling back.

"I don't! They're store bought." He chortled. "Expensive, too, but smart business folks like me don't worry about money because we always have it. Not like all those panderin', snot-nosed stockbrokers and bankers out there scrappin' out a livin' on a salary."

I was giving serious thought to what he had said because I knew he was a successful businessperson and very wealthy, someone to emulate if I was serious about becoming wealthy myself, which I was.

"So you're suggesting I use the money I make off of selling the stock to open a business?"

He reached over with the cane, tapped the bottom of my sneaker and touched his nose with his forefinger.

"And you say wholesalers make all the money?"

He nodded, slowly, with his eyes closed. The rim of his hat hit the back of the wall and almost fell off. He adjusted it again.

"How do you get into wholesale?" I asked.

He opened his eyes and looked at me.

"You know all the guys who sell you this crap." He pointed all around the store with his cane.

"Wait a second!" I said. "You're telling me to wholesale adult items?"

"It's what you know! Always do somethin' you know."

"I thought it was 'always do something you love.'"

"Bullshit!" he snapped. "Nobody loves anything but frolickin' and only whores make money doin' that! All you need is somethin' you can tolerate. And make time for your family. Lots of time! Your family will give you love. In *time* you might learn to love your business but I never did. I bought, managed and sold. Bought, managed and sold. But I never liked it. It's a pain in the ass because of all the knuckleheads you have to deal with, realtors, bankers, buyers low-ballin' you, trying to steal the property. But it always gave me plenty of family time. I'll be sellin' this building soon."

I sat there quietly, thinking about what he had said. I knew he had a good point. I had been in the adult industry for many years now and knew the products well, what they wholesaled for, what they retailed for. I did have a good relationship with all of our vendors, who drop shipped items to the store after I placed the orders over the phone. We chitchatted all the time and they seemed to like me. I had all of their names and phone numbers. All I needed to do was call them and ask if they'd connect me with the importers from whom they themselves bought items for pennies, as Mr. Richardson had said. But why would they do that and have *me* as competition? I wasn't convinced. It had to be much more difficult to break into the wholesale business than getting the numbers of an importer or two. Also, I did have my degree in economics. I hadn't gone to college all those years for nothing. There had to be a good job out there in the city waiting for me.

"Well!" Mr. Richardson snapped, knocking me out of my reverie. "What'd you get all comatose on me for?"

"I was just thinking," I said.

"About what?"

"About your suggestion of me going into business, but also about me wanting to get into finance. I'm conflicted."

"So the hell isn't everybody else. Let's talk about the timeline for you getting all this crap out of here."

I looked around the store and then back at him.

"I know rent was due on the 15th," I began, "and I haven't paid it, and you say you're not going to charge me as long as I get all of this stuff out of here by August 31st. Is that still the deal?"

"That's still the deal," he said, "and you can continue to stay in the studio upstairs rent free until you find a new place. But make it quick. If I find a commercial tenant for this space, you have to go. Whelan made that studio up there without my permission. That space is supposed to be dedicated storage space for whatever business is operating down here on the first floor."

"No problem," I said. "I'll have everything out of here and in that storage unit on 7th Street by the 31st. I promise."

He gave me a questioning look and said:

"All cleared out, all scrubbed up spic n' span, keys in my hand in just nine days?"

"Yes." I nodded.

He smiled and tapped the bottom of my sneaker with his cane.

"Then I'm not going to charge you for September. Get that pain in the ass Rye to help you out. Does he still come sniffin' around?"

"He's my best friend. He comes here all the time."

"I know, I know," he said, "You're both fine young men but pains in the ass too, the both of you."

I liked Mr. Richardson.

Chapter Eleven

I did just what I said I would: by Friday, August 31st, all of the items were out of that store, into the storage locker on 7th Street, the place was thoroughly cleaned, including mopping the floor, wiping down the glass counter and disinfecting the bathrooms, and the keys were in Mr. Richardson's hands. Rye had helped me on the weekend and on his two days off from the music store, which was Thursday and Friday. In return, I treated him to lunch on those four days at the **Happy Dragon** next door. On the last day, he asked me if I would talk to one of the waitresses there, Feather Fan – cute face, brown eyes, red lips, shiny hair going straight down to the shoulders, black skirt above the knees and silky white blouse, the owner's oldest daughter. He wanted me to try to hook him up with a date. He was too shy to do it himself, even though he knew her well. I knew her well, also. We ate lunch there all the time. I had even gone out on several dates with her when I first started working at **The San Andreas Fault Videos**, but nothing ever came of it because she didn't think her mother and father would approve of the type of business I was in. We had gone out together secretly.

So I spoke to her softly at the cash register while paying the bill, pointing over to Rye who was still sitting at our booth with all the dirty plates and empty soda glasses, him peering back at us nervously as he kept adjusting his wireframe glasses, but she just shook her head with an embarrassed smile.

The next day, Saturday, Rye and I met in front of **Virgin Records** on the corner of Market and Powell Streets. It was his alternating weekend off but he had forgotten to pick up his paycheck that Friday and went inside to get it. I followed him in and looked around at the posters on the walls, poking through the myriad and sundry music CDs in the rectangular racks throughout the store, while he went into the office in the back. We were only in there for a few minutes.

"Got it!" he smiled, holding up a white envelope. He folded it in half, stuck it in the back pocket of his jeans, adjusted his Yankees baseball cap and we left the store. We then walked the noisy streets – honking cars, swooshing buses, squealing breaks, cell phone talkers, pushing walkers, children running, mothers calling, teenagers laughing, a million shoulders passing – and we visited several high-rise apartment buildings in the financial district. It took half the day because all of the apartments I looked at, and some of them were very nice, were very expensive. But I finally found a place on Bush Street.

"This place is rad," Rye said, walking from the living room into the kitchen and opening the cupboard doors above the stove.

"We're running a special," the building manager said. She was standing next to me on the burgundy living room carpet. Her name was Shirley. She was middle-aged, voluptuous, brown hair in a strict bun held tightly together by a pair of bone-white chopsticks, freckly face with thick, black glasses. She was wearing a tightly fitting, navy-blue woman's business suit, stretchy pants and rose blouse beneath the vest.

"No rent for the first month," she sang.

"Sounds great," I said, looking around at the empty space and cream-colored walls.

It was amazingly small. The living room was shaped like a trapezium, just big enough for an I-KEA sized sofa and chair, a surfboard coffee table and a small TV. The kitchen to the right was walk-the-plank narrow. It had an overhanging, green-tiled counter top that could fit chairs or barstools underneath, so I didn't need a table. There was a stainless steel sink, a green electric stove, dishwasher, microwave and green refrigerator. The linoleum floor was light green squares. There was a shoebox of a bedroom off of the living room, only big enough for a twin bed and one nightstand, with a folding-doors closet. The angled far wall of the living room, when the red curtains were flung open, had two sliding glass doors that led outside onto a catwalk balcony. Rye stood out there with me, both of us holding tight to the metal railing, the wind funneling fast through the high-sided corridor of buildings running along both sides of the street. It messed up our hair. We were on the 13th floor, the traffic muted and appearing as a parade of bugs way below us. Off to the right, there was a partial view of the city's skyline. All and all the place was cramped, but clean and acceptable, especially due to the rent: only eight hundred dollars per month.

"I'd like to have the place," I said.

"Right on!" Rye chimed.

"Are you working?" Shirley asked. "Because I'll have to do a background check."

"I am working," I said. I lied to her, but had a story all worked out already. Mr. Richardson had anticipated me being asked that question, so he gave me his cell phone number and told me to tell anyone who wanted to do a background check to call him, and he'd say that he had just hired me to be his new building manager and, even though I hadn't received a paycheck yet because my new employment didn't begin until Tuesday, that he would verbally confirm my salary as being thirty thousand dollars a year.

"What's the name and phone number of your new employer?" Shirley asked.

I told her and she wrote it all down on the application on the clipboard she was holding.

"You can call Mr. Richardson today," I said, "if you want to expedite the process. He's working right now over at his building on Market Street. He always answers his phone, even on weekends."

Shirley looked up at me and tapped the black arm of her glasses with the pen she was holding. Her chopsticks looked like TV antennas.

"Have you seen other apartments today?" she asked.

"Many," I said. "I filled out applications for them all and told the managers the same thing I told you about expediting the process, but they all said they'd wait until Tuesday after the holiday."

All of that was a lie as well. I hadn't filled out a single application because all of the apartments I had seen so far were way too expensive for me.

"I think I **will** expedite the process!" she said emphatically. "This apartment is difficult to lease out because it's so small. I'd hate to lose you."

She walked to the kitchen, which only took about three steps, and placed the clipboard and the pen down on the green-tiled counter top. She then pulled a cell phone out of her pants pocket and began dialing while looking down at the clipboard.

Rye and I went out onto the balcony again and held on to the railing.

The wind whistled.

I listened and could hear Shirley saying hello and then talking, asking questions about me. It lasted for about five minutes and then she called for me.

"Did Mr. Richardson give you the clean scoop?" I asked, stepping back inside onto the burgundy carpet.

Rye walked up to the side of me.

She nodded, smiling, holding the pen and the clipboard in front of her.

"Now, if you want the key today," she began, "you'll have to give me a check for two thousand four-hundred dollars. That's first month's rent, last month's rent and a security deposit."

"No problem," I said. "I have my checkbook right here."

I tapped the back pocket of my blue jeans.

"Let's go downstairs to my office to complete the process," Shirley said.

We left the apartment and headed down the red-carpeted hallway for the elevator.

The following day, Sunday, I hired a guy I knew, John Alder, one of Rye's roommates. For thirty dollars, he helped us carry all of my furniture out of the studio, down the two flights of stairs, out the front door of the clean but now empty store space, and into the back of my van. It took several trips, all morning and afternoon, but we finally got the last load onto the elevator and into my new apartment.

"Nice place," John said when we were finished.

He and Rye were sitting on my square-patterned, beige and brown sofa which was up against the long wall in the living room, and I was sitting in the matching chair against the smaller wall by the front door. I looked around the place just to get a feel for it. It was tighter than hell with all the furniture in there. I'd have to get used to it, though. It was all I could afford. But at least I was in the Financial District and not back in the Tenderloin where Rye lived.

"It's small but okay for one person," John said, looking around. He had his right arm extended over the back of the sofa and he used the fingers of his left hand as a comb to try and fix up his hair; he had gone onto the balcony earlier.

"I wish I could afford to live here," Rye said. He had his Yankee's cap on the black coffee table in front of him.

John reached for the channel changer on the coffee table and turned on the TV. Channel 10 News flashed on the screen.

"Shit," he complained, "it's 5 o'clock. I have to go. I'm using the money you gave me today to take Lisa out to the **Happy Dragon** for Chinese food."

Lisa was his girlfriend. She lived in the same building as him and Rye but in a different four-bedroom apartment with five other women as roommates.

He turned off the TV.

I turned to Rye.

"Are you up for Chinese food again?"

He shook his head.

"Why?" I asked.

Silence for a few seconds – then, while putting his cap on his head he said: "Feather Fan."

"Okay, we'll go to the **Leaning Tower** and have pizza," I said.

Rye smiled and told a joke:

"What did the hungry female porno star holding a casserole dish say to the arsonist holding his giant torch in his hand?"

John and I both shrugged.

"Come on baby light my fire."

We left the apartment and I locked the door.

"What's the rent by the way?" John asked in the hallway beside the elevator.

"Eight hundred dollars per month."

He let out a loud whistle to let me know he thought that amount was steep.

"You're not even working," he said. "You'd better get to selling that stuff."

The elevator dinged and the door opened.

"I better," I said.

The next day was Labor Day. I did nothing but relax in my new apartment all day watching TV. But the following day, Tuesday, I had to walk fifteen city blocks all the way from my apartment to Mr. Richardson's building, because it was impossible to find street parking at my new place. Mr. Richardson said I could keep parking on the paved area behind his building for now – and he wasn't charging me anything, either – but when a new commercial tenant moved in, if they required all of that space back there for parking their own vehicles, I'd have to find someplace else to park the van.

I drove the van to 7th Street, passing the county jail and going under the highway overpass. I then reached the long, grey-cinderblock building where all the storage units were. Turning left onto the driveway, I stopped in front of the electronic gate opener, rolled down my driver's side window, reached my left hand out and typed the numeric passcode out on the key pad. The gate opened suddenly with a jerk, and then slowly rolled all the way open. I drove down the driveway into the big cordoned off courtyard, surrounded on all sides by cinderblock walls and a myriad of orange, rollup doors. The security gate closed behind me. I stopped in front of my unit, *212* in large black letters on the orange door.

I got out of the van and walked across the courtyard to the office. Inside, Krill, the manager, was sitting behind the white counter watching some show on a small screen TV.

"Doe-bray-ootra," he said, rolling the "r", in his deep, Russian accent. He then turned down the volume on the TV.

"Good morning, Krill."

His real name was Kirill Kolar. He had long, unkempt hair, blondish-brown, and a goatee of the same color. He was wearing a pair of grey sweatpants and a grey sweatshirt with the arms ripped off. He was a big guy, too, the same height as me, 6ft, but muscular. Not weight lifting muscular either, just naturally thick arms and a thick neck. He had a mean looking face, with one long scar running straight down the left cheek; another one running through his right eyebrow at an angle, up to the middle of his furrowed forehead. I never asked him how he had gotten them, even though I had known him now for many years. I figured it was best to just leave some things alone. Hidden histories, revealed, had a way of stirring people up.

He stood up, walked towards me, and set the bottoms of his large hands on the countertop.

"You have Septembra rent check?" he said, rolling the "r" in September.

"I do."

I passed him one of my own personal checks written out for two hundred dollars.

He took it with both hands, looked it over and looked back at me questioningly, his damaged right eyebrow all furrowed.

"What's this? No San Andreas Fault check?"

"I have some bad news for you. Whelan passed away last month."

"Wheleen go away?"

"No. He died."

He nodded and then asked: "What from?"

"Prostate cancer."

He made a clicking sound with his tongue and cheek.

"It is too bad. Cancer –"

He looked up at me and said: "We should close account."

"Not yet," I said. "I have to sell all that stock in there first, and there's a lot of it. I don't have any place else to take it."

"We close account, reopen in your name – very simple."

"But then I'll need to sign a minimum 3 month term with you and I think I'll have all of this stuff sold in a month."

"Okay, okay," he said, nodding. "I give you to Octobra" – again he rolled the "r" – "Then I have no choice. I must close the account."

"No problem, Krill. I'm driving around the city today to see if I can find some buyers."

We shook hands.

"See you later," I said, heading to the door.

"Dos-Vah-danya."

I opened the lock on *212* with my key and rolled the orange door up all the way with a loud clang! Sunlight poured into the storage locker and I could see all of the cardboard boxes in there piled up on top of each other. There was one passageway through the middle of the two great piles, and a passageway on either end of the two great piles.

It took me exactly two hours to go through the various boxes, the ones I needed to rummage through, to make sure I had one representative of all of the different types of products the store once carried. I also pulled out all of the paperwork from the plastic pockets on the top flap of those boxes, which detailed the types of items contained in each box, their quantity and the wholesale price Whelan had paid for them.

I piled the actual product onto the ribbed floor in the back of the van and threw the paperwork onto the passenger bucket seat. I then rolled down the clanging orange door, locked it, and drove off in the van. It was 10am, bright and cold outside because of the wind.

I knew the section of the city where tons of adult retailers were, just east of Chinatown. I headed there. When I got to Broadway, I pulled up next to the first XXX Adult retailer that I saw – *La Castor Velu*.

The entire curb of the sidewalk, for as far as the eye could see in both directions, was painted yellow: freight loading and unloading only. I was there as a vendor, I said to myself, and I was driving a van with stock in the back. I figured that gave me some time.

La Castor Velu had no windows, just brightly painted red bricks stretching half-a-block, a gigantic marquee filled on both sides with large black XXX's and the coarse, humorous names of the movies they were peddling, and one narrow glass entrance with brown paper covering it lest Puritan eyes, unintentionally peering into the Devil's furnace, have their retinas singed and cleansed, revealing the enlightening, glorious truth!

I opened the door and stepped inside.

It was dark. So I held the door open and looked around. It was vast: half a football stadium lined with rows of white wire racks filled with Adult CDs; the entire wall in the rear of the store, maybe 70 or 80 feet long, dedicated to the most colorful and mesmerizing collage of both straight and gay porno magazines; long glass counters, rectangular and clean, skirting the edges in various places, filled with all sundry of sexual gadgets and toys, lotions and gels in gleaming bottles on top; there was a big wooden crate, the size of a dumpster, in the very center of the floor, filled in a gigantic heap with blowup dolls of every color, all deflated and neatly folded into convenient square boxes for hiding in a brown paper bag and carrying covertly to one's car.

I was impressed.

"Close the door."

I heard a French accent.

I looked to the left at the winding corridor of velvet barrier ropes strung across silver stanchions, that lead customers first to the cash registers and then through the rectangular theft detectors prior to leading them to the door. Behind the glass counter beyond the velvet barrier of ropes, there was a man sitting behind a large, electronic cash register. He had short, grey hair, finely trimmed beard and moustache, was wearing a sporty, black leather jacket with a blue-white-red oval patch across the right breast that said Viva La France!

"Allez-y," he said, in an even tone. "Close the door or get out."

I let the door close behind me. I then walked through the maze of long and twisting velvet ropes, trying to reach him. It seemed to take forever and I felt like an idiot because he and I were the only ones in the store.

"Good morning," I said, placing my hands on the glass counter top, close to the back of the register.

"Bon jour."

He was very calm, sitting on a stool with his hands folded in the lap of his brown slacks, looking down at me curiously. The floor on his side of the counter was elevated. He had blue eyes.

"I worked for Whelan Kearney for eleven years at *The San Andreas Fault CDs*," I said.

"Voila!" he exclaimed, jumping from the stool to his feet, pressing his legs against the counter and leaning over so he could get a better look at me. He wagged his finger at me, smiling. "I knew I recognized you!"

"You've seen me before?" I asked.

"In this industry" – his accent made it sound like he had said '*in dust tree*' – "we spy on one another all of the time."

He thrust his index finger into the air.

"I've been to Whelan's store many, many times," he continued, "in a baseball cap and sunglasses, of course, to see what kinds of items he was carrying on the shelves, to see if he had found anything new, exciting. I haven't gone for about a year now but I recognize you. Hard worker. It's difficult to find good help in this industry. Everyone's either a sex addict, flunky or drug fiend. They steal, I fire them, help wanted ads in the newspapers all of the time. Mon dieu!"

He threw his hands into the air then reached out to shake my hand.

"Pelage Trappeur," he said. "But do call me Pelli."

I shook his hand.

"Cree Quinn," I said.

He looked down at me thoughtfully while rubbing the bottom of his steely beard.

"It would be magnifique to have someone like you working here."

He stretched out both hands as though to hug me, then crossed his arms.

"But Whelan will not allow it I suppose. But what brings you here?"

"Whelan passed away not quite a month back, near the beginning of August, and **The San Andreas Fault CDs** is closed now and out of business."

His blue eyes popped out their sockets and his jaw hung low. He held out his hands and began gesticulating wildly.

"La raison?" He shook his head. "How?"

"Prostate cancer," I said.

"Le cancer prostate!" he said sorrowfully, looking at me and shaking his head. "This is bad news indeed. Too much fatty, fried food in this country, cholesterol, lipids, causing the cancer, the heart attacks."

He used all ten of his fingers to poke the chest of his leather jacket.

"Me too!" he exclaimed passionately. "I am on the high blood pressure pills, two a day each morning with my orange juice. C'est la vies. But what of his wife?"

"A week after he was buried, she jumped off of the Golden Gate Bridge."

His mouth swung opened and he covered it with the palms of both hands.

We both stood across the counter from one another, motionless and silent for several seconds.

He finally took his hands away from his mouth.

"I did not hear this news." He shook his head. "Shocking. I am so busy here at the store, working all of the time, sometimes 12 hour days, 7 days a week. I must be vigilant because the workers steal and the customers steal and the vendors steal. This is something that just got by me. Mais je suis desole. I am sorry for the loss."

"Thank you," I said.

"But why is the store closed? Did Whelan not leave it to anyone?"

"He left it to me," I said.

"And why have you closed it? Not to be insensitive at all, it is better for me that you did close this store because there is too much competition in this town, but you had a gift handed to you. A business of your own! It is the only way to get rich in this world. This is why I left Paris thirty years ago to come here when I was a young man, to start a business. Don't you want to be rich someday?"

"It's my dream."

"Then you need to own your own business, and you had one handed to you on a silver platter."

"Look," I began, "working at the store was fine while I was in college. I needed the money. But I've graduated now and I felt the store was holding me back. I have other plans for myself. And you're not the only person to tell me that I need to start a business. I'm giving that idea a lot of thought. But there's no way it's going to be an adult retail store, working my ass off every single day of the week, all hours of the day and night for the rest of my life – no free time, no fun, no parties, no women."

He poked the air with his index finger and smiled at me.

"Ah ha! It is the women you did it for."

"That had something to do with it too," I agreed. "I would like to find somebody who is right for me and get into a serious relationship. That store was a relationship killer!"

"Okay," he said, nodding in agreement. "But now that you have closed the store, what have you done with the left over stock?"

"That's the reason I came here to see you today. Will you come outside to my van so I can show you the items I'm trying to sell?"

There was no one in the store besides us, so we both walked outside and he locked the front door.

I quickly checked my windshield to see if I had a ticket.

I did not.

"Thank God!" I said to myself.

I then opened the back doors of the van and showed him the items sprawled all over the ribbed floor.

We were out there together at the back of the van for about ten minutes. He picked up some of the items and held them up, turning them over in his hands. A meter maid pulled up to us in her little golf cart and told me I had been parked there for thirty minutes, and needed to leave or get a ticket. So Pelli said I could park on his small parking pad at the rear of the store, which I did.

While I was moving the van, Pelli unlocked his front door again and moved to the rear of the store to unlatch the backdoor deadbolt, letting me in that way. We then returned to the places we had originally been, him on the elevated floor behind the front counter and me on the customer side of the counter with my hands resting near the back of the cash register.

I had brought the stack of paperwork in with me this time, the yellow invoices listing the various names of the items, their quantity and wholesale price. It took me about twenty minutes, using a calculator that Pelli had on his counter, to add up what Whelan had paid for all of that stock. The final tally: eighty thousand dollars.

I thought that was a lot so I whistled incredulously.

"No, monsieur," Pelli said, shaking his head and gesticulating with his hand. "You believe it to be a lot of stock, but it is not. You would be surprised how quickly items move in here. Look at the size of this store. I have thousands of customers roaming through here on a weekly basis and I have empty shelf spaces all of the time. I am just too busy watching my employees and the customers. I often times simply forget to reorder stock. That would be a great business for you right there, Cree."

"What would be a great business for me?"

He stood motionless, gazing into my eyes, mouth wide open and face all a glow with the intuition that he had hit upon a great idea.

"You, Cree," he began, still gesticulating, "driving around in that van with the back all filled with stock. You could provide a personalized wholesaling experience, visiting all of the adult retailers in the area and filling their empty shelf spaces. You come into the store, do the inventory yourself, get the product from your van, you tear the bags and boxes open, you price the product and you stock it on the shelves. You do it all for us so we can focus on running our businesses. There is no one doing that at present. We have to phone in our orders, and the drop shippers, they add a shipping charge, which we have no choice but to pass on to the consumer. If you could somehow get in with an importer, even if your prices were a bit higher than the big wholesalers, I would buy from you for this type of personalized service and I am positif other retailers would do the same."

He was looking at me and I was looking back at him. It did seem like a good idea. If no one else was doing it, then I'd be the first. It was always a good thing to be the first. And I liked the idea of making a living by driving around all day. Sitting in one place bored the hell out of me. I don't know how I had ever made it through those eleven years with Whelan.

"It does sound like a great idea," I said.

"A magnifique idea," he said. "Do you have the money to get started?"

"That depends," I replied. "How much of my stock are you going to buy and how much are you willing to give me for it?"

"How about I purchase all of it?"

I looked at him incredulously.

"All of it? You want to buy all of it?"

"Yes," he said, "if the price is right. I could use it no doubt. My shelves get low after the weekends."

"Well," I began, "what do you think is a good price? I mean, Whelan paid eighty thousand dollars for it all, so it definitely has a retail value of at least one hundred sixty thousand dollars."

"So what do you want for all of it, Cree? You tell me they are all brand new items still in boxes. So maybe the quality is not an issue, and my need for the items is not an issue, just the price you are going to charge me."

"Will you give me half what Whelan paid? Forty thousand dollars."

He smiled at me, reached down and placed a hand on my shoulder.

"Yes," he said. "I will give you forty thousand dollars for it all. That is a fair price. I will have to drive to the storage unit on 7th Street with you before I give you the check so I can verify the condition of the items. Is that acceptable?"

"Yes," I said.

We shook hands.

"We will go to the storage locker together this afternoon," he said, "when my night manager comes in. He is the only one I trust around here."

He tilted his head and gave me a serious look.

"Cree, I think you should consider carefully this idea of being a personalized wholesaler. It is a money maker, I think very much so."

I nodded.

"I am thinking about it," I said. "I think I'll make a few phone calls tomorrow to some of the wholesalers Whelan and I once worked with."

He laughed at me.

"Do not waste your time talking to wholesalers," he said. "They will not assist you."

Reaching into the draw beneath the cash register, he pulled out the heavy San Francisco Bay Area Yellow Pages, plopping it onto the counter in front of him. He then flipped through the pages, quickly at first, then more slowly, scrolling down each page with his index finger, until finally finding what he was looking for. He then spun the book around with one deft movement of his hand. The opened book was right in front of me now. Pelli was pointing to one of the smaller, square, black print ads.

"There is an importer right there," he said, tapping the page. "I do not know this gentleman personally but I know of him. He will not sell product to me because I am a retailer. He only sells to wholesalers who guarantee they can move large amounts of his imports, and he has these wholesalers sign monthly purchase agreements with him specifying how many pallets of stock they are willing to buy on a monthly basis, and that determines your price point – the more pallets you purchase from him each month, the lower your price point. He is one of the biggest dealers in adult products on the entire west coast of the U.S. My drop shippers speak very highly of him because he is honest."

I looked down at the ad that Pelli's finger was pointing to, and I read it: **Lee Industries – Imports and Exports**, 212A-212B Harbour Way South, Richmond, CA, and then a phone number.

Pelli ripped the entire page out of the phone book and handed it to me.

"Give Mr. Lee a call," he said.

The yellow page crinkled in my hand as I grabbed it. I then held it close to my eyes so I could read it again. 212A-212B – The same number as the storage locker on 7th Street. Was it fate? Just a coincidence probably, I said to myself. I was also concerned. I didn't like at all the idea of having to sign an agreement with someone to move X number of pallets of stock each month. He would have to put me on some type of a startup program, give me a little time to drive around and open some more accounts before I signed any agreement. Otherwise I wasn't going to do it. I couldn't waste the forty thousand dollars I was getting. I had monthly rental payments I was responsible for now. I did honestly believe that both Pelli and Mr. Richardson were correct, that if I really wanted to be rich, I needed to start my own business, but it had to be done right, and slowly.

I guess Pelli saw the lock of concern on my face.

"You are just calling to speak with him, my friend."

He placed his hand on my shoulder again.

"You are not making a commitment yet. That will come later if the terms are tres bon – favorable. Everything begins with words. It has been that way from the beginning."

And there it was: the third and final event that caused me to seek a meeting with Mr. Lee.

Chapter Twelve

I was in Berkeley now, passing the exit to University Avenue. Traffic was still heavy but moving. On my right, above the cardboard box and through the van's passenger window, I could see the smooth water of Berkeley Aquatic Park. Beyond that was the wrinkled deep blue of the bay. It was beginning to get cooler now because I was in the greater Metropolitan area, surrounded by the ocean and the bay, where the deep waters brought cold tidal currents. So I turned off the air-conditioner. I also turned up the volume on the radio because the commercials were over and Mike and Ike were back on the air.

"Okay, we're back," Ike said, his voice coming loud and clear through the radio's speakers. "We're going to be speaking with Lieutenant Ajax Papadopoulos of the United States Coast Guard this hour. How are you today, Lieutenant Papadopoulos?"

"Just fine," he said with a deep voice, "happy to be here."

"Lieutenant Papadopoulos," Mike began, "we have on the symbolic weaving loom a fabric with a pattern that is turning out to be not quite as geometric as the consumer would like, but rather an unusual cross webbing – a sticky wicket, as the English would say – where all of the agencies whom the public perceives might have a hand in the picking up of this turd and disposing of it, are pointing fingers at one another, accusing the other guy of being responsible for the dirty task --"

He paused, then came a refreshing exhalation as though he had taken a quick drink of some liquid.

"And for those of you just joining us," Mike began again, "we have been talking at length today about the dead killer whale that has washed up against the base of the Golden Gate Bridge's northern pylon, the Marin County side pylon. We had with us last hour Dr. Waverly Seymour with the California Academy of Sciences, who had visited the whale's carcass in a boat with some other scientists to retrieve blood and tissue samples, and she reports that the animal, who we have named Dick by the way, with Dr. Seymour's tacit approval I might add, is grounded out there on a new sedimentary layer of rock and soil caused by recent seismic and then subsequent rock slide or avalanche activity. She says that someone, some agency responsible for marine safety, needs to tie a rope around Dick's tail and tow him far out to sea, from whence the fallen fauna floated, in order that nature might commence in the decomposition of the body. Otherwise this beastly Dick is just going to jiggle out there in the open oceanic currents for god knows how long. Is the Coast Guard going to get involved in this situation, Lieutenant?"

"The Coast Guard is and *has* been involved in this situation from the very beginning," Lieutenant Papadopoulos said. "It was our cutter the U.S.S. Ohlone that first spotted the floating carcass last Tuesday, July 17, at approximately 6:45am. The initial report had it floating one mile west of Seal Rocks, the tidal current carrying it at a speed of approximately 3 knots in a northeastern trajectory. Therefore we were able to predict an imminent beaching that day of sometime between 8am and 8:30am, projecting it to occur somewhere between the Kirby Cove Campground and Battery Spencer on the Marin County coast, just west of the Golden Gate Bridge."

"That's interesting," Mike said. "So the Coast Guard sees the carcass a mile offshore more than an hour before it strikes the bridge?"

"According to the report, yes," Lieutenant Papadopoulos said.

"Couldn't the U.S.S. Ohlone have done anything to prevent its stranding? Maybe blast it into a million pieces with machine gun fire or rockets?"

"The Ohlone had to follow orders. The crew was given orders to reconnaissance and report only."

"I see," Mike said. "So the Ohlone is following this thing for an hour and a half, basically, and the crew actually watches as it strikes the bridge."

"According to the report."

"What happened next?"

"After the carcass struck the cement base of the northern pylon at approximately 8:15am that morning, five radio contacts were made: first to the Coast Guard holding station at Treasure Island, where the stranding was reported to Captain Kofi Fredericks, the facility commander, with a request put in that a response boat be dispatched due to possible safety and commerce concerns; second and third to both the San Francisco County Sheriff's Marine Patrol, and the Marin County Sheriff's Marine Services, informing both of those law enforcement agencies of a possible marine hazard. The fourth and fifth radio contacts were made to both the Marine Mammal Center and the California Academy of Sciences, relating to those organizations the stranding of the whale and its exact location. A sixth contact was made via telephone to the Golden Gate Transit Authority, who operate and maintain the bridge, with Captain Fredericks personally informing them of the event. So as you can see, we headed up this effort."

"Without a doubt," Ike said, "the Coast Guard has responded quickly and professionally to this situation. My hat's off to you guys."

"We believe we have responded appropriately to this situation," Lieutenant Papadopoulos said.

"But are you going to tow Dick's carcass out to sea?" Mike asked. "And if not, who is? It can't just stay there stinking up the place. Aren't all those seagulls creating a hazard to oceanic commerce?"

There was a pause.

"Let me start by saying this," Lieutenant Papadopoulos began. "Our primary obligation, the Coast Guard's mission, is to protect the maritime economy and environment and to save those in peril on the sea. We accomplished that mission through our initial reconnaissance effort and our subsequent communiques to the appropriate authorities as to the location of the stranding."

"Okay," Mike said, "let me put it another way. If the Coast Guard chose to, could it not take on the responsibility of towing Dick's body out to sea?"

"Several things at issue here. Could we take on the responsibility if we chose to? Of course, but we don't believe we should. Here's why. And I want go all the way back to nineteen years ago, way before I ever joined the Coast Guard. Captain Fredericks, who is an outstanding commander by the way, and has worked his way up through the ranks for the past thirty years, over half of his career spent right here in the Bay Area, told me this story and he asked me to bring it up today on your show. Back in the Fall of 1988, when he was an Ensign at the San Francisco Air Station, he informed me that an eighty-ton blue whale washed up on the beach here at Fort Funston. Do you guys remember that incident?"

"I don't," Ike said. "I moved to this radio station from station 102.7FM in Seattle back in 1998, so that was ten years before my time here."

"I remember it!" Mike said. "That thing was something like seventy-two feet long. It was a monster compared to Dick. The Coast Guard back then said they were going to tow it out to sea, but then changed their mind because they thought it might damage their boat."

"That's right," Lieutenant Papadopoulos said. "That's the number one reason we don't want to tow Dick out to sea — we don't want to damage any of our boats. Secondly, we would like to remain consistent in our response to any such beaching in the future. This job is better handled by a tugboat which is specifically designed to haul large, heavy objects through the water. The third reason we don't want to do it is because it would be a distraction from our primary mission. It's really the Golden Gate Transit's responsibility to take care of this problem. They are the authority responsible for maintaining and repairing the bridge, and the northern pylon is a part of the bridge's superstructure."

"That's a good point," Ike said.

"That is a good point," Mike agreed. "But Pricilla Pan with Channel 10 News spoke to the folks at Golden Gate Transit on Wednesday, and here is what their public relations officer, Cleary Muddy, had to say. I have the transcript right here in my hand. Mr. Muddy said that their organization was responsible for maintaining only the actual bridge itself, and he gave examples: the cables, roadway, sidewalks, tollbooths, suicide barriers, the pylons right down to the bottom of the seafloor. The whale, he said, was not actually attached to the bridge in any way, just its stomach pressed hard against the base of the pylon. While that might constitute a partial obligation on the part of his organization, they certainly weren't responsible for the tail section of the animal, which floated freely in the water. That part of the animal, according to Mr. Muddy, was the Marin County Sherriff's Marine Services responsibility. 'We're not going down there with a chainsaw to cut that thing in half,' he said. 'When Marin County removes the section of the whale that they're responsible for, well, both halves are connected, so they might as well just get rid of the entire thing while they're at it.'"

Both Ike and Lieutenant Papadopoulos laughed.

"It's amusing!" Mike agreed. "And it gets better. Later on that same day, Channel 10 News drove over to the Marin County Sherriff's Maine Services office in Sausalito and interviewed the director over there, Captain Mince. I have *that* transcript in my hand as well. Here's what he had to say:

"'Imagine being in a helicopter hovering over the Golden gate Bridge.'"

"What?" Ike interrupted.

"Hear the man out," Mike said. "I know it starts off surreal but Captain Mince was trying to make a complicated point through the use of a visual device. Anyway, let's start again. Captain Mince said, 'Imagine being in a helicopter hovering over the Golden Gate Bridge. The bridge itself constitutes a border, a line of demarcation. Everything on the bay side of that line, including one mile off of Marin County's shore on the *inner* side of the bay, is the responsibility of the Marin County Sherriff's Marine Services division. Everything on the other side of that line constitutes Open Ocean, which is patrolled by the San Francisco County Sherriff's Marine Patrol. Therefore *they* are the agency responsible for removing the carcass.' He went on to say that, 'Had the whale floated just another twenty more feet, and got stuck against the opposite side of that same pylon, the inner bay side, then his agency would have been responsible for its removal. But since it was stuck against the open ocean side of that pylon, they had nothing to do with it.'"

"Amazing!" Ike said, laughing loudly

"We do have a situation here," Lieutenant Papadopoulos agreed.

"It gets better," Mike said. "Yesterday, Pricilla Pan interviewed Captain Addle with the San Francisco County Sherriff's Marine Patrol, and here's what *he* had to say:

"'Although it is the responsibility of this law enforcement agency to patrol the shore along the open ocean side of Marine County, we are not responsible for any cleanup efforts, which is what this situation constitutes. The carcass is not in any way affecting the deep section of the waterway below the bridge, where cargo vessels traverse, posing no threat to commerce. Therefore,' he went on to say, 'the problem really was one of ascetics, not safety. Since no law enforcement agency concerned itself with ascetics, the responsibility for the removal of the whale rested primarily with the California Coastal Commission, since it was their stated mission to protect, conserve, restore and maintain the beauty of the bay for future generations.'"

"Wow!" Ike exclaimed. "Captain Addle throws a whole new player into the game."

"Do you agree with Captain Addle, Lieutenant?" Mike asked. "Is the California Coastal Commission responsible for the removal of Dick?"

"I can't comment on that," Lieutenant Papadopoulos said. "I can only comment on what Captain Fredericks had briefed me on. The California Coastal Commission never came up in my briefing."

"Well," Mike continued, "I called the office of the California Coastal Commission downtown prior to the show. They didn't want to be quoted officially and asked me not to use any names, but here's what the individual I spoke to had to say. She told me that *absolutely* they were concerned with the ascetics of the bay but only in the form of land rights issues. For instance, if you, Ike, wanted to set up a fishery somewhere along Treasure Island, they wouldn't allow you to do that because it would be an eyesore. If big oil wanted to erect some more storage tanks along Richmond's shore, they wouldn't allow that for the same reason. The killer whale issue was a natural phenomenon, she told me, and would be dealt with by nature, and she mentioned the lightning storm that's going to be coming through San Francisco early tomorrow morning. I told her, 'Yeah, the storm might just free the beast from its position against the pylon's base, but that didn't guarantee it would wash the carcass out to sea. It was just as likely to be carried into the bay and get beached on one of the many beaches skirting the bay.' She said a beaching wasn't the concern of the California Coastal Commission, but was more than likely the jurisdiction of the United States Coast Guard, who should preemptively tow the carcass out to sea to *prevent* any beaching."

"So we're back to square one," Ike said.

"Back to square one," Mike parroted, "with no less than five different agencies – the U.S. Coast Guard, the San Francisco County Sherriff's Marine Patrol, the Marin County Sherriff's Marine Services, Golden Gate Transit and the California Coastal Commission all denying responsibility for the removal of Dick's carcass. Not to pass aspersions on you, Lieutenant, because I know you have nothing to do with it, your superiors make the decisions."

"We've fulfilled our portion of the responsibility," Lieutenant Papadopoulos said.

"Well," Ike said, "The Coast Guard has done a hell of a lot more about the situation than anybody else. Thanks for being on the show with us today."

"Yes, Lieutenant," Mike said, "we really appreciate your time today and our hat's off to everyone in the United States Coast Guard."

"Thanks, guys."

I turned off the radio.

I was in Emeryville now and making that fast, twisting right turn on the larger-than-life hot wheels portion of I-80, being funneled in the direction of the Bay Bridge. The myriad tollbooths to get onto the bridge, way up ahead, were clogged with thousands of vehicles, idling, humming, revving, honking. It was going to take me another hour to get over that bridge, then another 20 minutes to get to *La Castor Velu*, who knows how long chatting with Pelli in order to get those two blowup dolls I needed, and finally another half an hour, with city traffic, to get to the Golden Gate Bridge.

I looked at the clock on the dashboard.

It was 2pm.

I wouldn't get to that whale until after 4pm – only 12 hours until the storm.

Traffic moved slowly.

I was in the far right lane close to the water.

The bay was black and glassy in parts, blue and choppy in others, with low rolling swells the length of school buses splashing hard against the gravely grey shore.

Through the passenger side window I could see across the entire five miles of the bay's eastern shore, all the way to the giant white cargo cranes at the Port of Richmond, which looked one inch high from where I was on the Bay Bridge onramp, and the tiny yellow rectangles behind them that were the warehouses.

Two days after getting my forty thousand dollar check from Pelli for all that stock I had inherited, and depositing it into my checking account, I called Mr. Lee and introduced myself to him over the phone. After telling him why I was calling, he said he didn't usually take on a guy like me to be a wholesale distributor because I didn't have an established territory, but because of my eleven years in the adult industry, which gave me an expert understanding of the products that Mr. Lee primarily imported, and the fact that I had told him about Pelli, how he had envisioned a new type of personal, wholesale delivery concept for the adult industry with *La Castor Velu* being my first account, he said I could stop by the warehouse and we could at least discuss the possibility some more. The meeting was set up for Monday, September 10th, 1990.

Getting to Mr. Lee's warehouses was simple. I was still living in San Francisco at the time so I took the Bay Bridge east all the way to Richmond, around the cloverleaf at the Cutting Blvd exit, west down Cutting Blvd past the John F. Kennedy High School and the Martin Luther King Jr. Memorial Park, then left onto Harbour Way South.

I parked on the expansive, graveled lot in front of the two warehouses. *212A* was to my left and *212B* was to my right. The buildings weren't very high, maybe a little over 25ft at the peak of their slanted roofs, but they were wide and long like zeppelin hangers at some airport, built on cement slabs with corrugated, metal siding, the color of weathered mustard. I got out of the van and walked toward *212A* where Mr. Lee had told me the office was located.

Gravel crunched with each step.

It was cold out.

Winds from the bay whipped my left side.

It was noisy, too. Men in black boots and jeans, each wearing a beat up canvas jacket with round union patches on the chest and arms, were standing at the docks not far away, shouting obscenities at one another. It was mainly a mass of mumbles, but I made out some sentences:

"Get that rope, idiot!"

"Marvin, you ass!"

"Where the f – is Jimmy with that f-ing fork truck?"

Chains clanking, wheels rolling, men running, the wind howling – all the while the monster cranes ceaselessly loading and unloading the various cargo ships that were lashed tightly, by gigantic ropes, to the slips of the pier.

There were two swinging glass doors. I pushed open the one with **212A** in black letters on it, and stepped inside.

The door closed behind me.

The smell hit me first: lavender incense.

The lighting was low. It took a few seconds for my eyes to adjust.

It wasn't really an office, just a big squared off area surrounded by industrial racks – grey, metal and high – their shelves overflowing with an array of adult toys. Through the openings in the back of the racks, I could see the rest of the warehouse, a monstrous maze of the same type of racks, their shelves, too, an avalanche of cardboard boxes, filled, ostensibly, with sexy things. A veritable sexual haven!

"I am Mrs. Lee."

There was a woman standing up behind the only desk at the rear of the squared-off area. She was short, somewhat plump, raven black hair which was obviously dyed because the woman looked ancient, all wrinkly with large age spots on her hands and face. She had her diminutive hand held out toward me. I moved closer to her and we shook hands. She had a calming smile. She wore no makeup. Her clothing was simple but neat, a beige sweater and brown slacks. Her simple slip-on shoes were black with a green, lotus flower pattern.

"Are you Cree?" she asked softly. She continued smiling at me with her head askance.

"Yes," I said. For some reason I felt very calm, as though I might lie down on the cement floor and take a nap.

"Mr. Lee is in the warehouse," she said. "I will get him. Wait here."

Her opened hand motioned to a wobbly coffee table with two beat-up, old wooden chairs around it.

I went and sat down.

I looked around at the products on the industrial racks. It was all the same type of stuff I had sold all those years at *The San Andreas Fault CDs*. I thought way back to *Naughty's*, the place in Boston my buddy Badley had taken me to when I was 14 years old. I hadn't thought about that for a while. It made me smile. I wonder what had happened to old Badley.

A man turned a corner and stepped into the room. He moved quickly and determinedly toward the coffee table. He was short, maybe 5ft at most, not heavily built but rugged looking as one who has worked hard his whole life might appear. He was old, with greying hair, black shoes, black slacks, white-collared shirt buttoned up to the neck and rolled up sleeves, no tie. He was smiling at me.

"I am Mr. Lee."

He held out his gnarled hand.

I stood up, but still had the nagging urge to lie down and take a nap.

"I'm Cree Quinn."

We shook hands.

His small frame was deceiving: he had a powerful grip like a vice.

Mrs. Lee was back behind her desk now, doing paperwork.

Mr. Lee and I stood across the coffee table from one another. To our left, on the middle shelf of an industrial rack, were several small bowls of fruit and a burning incense, smoke curling at an angle, skyward, with a picture of a Buddha taped to the wall behind the shelf.

"I have been thinking," Mr. Lee began, "of what you told me over the phone last week. This idea of yours – a mobile wholesaler giving personal service, not just drop shipping but visiting the stores, opening the boxes, pricing the items, filling the empty shelves for the owners so they can focus on other issues –"

He was looking up at me, his scrutinizing brown eyes searching my face for the truth. He began nodding.

Smoke wafted between us.

"Yes," he said. "It is a good idea. You need a niche in order to break into the market. That niche must be something that everybody needs in order for you to stay in business, otherwise you disappear. *Lee Industries* will not disappear. It is my family who own the factories in Hong Kong who make these products. That is where they are shipped from."

He motioned his opened hand around the room, toward the racks and the products. He then continued:

"My father sent me here long ago to handle the distribution in America. That was 53 years ago. My father came here with me and stayed for one year, with my uncles back in Hong Kong in charge of the manufacturing process until his return. He joined the Chinese-American Club here, whose members helped us find suitable warehouses and assisted with the paperwork required by the state and federal offices here in Richmond. My father then found me a wife and we have been married now for 52 years."

We both turned to Mrs. Lee behind her desk. She did not look up at us, but continued working, writing things down on a piece of paper, but she was smiling that confident smile that all women have, knowing that men can't live without them.

Mr. Lee turned back to me.

"Do you have a wife, Cree?"

"No."

He let out a disappointed grunt and looked at me incredulously.

"How old are you?"

"29 years old," I said.

He laughed, smiling at me.

"You are getting old, Cree. Start looking."

He gave me a friendly pat on the arm.

Mrs. Lee peered up at me from behind her desk, smiling, and then went back to her work.

"I am looking," I said, smiling back.

He searched my face, intently, one last time, and suddenly all of the muscles in his body relaxed simultaneously.

"You are a good man," he said, nodding. "Okay then –"

He motioned with his opened hand toward the inner parts of the warehouse.

"Come with me," he said. "I will show you around. You will see my prices. Very low. No one can beat my prices. I also need you to come up with a business plan. I need to know how you are going to get more accounts. *La Castor Velu* is a good start because it is a very big store, in one of the very best locations in San Francisco, and Mr. Pelli over there requires lots and lots of items on a weekly basis, but you are going to need a whole lot more accounts if you are going to move the amount of stock that I want you to move."

"Mr. Lee –" I began. I had my hands folded in front of me. I was a bit nervous.

He was looking at me curiously.

I went on:

"I've been told you have your wholesalers sign an agreement with you to move a certain number of pallets of stock each month."

"Do not worry about that right now," he said. "You will have to buy a lot of stock off of me up front if you want me to grant you wholesaler status, and yes, eventually you will have to sign an agreement with me, what I call a volume commitment, pledging to move a certain number of pallets each month in order to maintain your wholesaler status. I require this of all my wholesalers because this is the only way I know how much stock to have shipped to me on a monthly basis from Hong Kong. But after your initial purchase, I will not ask you to sign a volume commitment for about one year. That will give you enough time to open plenty more accounts."

He gave me a serious look.

"If you work hard, Cree, you will succeed. If you are lazy, you will fail. Understand?"

"Yes," I said.

"Good. Now come into the warehouse and let me show you what I have. I will help you with your business plan. I know what you need to do in order to get new accounts and be successful. You will need to be on the computer every evening when you get home, searching for the addresses of adult retailers. Not only in San Francisco and the Metropolitan area here, but everywhere you can drive to in a day. And every morning you need to be on the road going to visit those places, speaking with the owners and managers, letting them know that you will be visiting them each week, month, or every two months – whenever they need you to be there – letting them know about the personal service you will be offering. You will have to invoice them. That means they have 30 days to pay you, because that is what all the drop shippers offer, so you must offer the same. So it will be a long time before the money starts coming in, especially because you only have one account right now, and it will take much time to build up more accounts, because the owners might not trust you on your first visit. You might have to make two or three visits before they see that you are honest and intend on keeping your word about visiting them on a consistent basis. Consistency is the key word. Without consistency, there will be no trust. If they do not trust you, you fail. I hope you have enough money to rely on while you're getting this business started." He gave me a questioning look.

"I have some money saved," I said. "It's definitely enough to get me started."

"Good. And your van – does it have shelving?"

"No. But it's an extended Chevy cargo van. It will hold a lot of stock. I can just pile it all in the back."

"No," he said. "You will install shelving with draws in the back of your van. Lots of draws! You will mark the draws and you will store the same items in the same draws at all times. This way, if an owner says they need five of a certain item, you know exactly what draw to look in and you don't spend fifteen minutes searching through a big pile looking for it. You must be organized. Do you understand me?"

"Yes."

"Being organized is the only way. Or it takes you too much time to service shops and you do not see as many customers in a day as you need to, and then you fail because you cannot move your stock fast enough. Do you understand me?"

"Yes."

"Good. You have much to learn, Cree. But do not worry. I will teach you."

I spent three hours there with Mr. Lee that day. We walked through his warehouse and he showed me the many items his family members in Hong Kong manufactured. They weren't just adult products, either. They manufactured all kinds of things like toys, games, key chains and locksmith supplies. Mr. Lee also imported items from non-family members as well, manufacturers from all over the world who made things like women's and men's clothing, sneakers, shoes, purses, cosmetics and jewelry. The non-family items were stored in the other warehouse, 212B.

We talked extensively about my business plan, going over and over again the work ethic he expected from me and the things I needed to do in order to be successful. He told me it would be simpler for me to begin my business by offering stores only a few items at first, the staple items that all adult retailers required, such as triple-X cds which came prepackaged, a variety of the latest titles in a box of 12; porno magazines, which also came prepackaged, a variety of the latest straight or gay issues in a bundled package of 24; and a few of the sexual toys such as dildos and blowup dolls. That way I could at least get my foot in the door with these retailers and then introduce new items to them on a later date, as my business grew.

He asked me where I had gotten the money I was going to rely on to get my new wholesale business up and running. So I told him about me having sold all that stock the week prior to Pelli. The story made him upset and he chided me, loudly, right there in front of his employees, who were working all around us, as though I were a naive son of his. He claimed I had allowed Pelli to rip me off, accepting forty thousand dollars for items that should have wholesaled for eighty thousand dollars. He told me never to undercut his pricing ever again. The retailer, he said, once they purchased the item from the wholesaler, could set the price at whatever they wanted to for the customer, because retail pricing was different for each store depending on many factors such as location, clientele and business expenses. But the wholesale prices of his items were set by him, Mr. Lee, and all of his wholesalers had to agree to that; he would not have one of his wholesalers undercutting another. It was bad for business.

I apologized.

He said it was okay this time because I didn't know.

As he continued with his tour, I looked around at all of the people working there. There were both men and women, all of Asian descent, of various ages, some of them looking quite young, either stacking boxes onto shelves or unloading boxes from shelves and piling those boxes onto pallets; others would then tightly stretch-wrap together the piles of boxes on those pallets, and finally one person would use a battery operated dolly to move the pallets to the back of the warehouse. There were five separate truck depots in a neat, rectangular pattern along the back wall. One of the depots was opened with a truck backed up to it. There was a middle-aged man on an orange fork truck back there, red and black squared flannel shirt, unbuttoned, black tee shirt beneath, working gloves, loading the stretch-wrapped, stacked pallets onto the truck.

We were approaching two workers, a man and a woman, who were stacking boxes onto a high shelf. The woman looked at me and smiled. The man totally ignored me.

"Hi," she said shyly as we got near. She was young, maybe 25 years old, with long black hair and a smooth complexion, wearing loosely fitting jeans and a red sweater.

"Hi," I said.

Mr. Lee said something to her in Chinese and she quickly went back to work.

"That is my granddaughter, Creamette," he said, after we had passed them. "The young man working next to her is her brother, my grandson, Tyco."

"Oh, really," I said.

"Yes, Cree —"

He motioned his opened hand all around the warehouse.

"*All* of these people you see working here are my family." He said it with a smile, obviously proud of his gargantuan effort at procreation.

He continued:

"These are my and Mrs. Lee's sons, daughters, sons-in-laws, daughter-in-laws and grandchildren."

I was actually kind of amazed.

"All of them?" I asked.

"All of them."

"How many of them are there?" I asked.

"Eleven of us here," he said, "which includes me and Mrs. Lee, and 8 over at the warehouse next door."

"That's 19 people in total!" I said.

"Yes."

He stopped walking, looked around the warehouse and pointed to the man on the fork truck.

"That is my second son," he said. "His name is Gang. It means 'strong.'"

He then pointed to a middle-aged woman carrying a box down the aisle adjacent to us. She was wearing a white sweatshirt, a pair of tan, farmer's overalls with one of the straps undone and hanging down her side, and she had a green and black kerchief around her head.

"That's one of my daughters. Her name is Lan. It means 'orchid.'"

"That's amazing," I said.

We stood there together silently, in just about the very center of the warehouse, industrial racks filled with boxes and loose product all around us, and Mr. Lee's family members working diligently, rushing here and there.

"This is our life," Mr. Lee finally said.

He gave me a long and serious look, his brown eyes peering straight into mine.

"Family," he said. "They are the only people in this world you can ever truly trust. Remember that, Cree."

"I will," I said.

I bought twenty thousand dollars' worth of items from him that day, large quantities of the few items he was starting me out with. He told me what to sell each item for and told me the items should gross me somewhere around twenty five thousand to twenty six thousand dollars, netting me somewhere around four thousand dollars after deducting my costs, such as what I had paid for the products, an estimation of monthly expenses such as gasoline and vehicle repair, and the free items I would initially have to give owners and managers in order to get in on their good sides and have them start trusting me. I asked him why my return was so low and he told me it was the nature of the particular items I was purchasing; I was purchasing staple items, products the adult retailers required the most because they were the items most sought after by the consumers. Because all of the retailers required these items all wholesalers carried them, and were forced to keep their markups low on these items or lose the retailers they serviced to other wholesalers. But I would always make at least some money if I stuck to the staples, he told me, and if I worked hard and opened up hundreds of accounts, organizing the accounts into efficient routes, eventually hiring employees to help me run those routes, I would eventually prosper and become wealthy through bulk sales.

"I will ship your purchases to you at this address," Mr. Lee said in the office. He was holding up the piece of paper upon which I had written down the address of the storage locker on 7th Street in San Francisco. I had paid Krill for the whole month of September so I didn't need to put it into my name until the following October.

"That's right," I said.

We were sitting at the wooden chairs across the coffee table from one another.

"I will not charge you a shipping charge," he said, writing something down in Chinese on my invoice. "But the stock will not arrive for about a week."

He looked up at me with the ink pen between his left fingers.

"While you are waiting for the stock to arrive, you need to go to a hardware store and buy a large, thick piece of plywood. Cut it with a saw so that it will fit around your wheel wells, and make sure it is big enough so that this one piece covers the entire floor in the back of the van. Just one piece you use. Do you understand?"

"Why?" I asked.

"Just listen!" he snapped. "I will tell you why soon and you will know."

Mrs. Lee smiled behind the desk as she toiled away at her paper-work. A new incense had been lit and the smoke curled into the air and filled the room with the sleepy lavender.

"After you get the wooden floor down, go buy some cabinets with draws, as many as you can fit back there. Okay?"

I nodded.

"Make sure you secure those cabinets by screwing them into the wooden floor. Use many screws to do this. When you go out on the road, you do not want to run out of stock. So you have to bring as much product with you as you can each day. So you will fill those draws up! Do you hear me?"

I nodded again.

"Those cabinets will be heavy filled with all that stock. One of these days you will be driving and need to stop short; maybe a dog runs in front of your van or the light turns red. If those cabinets are not secured to the floor, they will come flying to the front of the van and crush you to death! Do you hear me?"

"Okay," I said. "I understand now. The plywood floor is for safe-ty."

"Make sure to do it," he said, wagging the ink pen at me.

"I will."

Mrs. Lee smiled again.

A middle-aged man, appearing in his fifties, opened the front door and walked into the office. He was average height, trim, had short, neatly combed hair. He was wearing a grey herringbone jacket and matching slacks, shiny shoes, white collared shirt and orange tie with square pattern.

He moved fast, walking right up to Mrs. Lee, stopping in front of her desk and talking to her in Chinese. His voice was raised and it sounded like he was upset. I watched the interaction as Mrs. Lee spoke back with an even louder voice than his, obviously agitated, dismissing him with a derisive wave of her hand.

He brushed his hand back at her then walked towards Mr. Lee and me.

He spoke to Mr. Lee in Chinese in the same loud, agitated manner with which he had accosted Mrs. Lee. Mr. Lee ignored him and continued with my paperwork. The man looked at me, gave me an indifferent nod and disappeared into the warehouse.

"That is my oldest son, Ning," Mr. Lee said, still writing Chinese characters on my paperwork. "He is angry because we do not do things the way he wants us to."

He looked up at me and smiled.

"Ning thinks we are old fashioned."

He laughed loudly, looking over at Mrs. Lee, who also began laughing.

"He is probably right," Mr. Lee said, turning back to my paperwork, writing furiously with the ink pen. "When I am gone from this world, Ning will be in charge of this place, and then he can run things the way he sees fit. But not until."

Chapter Thirteen

"Five dollars," the tollbooth collector said loudly, over a concussion of idling engines and wheels coming to a grinding halt along the gritty roadway. He was overweight, in a light blue uniform, holding his hand out the window of the booth. I could only see his upper torso. He had those yellow, spongy plugs in her ears.

"What you drivin'?" he yelled.

"A Chevy cargo van," I shouted back.

"How many axles?"

"Two!"

"Okay, that's right, five dollars then."

I passed him a five, rolled up the window and, when the light turned green, drove through the booth into a jumble of cars, all of us jockeying fast for the five funneling lanes heading for the long ribbon of roadway of the Bay Bridge.

I was still in the far right lane on the upper section of the bridge. Way below me was the water of the bay, passing me by like a wrinkled blue canvas.

Traffic was moving now. The tollbooths had sieved us out into a flowing juice like whole tomatoes crushed in a caldron. The afternoon sun, a white ball angled high in the sky ahead of me, began straining my eyes unless I tilted my head in a certain direction.

The clock on the dashboard read 2:45pm.

The Bay Bridge had two spans: the boxy meat-and-potatoes span that traversed the 2.25 miles from Oakland to Yerba Buena Island in the very center of the bay, and then the elegantly arched suspension span that traversed the remaining 2.25 miles from the island into San Francisco.

Because the traffic always flowed well on the meat-and-potatoes span, I arrived relatively quickly at Yerba Buena Tunnel, which cut through the cliffs of the island, connecting both spans. I was happy to be there because the sun was no longer glaring in my eyes. The light inside the tunnel was always an unusual hue, a greenish-yellow mist, as though all bridge users were actually guinea pigs undergoing some type of government radiation therapy.

I passed beneath the Treasure Island exit sign that hung from the tiled ceiling above, swooshing along the level roadway of the tunnel until arriving into the sunlight once more. The towering silver pylons that held up the Bay Bridge's elegant span were in my sights now, along with the vertical weave of grey cables, all hanging neatly from the main cables above. The elegant span arched so high above the water, it was frightening to look down. It was like one of those carnival rides when you were a little kid, the ones the big kids rode that shot way up into the sky and did gigantic looping circles, spinning upside down, so you couldn't take your glasses or keys on the thing, and women couldn't take their purses, or you'd lose everything, and you'd beg your mother to let you on the thing, and she'd say no, but you'd bug the crap out her through persistent whining, so she'd final break down and let you on, and then you'd practically shit your pants halfway through the ride, clutching that metal bar locked across your lap like death: that's how high above the water the elegant span went. The elegant span had a problem, too. It was where all the traffic started bunching up again.

We flowed like cold honey in a narrow tube; nothing but long, viscous lines of cars struggling to squeeze uphill, to the peak of the arched roadway, and slowly dripping like tree sap onto the other side and out of sight.

I reached over and placed my right wrist on the edge of the cardboard box which was still sitting on the bucket passenger seat beside me. I used the tips of my fingers to push the opened flap down. It rose again, so I pushed it down again, and then again, trying to distract myself. I wasn't there yet, but the whale approached. I wanted to do it. Was eager to do it and get it done and over with. I needed that one hundred thousand dollars. It wasn't often one got the chance to earn that much money in a single *pop!* The anxiety of anticipation was like a vice, squeezing my head. I was tight with tension, like an over-twisted guitar string, conflicting feelings of excitement and fear upsetting my stomach, like Malachi's prediction of a great and dreadful day!

I needed a better distraction.

I turned my attention to the city ahead, which I could clearly see through the right side of the windshield – its lovely vista, a cubist canvass of stone, metal and glass, all a glow now with the afternoon sun.

San Francisco had a unique skyline. All cities do, I suppose, but I loved the city of San Francisco. It was the place that had harbored me after my self-imposed exile from Lynn and my parents; the city that nurtured me as I developed into a new person, a better person, layer by layer, like a new continent forming from a divergent plate boundary as Whelan had said. So the sight of the city filled me with those feelings of joy, contentedness and a ting of sorrow, that going home always inspired within one, even though I hadn't lived there for seven years now; it was the only city on earth that did that to me, and in that way came the skyline's personal uniqueness for *me*. There just weren't enough words in the English language I guess. I use the word unique to describe a skyline, when really I needed a word to describe my feelings. The city's skyline was an emotional-blender, each and every building there, just about, inspiring a personal memory of the past.

The San Francisco Ferry building with its ornate columns and giant clocks was always the first structure in the city that caught my attention. Lani and I had gone there often, mainly to dine at the seafood restaurant on the first floor. It had many large windows looking out onto the bay and it was beautiful to see the Bay Bridge all lit up at night. It was where we had our first date.

The cylindrical glass high-rise at 101 California Street was next. That was where all the big stock brokerage firms were located. It always glowed elegantly like a fashionable diamond in the afternoon sun. It was where I had almost gone eighteen years earlier, before getting into wholesale distribution, to apply for a job as a stockbroker.

The Transamerica Pyramid, with its triangular top, was the tallest building in the city, and located in Chinatown. Lani and I had gone to Chinatown many times on the weekends to look around at the odd and touristy items in the countless gift shops and boutiques there, and to have lunch at one of the many authentic Chinese restaurants there.

The buildings I thought to be the most artistic of all in the city were the four Embarcadero towers; delicate, windowed wafers in a rect-angular stack, rising into the sky like ancient fossil silt deposits now risen out of the earth, ready to be split open to reveal their hidden treasures. They always reminded me of my very first day in the city, twenty-nine years earlier, because it was where the oil company repre-sentative I had hitched a ride with from Sacramento had dropped me off. Those ten years that Lani and I had lived together in San Francisco, we had gone to the Embarcadero Center countless times to shop at the mall there, eat at the various restaurants, and have fun during the holiday season, ice skating on the big rink they'd set up each October through January on the stone plaza by the disjointed ductwork water fountain.

My two favorite buildings of all in the city, however, were, in sec-ond place, the high-rise masonry building on Market Street that Mr. Richardson had once owned; he had sold the building fifteen years ear-lier and then passed away two years after that. Seeing that building was always very emotional for me, reminding me of my eleven long years of working with Whelan at the store; fond memoirs of Becca and their home in Sausalito; and my college years. Those bad things happened, of course, but I lived in the interstices, in the good memories between the bad ones. The bad memories had perforations. I could tear them off and throw them away. Not really. It was more like throwing them into a deep and black reservoir I kept in the furthest recesses of my memory, and then leaving them alone for as long as I could. The reservoir was there, and I occasionally fished it, but not often. And I refused to eat the fish I caught there. It was the only way for me. Otherwise, I'd go mad.

My undisputedly most favorite building of all in the entire city was the old Flood Building in the retail district downtown. Not because the building was historical and 1800's looking. Not because of all the stores, restaurants and bars in the area making it a magnet for thousands of tourists and denizens alike at all hours of the day and night. Not because the cable car ride started outside in the front of the building, with its circular, railroad-track turnaround in the brick plaza. Not because of all the street performers who gave their funny-juggling-mime shows there in the plaza. All of those things helped to make that part of the city an extremely exciting and dynamic place. The reason the Flood Building was my favorite was because there was a very special club there. It was called **Biting the Hand That Feeds You**, or **Bites** for short, and it was where I had met Lani for the very first time.

"I need a drink," Rye said.

We were in my apartment on Bush Street, killing time until it was late enough for us to go out bar hopping. Rye didn't have any gigs scheduled for the evening and I had finished my Sacramento route early that day.

I was sitting on the chair in the living room, my left leg over the chair's arm. Rye was on the sofa, his Yankees cap on the coffee table. We were watching the 5 o'clock news on Channel 10. Firefighters from all over California, Nevada, Oregon, and the Naval Air Station in Alameda, had just gotten that big fire in Oakland under control on Wednesday, and the news people had just given a tally of the number of buildings – single family homes, condos and apartment buildings alike – that had burned to the ground: 3,791. I thought they'd never get that fire out. I thought the whole state was going up that year.

The last story before the news ended was Pricilla Pan reporting from the county jail. A man had been arrested for jumping into one of the enclosures at the San Francisco Zoo, who then chased the zebras around for twenty minutes. He said he had done it for fun. He was also high on crystal meth.

It was Friday, October 25, 1991. Over a year had gone by since my first meeting with Mr. Lee. I had been on the Internet every single day since then looking up the names and addresses of adult retailers all over northern California and western Nevada; during the days, I had driven all over the place in my van, filled with stock neatly categorized in the metal-basket draws I had in the back, safely screwed into the heavy piece of plywood I had laid down on the floor back there. I had driven way up north to Reading, as far south as Santa Cruz, east to Reno and Sparks. In that time I had spoken to about a hundred storeowners and managers and, through professional conversations, introducing my personal wholesaling idea to them and occasionally gifting them some free items as goodwill, I had established over 40 permanent accounts. I had also signed a volume agreement with Mr. Lee. I was committed to moving two pallets a month. It was just a beginning, Mr. Lee had told me. He expected me to commit to moving more pallets, in the very near future, as my accounts increased. A pallet held an average of 64 boxes, times 2, that was 128 boxes total I had to buy from him each month. An average box was a 3ft long, 2ft wide by 1.5ft deep. The number of pieces inside a box varied depending on whether it was sex toys, magazines or CDs.

"Come on," Rye said. "Let's go have a drink."

He put on his Yankees cap.

The news was over so I turned off the TV.

"Where do you want to go?" I asked.

"How about *Jolly Mollies*?" He adjusted his glasses. "I like how they keep those bowls filled with peanuts and how you can throw the shells on the floor. By the end of the night, it's like walking on dead bugs over there. Speaking of bugs – why don't elephants like devil beetles crawling up their trunks?"

I shrugged.

"It bugs the hell out of them."

"Is there even such a thing as a devil beetle?" I asked.

"Who cares? It's just a joke. Lighten up. You're always so tense. Is Mr. Lee coming down on you again?"

"Yeah – in five more months he wants me to up my volume commitment to three pallets per month."

"That's a bitch."

"Why won't you work with me? You're the only one I trust. I'll pay you well."

"There's no way, Cree. I can't be driving around all day on the highway. I need to be here, downtown, interacting with people and observing the stupid things they do. That's the only way a comedian can come up with good material."

"Okay, no problem," I said.

"So what about going to *Jolly Mollies* tonight?"

"No, I'm bored with *Jolly Mollies.*"

"There's a new place at the Flood Building by the cable cars. It's called ***Biting the Hand That Feeds You.***"

"What kind of name is that?"

"I don't know," Rye said. "Who cares? Let's give it a try. I've never been there but I hear it's a great place: lots of women."

"Is it a new comedy club?" I asked.

"No, it's one of those theme clubs. You know – where you have to wait in a long line and then pay to get in, and there are bouncers all over the place. They have a dance floor, a karaoke room, colorful lights and a huge square bar in the middle of the place where you can just hang around and drink if you just want to people watch."

"How do you know all this if you've never been there?"

"John told me about it. He's been going there with Lisa every weekend for the last two months since the place opened. Lisa loves dancing."

"How does John have money to take Lisa to a club like that every weekend? I thought he was broke."

"Oh, I didn't tell you. He was promoted to manager at ***Bay Gourmet Sandwiches*** about three months ago. He's doing alright now. He and Lisa are going to find an apartment and live together. They're even talking about getting married."

"Lucky bastard," I said.

"Come on," Rye said. "Let's give it a try. You need to get out. You're tense."

"Okay," I said. "We can give the place a try. But if I don't like it there, we'll go to ***Sheryl's*** in the Tenderloin and have steaks and lappers."

Lappers were shots of whiskey and then a bite out of a piece of honeycomb. They had chunks of real honeycomb in big jars on the bar there, just like bars in the Old West had jars of pickled eggs. You paid them $5.00 and the bartender, usually a big breasted woman, plucked you out a piece of honeycomb with a pair of silver tongs and put it on a saucer for you. The honey always dripped down your mouth so you had to lick it off your lips.

We went to this Greek restaurant first called **The Last Stand**. It was a few blocks away from my apartment on Bush Street. Gino, the owner's son, in white t-shirt and apron, was in front of the window with a big knife, slicing the spitted, rotating meat. They served what they called the *Fiery Flaky Gyros*. It had slices of meat, jalapeno peppers, lettuce, tomatoes, scallions and a special sauce on it, all wrapped up in that warm flat bread they handmade there. It fell apart as you ate it, but it was some-kind-of-wonderful eating it. That was what we called our pre-dinner, so we weren't drinking on an empty stomach. We'd have a real dinner latter on in the evening.

By the time we got to **Biting the Hand That Feeds You**, it was only 8pm: still too early for the real partiers to be out. So the line to get inside wasn't very long, about ten people ahead of us.

We waited on the red bricks of the plaza. I could see the club's blue awning and blue double doors up ahead. It wasn't just us, either: hundreds of people swarmed the plaza, entering and exiting the various restaurants, bars and retail stores all around us. The cable cars were running. One was spinning around on the turnabout with hopeful riders standing all around it, waiting to get on to take the trip to Fisherman's Wharf, where the other turnaround was. And even though it was nighttime, the entire city glowed in a yellow hue from the myriad street lights and building lamps everywhere: the busy roadway, the sidewalks and the stone facades of the tall buildings running all up and down Powell Street, were all clearly visible.

The temperature was mild. I had on a short sleeve shirt, a pair of blue jeans and sneakers. Rye was dressed the same way he always dressed. The three women ahead of us – a blond, brunette and redhead – were all dressed nicely in short, stylish, polyester evening gowns, shapely legs glittering in clinging nylon stockings. Some of the men in line wore pressed slacks, buttoned shirts and shined shoes. One guy even had on a suit and a tie.

"It smells like burning wood," Rye said.

The line to get into the club started to move.

"I know," I said. We were walking beside one another, looking at the women ahead of us who were chatting and laughing.

"The fire," I said.

I handed twenty dollars to the doorman.

That paid for both of us.

We stepped into the club.

We made it just in time to see the three women, who had been ahead of us in line, slip into the crowd, the hems of their gowns swishing around their thighs as they disappeared.

Lights were flashing. It was loud, but not deafening. The dance floor was on the right. It was large, square and reflective like a burnished aluminum. There were many couples on it, men and women, swaying their hips together sexily to the beat of the music.

There was a long, silver bar on the other side of the dance floor, with people seated along the line of metal stools, a myriad of backs to us in colorful shirts or flesh revealing straps, their conversational faces revealed to us in the reflection of the vast rectangular mirror on the wall behind the bar. The walls were all purple. Hanging from the ceiling were hundreds of lights – in round, oval and square metal casings – flashing red, blue, green and yellow with the cadence of the song.

Rye put his mouth close to my ear.

"Can you see John and Lisa anywhere?"

"No," I said, looking around the room. "We might never find them, this place is so big."

"Let's go check out the other rooms."

I nodded, following him, pinning my arms to my sides, but still unable to avoid, and gently brushing as I passed, a legion of other arms and chests and backs as we moved through the crowd of young men and women blocking the room's egress, some of the women dancing rhythmically by themselves in the crowd, all of them watching the couples on the dance floor move their bodies.

We moved down a wide hallway of rag-rolled salmon and white. The ship anchor chandeliers, hanging high up on the arched ceiling, were all a-sparkle with crystal.

Turning left, we entered a more sedate room. There was a low volume techno music being piped in through speakers in the ceiling. The atmosphere was more conversational. Da Vinci, Michelangelo, Renoir, Degas – prints no doubt but colorful and eye-catching nonetheless – filled the walls in ornate frames. There was furniture everywhere: tall backed walnut chairs with cushioned seats circling around glass coffee tables in the middle of the room; suede ottomans and sectional leather sofas against all the walls. People were sitting everywhere, holding mixed drinks or bottles of imported beer. There were a myriad of conversations occurring simultaneously, between men and women, women and women, men and men. Drinks filled the tops of the coffee tables as many found it necessary to gesticulate while articulating their complex points of view. There was a bar at the rear of the room, no stools, but two male bartenders in tuxedos; and three female servers worked the room in a flurry, their silver trays cluttered with drinks, all dressed exactly the same: tightly fitting nylon shorts, white blouses, top three buttons unbuttoned, and black platform shoes – ostensibly the club's uniform.

"This room is flush with material!" Rye said. "Look at that guy back there."

He nodded toward the back right corner of the room.

There was a guy standing up back there, bald head, fiftyish looking, talking to four other people who were all sitting on a leather sofa. We could only see the left side of the guy's face, but he was gesticulating with both hands in front of him, his face all scrunched up as he spoke, like he had eaten something sour. Throwing his hands into the air as he ended his soliloquy, all four people on the sofa began laughing hysterically.

Rye looked at me and smiled. I knew what was about to happen. He did it all the time, imitating the people around him he thought were funny, trying to produce, with his own words, emotional correlatives:

"Until finally the boss catches us one day –" He was squinting at me through his glasses, flailing his arms in the air – "me and his wife in the work restroom banging away like we're building a fence, and the boss says to me, 'Hey, Rye, I think you can do better than that!'"

"Let's try another room," I said.

"What? You didn't think that was funny?"

Across the hall were two rectangular doors – padded-blue-leather with gold buttons between the padding – on giant silver hinges. The neon sign above the doors, in glowing red letters, read: *The Sticky Fingers Room!*

"That's interesting," I said. "What do you think that means?"

"I don't know," Rye said. "Maybe they serve peanut brittle and salt water taffy in there. Let's go in and find out."

We pushed through one of the doors and entered the room as three other people were pushing the other door to exit the room.

There were hundreds of people inside: sitting on sofas and chairs by the door; crowded around the square bar in the middle of the room; sitting in booths at the far end of the room to the right of the bar, where the kitchen served up hot sandwiches, steaks, pizza and pub fries. To the left of the bar, at the other far end of the room, couples walked hand and hand into a darkened room through a door-less entrance. Everyone had a drink in their hand, talking, laughing, telling stories, looking around and people watching.

To our right, there was another door-less entrance leading into another darkened room. A screen of light projected onto the back wall in that room, with words on it. I suddenly heard singing. It was a karaoke room.

I walked to the doorway, looked inside and saw only one person: a woman, obviously a club employee, because she was wearing the club's uniform – tight nylon shorts, white blouse, top three buttons unbuttoned, and black platform shoes. She was standing in the very middle of the room, in front of a microphone set up on a stand, singing the song *I'll Take You There* by The Staple Singers. She was reading the words right off the wall. Her black hair hung in loose curls down to just above her shoulders. Her skin was smooth and tan like someone from the islands. She danced as she sang, moving her body to the rhythmic beat:

I know a place
Ain't nobody cryin'
Ain't nobody worried
Ain't no smilin' faces
I'll take you there

Her voice was melodic and feminine –

Lyin to the races
Help me, come on, come on
Somebody help me now
I'll take you there

Her hips moved as she danced –

Help me ya'all
I'll take you there
Help me now
I'll take you there

Rose-colored lips – full –

Ah, oh, oh! Aye!!!
I know a place ya'all
I'll take you there
Ain't nobody cryin'
I'll take you there
Ain't nobody worried
I'll take you there
No smilin' faces

Beautiful –

I'll take you...

She looked up for some reason, saw me looking at her and stopped
singing.

145

The music continued playing.

"Hi!" she said. She said it emphatically, but friendly, too.

"Ah-h, hi –"

She walked right up to me, smiling. She had good height, the top of her head coming up to my nose.

Rye stepped past me and entered the room.

"Hi!" he said to the woman.

"Hello," she said. "I'm Lani. I run the karaoke room here. The room is open. It's just a little early yet for people to start gushing away; not lubed up enough."

She laughed.

She was direct.

I liked it.

"We'll start filling up in an hour or so. Do you guys want to come in?"

"Sure," Rye said. "Just let us go get something to drink first, okay. I'm Taggart Reise, by the way."

He reached over and shook her hand.

"But everyone calls me Rye."

"I can get you guys drinks," she said. "What do you want?"

"Rad!" Rye shouted. "You guys have any good light beers?"

"We have a beer from Wisconsin called *Bessie the Cow Light*. Is that okay?"

"*Bessie the Cow* it is!"

She turned to me.

For some reason I couldn't think. So I just kept looking at her.

"Well don't just stand there staring at her," Rye said, "tell her what you want. You need a *Bartender's Guide* so you can tell her how to mix it?"

She laughed and looked from Rye back to me.

I still couldn't think. My brain wasn't working for some reason.

"I can get you something if you're drinking tonight?" she said.

"Are you nuts?" Rye exclaimed. "Tell her what you want so we can get this *me-see-Bah* rolling!"

"Sorry," I said, a little embarrassed. I could feel my face getting red.

146

"He's just over working himself," Rye said. "That's why we're out tonight. So he can loosen up. He can't get work off his mind."

"What do you do for a living?" she asked, looking up at me.

"He owns his own business," Rye said.

"Oh, really," she said. "What kind of business?"

"He sells adult items," Rye blurted out.

I couldn't believe he said it. After all the years I've known him, and all the trouble I've had with women because of my line of work. He couldn't just keep his mouth shut.

Well, it was out of the bag now.

"What kind of adult items?" she asked, looking at me curiously, her head askance.

"I'm actually a wholesale distributor," I began. I figured if I stretched it out and threw a whole bunch of industry terminology in there, it wouldn't sound so bad.

I continued:

"There is a company in Hong Kong that manufactures playful and curious items that are primarily retailed through certain businesses here in this country that are of an adult nature."

"You mean triple-X shops?" she said.

Holy shit! I was really getting nervous now. My stomach was starting to hurt.

"Well. Yes," I said. "We in the industry prefer to refer to them as adult retailers, like your corner grocery store is a food retailer."

"Go on," she said, laughing.

"Well, it's just that I, ah-h, I buy the items from the importer here in the U.S. and I sell the stuff to the adult retailers. That's all. No big deal."

"Give me an example of the things you sell," she said.

"Well, ah-h, they're, ah-h —"

Rye gave me a nervous look, and then quickly headed toward the karaoke machine that was beside the long, crescent sofa that circled the wall along three quarters of the room. He started fiddling with the knobs.

Lani was giving me a funny look.

There was no sense in holding off any longer. I was losing her.

147

"Sex flicks and porno mags," I blurted out.

I couldn't believe I was put in the awkward situation of having to tell her that, and now I was gazing at her in shock, holding my breath, waiting for her to walk away in disgust.

"No shortage of buyers for that kind of stuff," she said. "Sounds like a great business. Now can you tell me what you'd like to drink tonight?"

I couldn't believe it! She was actually smiling at me.

I let out a loud exhalation.

"Incredible!" I said.

"What's incredible?" she asked.

"It's just that – I thought you were going to be put off, that's all, by what I did for a living."

"It's not that bad," she said. "My father's a business man, too. He owns a restaurant in Hawaii. My whole family works there except for me. He says all businesses are good businesses, as long as they're not illegal."

"Your father says that, huh?"

"That's right," she said, giving me a half-smile and nodding. "And I always listen to my father. He's a good man. He loves my mother."

"If your mother's anything like you," I said, "I can see why."

She gently touched my forearm with her fingers then drew them back.

"What's your name?" she asked.

"Cree," I said – "Cree Quinn."

We shook hands.

"So your whole family runs their own restaurant in Hawaii," I said.

"Yep!"

"Is it a big place?"

"Pretty big, about seventy tables."

"That is a pretty big," I said. "It takes a lot of people to run a place like that. How many people in your family?"

"There are ten of us," she said, "my mother and father, me and my seven brothers."

"What the!"

That one shocked the hell out of me.

"Seven brothers?" I said incredulously.

She laughed.

"I know! It's a lot! But I know how to handle men because of it. Believe me. I'm the oldest. And I've kicked my brothers' asses many times. So don't try to pull anything on me."

We both laughed.

"So do you want something to drink?" she asked.

"Sure. I like dark ales. You guys have anything like that?"

"We have an import from Australia called *The Sheila's Brown Ass.* Is that okay?"

"Sounds good," I said, handing her my credit card. "Open up a tab for us, please."

"Sure."

She left the room and headed for the bar. I stood in the entry-way and watched her walk through the crowded club. I was breathing heavily now, like I couldn't catch my breath. There was a lot of noise – talking, laughing and a general reveling.

Rye stepped into the entryway beside me, put his arm around my shoulder, and then quickly drew it back.

"Sorry about that," he said. "I know your business is a touchy subject for you."

"No, Rye," I said, looking at him, smiling, giving him a quick hug around his back with my left arm. "You did the right thing."

That's why he was my best friend. He said things as they were and he didn't hold back. It was all out in the open now. No hiding or sidestepping around the truth. She knew what my business was and she didn't care. But I was a nervous wreck. Women did that to me. I don't know why.

She came back to the room with two bottles, one in each hand, passing Rye one and me the other, and handed me back my credit card.

"At the end of the evening," I said, "when they're tallying up the tab, please give yourself a big tip."

"How much?" she asked, looking up at me.

"I don't care."

She gave me a sly smile.

Rye and I began drinking.

Other people came into the room; a young man, about twenty-five years old, wearing slacks and a salmon-colored shirt with white collar and cuffs. The shirt was unbuttoned, reveling his smooth chest. He had a high-pitched voice and was very expressive with both his words and hand gestures. He was with three young women about the same age as him, all wearing painted-on-jeans and tight-fitting tank tops.

"Let's sing!" he said melodically, his arms around the shoulders of two of the young women.

"Yea-a-a-a!" all three women exclaimed in unison.

"Okay," Lani said, standing by the karaoke machine, "any requests?"

"*Don't Let the Sun Go Down on Me*," the young man said, "the new version by Elton John and George Michael."

"Good choice!" Rye said. "I like that one."

The young man looked over at us, smiled and gave us the thumbs-up.

Lani began pressing buttons on the machine.

The three young women sat down together on the far left end of the crescent sofa.

Rye and I sat down on the opposite end, by the entryway.

The young man walked up to the microphone in the center of the room.

Soon, the words to the song appeared on the back wall of the room.

The music began – coming from the speakers in the ceiling.

The young man began singing.

Lani went over to the young women and asked them if they wanted anything to drink. They nodded and smiled and told her what they wanted. The young man stopped singing, told Lani what he wanted, and then continued with his song.

Lani left the room, winking at me as she walked by. It made me smile and I wasn't quite as nervous anymore.

The young man continued singing. One of the young women, the one with short black hair and a silver hoop earring in her lower lip, stood up and sang with him.

"They're good," Rye said. He was sitting about three feet away from me.

"They are," I agreed, watching them standing in the middle of the floor together, arms around each other's waists, singing loudly and animatedly, making large, circular motions together with their hips.

The two young women who were still seated – one with long, crimson colored hair and the other with short, green colored hair – began clapping their hands to the beat of the music.

"You know," Rye said, "I can tell Lani likes you." He took a big chug of beer from his bottle.

"I hope so," I said.

"You hope so," he said sarcastically, wiping his chin with his hand. "Didn't you just see her wink at you? What'da ya think, she's going around all night winking at everybody? Of course she likes you. You got a serious problem, man."

He looked at me, laughed and shook his head.

"You never thrust people. You always think somebody's trying to scam you."

He was right about that.

Lani came back holding a silver tray filled with drinks, including two more beers for me and Rye, and she distributed them correctly to everyone. The young man paid with cash for him and the three young women.

The song was over.

The young woman with the crimson hair made a request and the words to that song soon appeared on the back wall, and she then took her turn singing.

It was like that for the next three hours, with more people entering the room, sitting down on the crescent sofa, making song requests and ordering drinks, with Lani moving from the room to the bar to the room again, her silver tray all loaded up with various cocktails and bottles of beer.

Different people sang, loudly and emotionally. Some were okay, some weren't. It didn't matter. Everyone was having fun, including me, and it was hard for me to have fun. The young man and the three women had left the room, but not before Rye, after downing a couple more beers, went over to the one with the silver ring in her lip and began talking to her. It was a no go. Rye always had a difficult time with women. I told him to lose the baseball cap because it made him look juvenile. But he wouldn't. It was just how he was.

There were many people in the room now. The crescent seat was filled. People were sitting on the floor, standing, leaning against the walls; everyone was holding a beverage.

A song ended.

The singer sat down.

Multiple, simultaneous requests were shouted out, but Lani didn't respond.

She walked over to me.

I had just finished my fourth brown ale; they were strong, being from Australia.

"Sing a song with me," she said loudly, over the din of everyone talking and laughing and carrying on.

I was sitting down.

My eyes drew the line of her shapely legs, tight shorts, silky blouse, the portion of her breasts that was exposed, and then I looked into her brown eyes.

The raucous room buzzed: a gaggle of voices playing in my head.

I made out words:

"No, Jim."

"I start Monday."

"Let's go to the bar."

"That f-ing bastard!"

"She said what?"

"Hi, Sally!"

"What about that fire?"

"They just got it out."

"The Oakland firestorm is what they're calling it."

"Come on let's sing a song together," Lani said again.

She was looking down at me, smiling.

"Okay," I said.

I stood up and we walked over to the karaoke machine.

"Any special request?" she asked, laughing at me.

"Why are you laughing?" I said.

I was smiling at her.

"No reason," she said.

"Well," I said, "my favorite song of all time is **Gimme Shelter** by the Rolling Stones. Do you have that one?"

She looked down at the machine, pressed some buttons, and soon the words to the song were a-splash on the back wall.

"I don't even need that," I said. "I know the words by heart."

"I do too," she said.

We walked to the center of the room together and stood face-to-face, lips almost touching as our mouths neared the microphone:

The music to the song began.

We started singing:

'Ohoo, a storm is threatening-g-g
My very life today
If I don't get some shelter
Oh yeah I'm gonna fade away

War, children, it's just a shot away
It's just a shot away
War, children, it's just a shot away
It's just a shot away

She danced, moving her hips –
I danced with her –

Ooh, see the fire is sweepin-n-n
Our very street today
Burns like a red coal carpet
Mad bull lost its way

War, children, it's just a shot away
It's just a shot away

War, children, it's just a shot away
It's just a shot away

Her eyes in mine; my eyes in hers —
We moved together, our arms, shoulders, hips —

Ra-a-ape! murder-r-r!
It's just a shot away
It's just a shot away

Ra-a-ape! murder-r-r!
It's just a shot away
It's just a shot away

No one else in the room —

Ooh, the flood is threatening
My very life today
Gimme, gimme shelter
Or I'm gonna fade away

War, children-n-n, it's just a shot away
It's just a shot away
It's just a shot away
It's just a shot away
It's just a shot away
I tell you love-e-e, sister-r-r, it's just a kiss away
It's just a kiss away
It's just a kiss away
It's just a kiss away

It's just a kiss away
Kiss away, kiss away

The music stopped and we stopped dancing.
Everyone in the room stood to their feet and clapped furiously.

Some of them were shouting.

"Yeah!"

"That was great!"

"You guys are good together!"

"Do another one!"

"You guys did great!" Rye said, patting me on the shoulder. His baseball cap was off and his glasses, too, and he was standing next to a woman. She was thin and cute, with short blond hair and a pretty smile.

"This is Betty," he said. "We danced while you two were singing."

He looked at Betty.

"This is Cree and Lani."

"Hi."

"Hi."

We both shook her hand.

There was a general din again as everyone in the room was talking simultaneously.

"I'm going to buy Betty a drink," Rye said.

"I'll – I'll go get her one," Lani said softly.

"No," Rye said. "You two stay here. We'll go to the bar. You ready, Betty?"

Betty nodded and smiled; a pretty smile.

Rye grabbed his cap and glasses off of the crescent sofa where he had been sitting and he and Betty left the room.

Lani and I stood there in the middle of the room, near the microphone, looking into one another's eyes.

"I have to go back to work," she said, breathlessly.

"Do you get a break tonight?" I asked.

"We're not supposed to fraternize with the customers. I'm going to get in trouble if I keep standing here with you like this."

She had a serious look in her eyes: afraid to let me go; afraid to hold on to me.

"When's your next day off?" I asked.

"This coming Monday," she said. "I always have Mondays and Tuesdays off."

"Do you like seafood?"

155

"I love seafood. I grew up in Hawaii. Seafood is a staple there."

"I grew up in New England. Seafood is a staple there, too."

We smiled at one another and laughed.

"Will you have dinner with me Monday night at **The Gloucester House?**"

"Yes," she said. "I've never been there. It's so expensive."

"I don't care how expensive it is. You're worth it."

"Stop," she said. "You're gonna make me cry."

Song requests started coming from the crowd.

"I have to go back to work."

"Do you have a pen?"

"No."

"I'll go borrow one from one of the bartenders. We need to exchange phone numbers."

"Okay," she said.

I borrowed a pen from one of the bartenders and a piece of paper as well. Lani and I exchanged phone numbers and then we said goodnight to one another. I then left the club. I didn't even go looking for Rye and Betty to say goodbye. I had to leave: the evening had reached such a crescendo for me; I couldn't stay there any longer. I wouldn't be able to leave Lani along. I couldn't stop looking at her. I couldn't stop talking to her and she needed to work.

Chapter Fourteen

The Gloucester House was a charming restaurant with a nautical theme: New England style mahogany booths with high backs; old fashioned diving equipment, copper head gear and rubber-canvass suits, mounted to the walls; along with lobster traps, ship's steering wheels and old fishing nets on the thick wooden ceiling beams. The walls were aqua-blue dotted by black-and-white photos of past sea captains in old black frames; and the lighting was a mellow glow of candles, mysterious and exciting, especially in the evenings when they blew out a bunch of the candles and opened all the curtains in the back, so everyone could see the Bay Bridge, with the rows of white lights lining the curves of the two main cables for its entire 2.25 mile length, all lit up like a Christmas tree. It was magic: nothing less.

"This way please," the hostess said pleasantly.

Lani and I followed her to a booth in the rear of the restaurant. It had a blue tablecloth and a lit candle in the center: private and romantic.

"This place is so beautiful," Lani said, sitting across the table from me. She was wearing a pretty dress, two tone blue, light blue on the top third, the middle third dark blue, and the bottom third light again. It had a delicate stitching where the colors changed, creating lines around her body. The hem was well above her knees, and it had a long, silver zipper up the back. She was looking at me, smiling that beautiful smile of hers, her black hair, all a curl, pulled back into a ponytail, with some of the curls falling gently down the sides of her glowing face. I couldn't stop looking at her.

"Are you going to say something?" she asked, shyly. "Or are you just going to look at me?"

"What would you like me to say?"

"Anything."

"I'm glad we're here together tonight."

"I am too," she said.

"Look at the bridge," I said, pointing out the window.

"I know," she said, turning and smiling at the sight of it. "It's beautiful."

Our server, Cheryl, came over and introduced herself, set a basket of freshly baked small breads on the table, handed each of us a menu and asked if we would care for a drink.

"Does your restaurant serve the Hawaiian Martini?" Lani asked.

"I don't believe I've ever heard of it," Cheryl said. "Would you describe it to me? I will have the bartender prepare you one if we have the ingredients."

"It is two parts vodka, one part vermouth, one part grenadine, two parts pineapple juice, shaken, and served with a pineapple slice and a little umbrella."

"Sounds delicious," Cheryl said. "I don't believe that will be a problem. We have all of those ingredients."

"Thank you," Lani said.

"And you, sir?"

"What type of brown ales do you carry?"

"We have *Nut Brown Ale* from England."

"I'll have one of those. Thank you."

She smiled and left our table.

I turned to Lani.

She was quiet now: thoughtful.

"So," I began, "here you are with me tonight, seven brothers in Hawaii, all big guys probably."

She laughed.

"They *are* big," she said. "You know, the Hawaiians are descendants of the Polynesians, and the Polynesians were large people."

"I know," I said, "and the greatest navigators the world has ever known."

"That's right!" she said, smiling. "How do you know that?"

"I went to college for eight long years."

"You're kidding me! Do you have a PhD?"

"No. It took me that long to get my B.S. in economy."

"Wow! Why was that?"

"I had a demanding job while I was in college. Also, I took a whole bunch of courses that weren't required by my major. But I'm glad I did. It's made me a more well-rounded person."

"I'm glad you did, too," she said. "It's nice that you know something about my people. Learning about other people, other cultures, it means you care. It also means you're intelligent."

"You sound very intelligent as well," I said. "You must have gone to college too."

"I did!"

"Where at?"

"UC Berkeley."

"Did you graduate?"

"Yes. I have an M.A. in History. I always wanted to be a museum curator or collector, but those types of jobs don't come around very often. That's why I have to work at *Bites*."

"Is it that bad?" I asked.

"Not really," she said. "The tip money is good. That's the only reason I can afford to live in this city. But I don't want to work there forever. I have bigger plans for myself."

I smiled at her.

"What," she asked, smiling back.

"You sound like me."

"Oh yeah?" she said, laughing.

"I worked for eleven years at *The San Andreas Fault CDs* on Market Street. It was the only job I ever had here in this city. I found it the very day I arrived here. And I never minded working there because the guy who owned the place, and his wife, became very good friends of mine. That job was the reason I could afford to pay for my education, and pay for the living expenses that I had at the time. But I always knew I was going to leave that job because I kept saying to myself that I had bigger plans. Just like you just said. So we have something in common: ambition; drive."

"We have something else in common, too," she said.

"What?"

"On Friday you told me you were from New England. My father's from New England."

"No kidding!" I said. "What a coincidence. What part of New England?"

"The Boston area."

"That's where I'm from too," I said.

Her mouth dropped open and she covered it with her hand.

"Are you serious?" she asked me.

"Yes. Where exactly in the Boston area was your father from?"

"He was born in 1933 a town called Lexington, in Massachusetts, just west of Boston."

"I'm familiar with Lexington," I said. "That's where the first shot of the Revolutionary War was fired."

"That's right," Lani said. "You know your history."

"You do too."

"Anyway, my father quit high school in 1950 when he was 17 years old so he could join the Army. He wanted to go to Korea and fight in the war. He lost the bottom half of his left leg in the war, from the keen down."

"That's too bad," I said. "How did it happen?"

"My father was infantry. He said on the front lines, the U.S. Army camps were just canvas tents with some barbed wire wrapped around the perimeter, protected by howitzers. At night, in the pitch black, the Chinese would come, wearing sneakers so they were silent, tens of thousands of them with bayonets fixed; no shots were fired so they could make it right up close without being detected, and they'd overrun the camps, stabbing everyone they could, hoping to wound rather than kill. It was their strategy, my father said. They were taking advantage of what they perceived to be an American weakness: Americans didn't leave anyone behind, and for every one wounded solider, three were needed for his or her care. They were trying to make it logistically impossible for the Americans to stay and fight by overwhelming their medical facilities. One night, my father's camp was overrun and two of them got him in the leg with their bayonets. One bayonet tore out his entire left calf muscle; the other completely severed his left knee joint. There was no way they could repair it."

"I'm sorry that happened to your father."

"Don't be," Lani said. "I'm not."

"Why do you say that?"

"If it weren't for that wound, I wouldn't be here today. They sent him to the Army Hospital in Honolulu for several surgeries, prosthesis fitting and physical therapy. He was in that hospital for over a year. My mother was a young orderly at that hospital. That's how they met. She used to bring him his food and clean his wound with sterilizing soap and wet towels. He never went back to the Boston area after meeting her. They've been married for forty years now."

"That is such a great story," I said. "Tell me more about your mother."

"Well, my mother was born in 1931 on the island of Kauai. It was the Great Depression and her parents, my grandparents, had lost their job at the sugar plantation where they both worked. So they relocated to the island of Oahu, where my grandfather found work at the pine-apple cannery there by the Honolulu harbor. My mother grew up in Honolulu. Her first job ever was that one she had as an orderly at the Army hospital. She started there when she was fifteen years old."

"Isn't it interesting the histories people have," I said.

"Yes, it is."

"I did some calculations," I said, "and I find that your mother was two years older than your father."

"Yes she was." Lani laughed. "Is that alright?"

"Of course. There's nothing wrong with it."

"How old are you?" she asked.

"I was born in August, 1961," I said. "I'm thirty years old. I hope I'm not too old for you because you look pretty young."

"You're not too old for me," she said, "and thank you. I was born in April 1963. I'm twenty-eight years old."

We looked at one another for a while.

"Well," Lani began, "you know all about my parents now. I told you about my seven brothers Friday and our family restaurant. What about your family?"

"I'm an only child."

"What about your parents?"

"They're both dead."

"How could you say it like that?"

"Well, they are. They both died of lung cancer a long time ago."

"Cree, I'm so sorry."

There was an awkward silence for what seemed to be a very long minute.

"Cree," Lani finally said, "would you like to tell me a little bit about your parents while they were still with you?"

I looked at her. I had to say something but I didn't know what.

"I like you, Lani. Could you please not ask me about my parents tonight."

"Okay," she said, "we can talk about them some time in the future. How about this: why'd you come to San Francisco?"

I turned to look at the bridge.

The past always comes back to haunt.

"Come on," she urged. "Why?"

"Why'd you leave Hawaii?" I asked, somewhat abrasively. I then shook my head. I needed to pull myself together. It was natural for her to want to know more about me. It's just that with regards to my past life in Lynn, my defenses were on a hair trigger.

"I'm sorry," I said.

"It's okay."

She brushed her curls with her hand then brushed the front of her blue dress.

"We're getting to know each other," she said. "I can see you need more time. I understand that because something happened to me that I've been keeping to myself."

"Do you want to tell me what that is?"

CUTTING OFF A WHALE'S HEAD

"I don't think I'm ready," she said.

"That's okay," I said. "It takes time for people to get to know one another."

"I agree with that," she said. "But since you asked, I will tell you why I left Hawaii to come here."

"Why?"

"Because I wanted to see more of the world."

"Me too," I said. "That's why I left Boston to come here. Another thing we have in common."

"How long have you lived in San Francisco?" she asked.

"Twelve years."

"In what part of the city?"

"Right here downtown," I said.

"That's odd."

"What is?"

"Well," she began, "I've been living downtown for ten years now. And you're telling me you've been living downtown for twelve years. Don't you think that's a little strange we've never bumped into one another before?"

"No," I said, "it's a big city. And besides, that job I told you I had for eleven years – I worked nights and weekends at that job. I rarely got to go out in the evenings."

"Oh!" she said. "That's why we never met before. Because even though *Bites* is new and I've only worked there for a little over two months now, every job I've had for the last ten years has been as a server. And I always have to work nights and weekends, just like you did."

"Another thing we have in common," I said.

"Yeah," she said. "It's strange, isn't it? We're from opposite ends of the world but we have so much in common."

She looked into my eyes.

I looked into hers.

We were both searching for something.

There was something about her.

She wasn't afraid.

She spoke her mind, just like Rye.

That Friday evening, she handled who knows how many custom-

163

ers – two hundred, three hundred – all by herself in that karaoke room, taking their song requests, bringing them drinks, all without a pen or a piece of paper to write anything down with; she did it all in her head and she never got flustered, she never fumbled once.

"What's the most important thing to you in the whole world?" she finally asked.

"My business," I said. "I have a dream. I want to become rich someday."

She frowned and sat back in her booth, obviously disappointed with my answer.

"I'm sorry," I said. "Sometimes I don't say things the way I mean them."

"It's okay," she said. "We just met. It's too early for me to ask you that question."

"But I want to ask *you* that question now," I said, "because I want to learn more about you. So would you please tell me what the most important thing in the world is to you?"

"My family," she said.

"You know what," I said, "I understand that because it sounds like you have a fantastic family. But what I don't understand is – and believe me, I'm glad you stayed in San Francisco making our date tonight here possible – but why didn't you go home to Hawaii after you graduated? You obviously miss them."

There was another awkward silence.

I didn't say anything because she was looking down at the table now and had her arms folded.

I could tell she was sad.

"Because I had a boyfriend," she finally said, looking up at me. "We met in 1985, the first year I had matriculated into the Master's program at Berkeley. He was in the English Master's program there. He wanted to be a writer so he studied literature. We fell in love and I let him move into my apartment here in the city. It was tight, but we didn't care. We had each other. He graduated one year before me. I guess he changed his mind about becoming a writer because he took a job as a loan officer with a bank, *The California First Loyalty and Trust*. We lived together for four years. We planned on getting married. At least that's what he told me. I believed him because I…"

Her voice cracked.

She looked down again.

"Are you okay?" I asked.

She nodded, but it didn't look like she was okay.

"I believed him because I loved him," she continued, "and I thought he loved me too. His company transferred him to another branch in Los Angeles. That was about two months after I had graduated. He told me he would go there first, find us an apartment, and then send for me when everything was settled, but he never called me. He changed his cell phone number and everything. And I haven't heard from him since. That was two years ago. I was so sad, and then so angry, for so long. I was angry at men. I didn't want anything to do with them and haven't been out on a single date since. This is the first one. And I was too embarrassed to go back to Hawaii and face my mother and father. Not just because of him abandoning me, but for me having my M.A. in History and not being able to find a job in anything but a club that makes me dress up like a sex toy."

She looked away, but I could still see the pain in her tightly closed eyes. And then a tear fell, and another.

"I'm so sorry all that happened to you," I said.

She turned back to me, still crying, rubbing the tears from her eyes with her hands.

I gave her my cloth napkin.

"Thank you," she said, using the napkin to wipe her eyes.

I reached my opened hand across the table.

She held it for several second and then let it go.

The tears stopped.

"I'm sorry for being like this," she said, handing me back my napkin.

I took it and set it down on the table in front of me.

"Don't be sorry," I said. "It's not your fault. It was his fault. And I'm going tell you something right now – he was a damned fool."

"Thank you," she said.

We looked at one another for a while, smiling, but I could see she was hurting inside. It made me feel bad. I didn't like when people were hurting.

Cheryl came back to the table and set our drinks down in front of us.

"Can I get you a new napkin?" she asked.

I looked down at my napkin. It had mascara and pink lipstick all over it.

"Please," I said, handing it to her, hoping the sorrow would be carried away from our table as well.

Lani looked at the napkin in Cheryl's hand and started laughing. She was back.

I sighed with relief.

"Is everything okay over here?" Cheryl asked.

"Everything's fine now," Lani said. "Thank you for asking."

"Are you ready to order?"

Lani and I looked at one another. We hadn't even opened our menus yet.

"We need a little more time," Lani said.

"Take your time," Cheryl said, smiling, and she left the table to go assist other diners.

"You handled that well," Lani said.

"What?" I asked.

"My little breakdown."

"I'm very sensitive to other people's feelings," I said.

"I know you are."

"How do you know?"

"I could see it in your eyes Friday. You have a sadness about you. You're probably not aware of it, but I can see it in your whole manner. Your facial expressions, how you move, how you try to protect yourself by being very careful with the words you use. *Pu' uwai Kaumaha, lu'ulu'u.*"

"What does that mean?" I asked.

"In Hawaiian, it means *sad heart*. It's what drew me to you."

We looked into one another's eyes.

Hers were moist.

I felt like mine were too.

"Cree," she said softly, "do you want to tell me why you have a sad heart?"

I continued looking into her eyes.

She was trying to smile.

I looked away at the bridge.

I turned back.

I had to say something, but I didn't know what. It was too soon and there just weren't enough words.

"Lani," I began, "I find that I am very fond of you, and it has happened very quickly. I know you want to learn more about me, and I want to tell you all there is to know about me. But please don't ask me to tell you about my sad heart tonight. I promise to tell you another time – is that a deal?"

She reached her opened hand across the table and folded her fingers into mine.

"Deal," she whispered.

I think we had fallen in love on that Friday we first met, and the dinner at *The Gloucester House* had just confirmed it. There was just too much we had in common, regardless of the geography that had separated our childhoods.

We saw one another as often as we could. I rearranged my schedule and did my closest routes on Mondays and Tuesdays, her days off, minimizing road time, so I could spend as much time as possible with her on those days. On Saturdays and Sundays, we had breakfast together and did lots of fun things prior to her going to work: movies, cable car rides to Fisherman's Wharf, walks through Golden Gate Park, trips to the art museum. I even rented a car once and we went shopping together at the mall in San Bruno.

In the evenings while she worked, I would sometimes go to *Bites*, to *The Sticky Fingers Room*, order a beer at the bar and then sit on the crescent sofa in the karaoke room, just so I could look her all night, and we'd share secret smiles. I tried not to talk to her too much, either. I didn't want to smother her. I didn't want to get her into any trouble. And it didn't take me very long to tell her everything there was to know about me, either. I held nothing back: I trusted her, and she trusted me, telling me everything there was to know about her.

I have heard that people have a soul mate waiting for them out there somewhere in this vast and lonely world. I never believed that and I still don't. It's not that soul mates are waiting out there to hopefully discover one another. Soul mates are forged in the fires of chance and opportunity: when people who are totally different from one another, accept those differences, and then poke around in the interstices to see where the hidden commonalities lie.

She moved into my apartment three months after that first date. It was cramped but we didn't care. We only required a single space, the space that held our hearts, intertwined and beating in unison now. We always sat together on the sofa or the chair while watching TV, her in my lap sometimes, arms around one another, looking into each other's eyes often, and speaking those kind, heartwarming phrases to one another that affirmed our love: *"How are you? Did you sleep well? Are you hungry? Is there anything I can do for you?"* This is what I had once referred to as the *touch of the miniscule*. What a damned fool I had been.

The sine wave point of view: I was now seeing things not only from the peak and trough of the sine wave, but from all points in-between, infinitely. Lani made that happen. She made **everything** happen. She made life not only bearable but wondrous. I had never felt that way before. I had always thought of life as being hard, capricious and something to just grudgingly endure. But it wasn't like that now. She changed my whole life. She had that magic in her – soft, soothing, streaming love – that a woman so easily can bring to a man. And there was also that other thing that I cannot deny: I was a beast for her sexually – the smooth, fleshy curves of her body; her hips; her breasts; her lips. We kissed always and amorously, open mouthed, breathlessly, and the ensuing sex sultry, sweaty, sweet. It was frightening how powerful a woman's influence could be – and glorious, too!

In 1995, four years after she had moved into my apartment, Lani and I got married at San Francisco's City Hall by a Justice of the Peace. Rye was there along with his girlfriend Betty, and so were John and Linda, who had themselves been married in Reno three years earlier. Lani and I then flew out to Hawaii so I could meet her family, her mother and father and seven brothers. There, we were married a second time in a traditional Hawaiian wedding, on the beach, a beautiful bright day, with Lani in a flowing white dress, me in loose fitting white shorts and a short sleeve shirt, lays around our necks, the preacher and musicians all in flowered shirts. There was a fire on the beach, dancing, the wandering ukulele player, kalua pig the center of the feast, everything! It was the best day of our entire lives! I got along with everyone in her family and they all got along with me, and I had finally gotten to see their restaurant in downtown Honolulu – it was called *Leilani Malone's*, which was her mother's name – the restaurant Lani spoke so happily of all of the time.

We stayed in Hawaii for one full week, staying at her parents' home, eating breakfast, lunch and dinner at the family restaurant every day. We'd walk the beaches hand-in-hand in-between times, swimming in the ocean in the late afternoons to avoid the high sun, her in a bikini, me in long shorts. The waves were towering and curling and we'd run straight into them together, practically drowning ourselves, but doing it over and over again while laughing hysterically, salt water coursing down our smooth, tanned bodies.

When we finally flew back to San Francisco, we decided that our apartment was too small. So we found a good-sized one bedroom on Powell Street, just up the hill from *Bites*. It had a large dining room with a moderately fancy chandelier in the middle of the ceiling. We bought a table that could accommodate eight chairs and, after Lani quit her job so she could focus fulltime on finding something that was better suited to her intelligence, we had great weekend parties in that apartment with all of our San Francisco friends.

I had been steadily building up my business and had accumulated 160 permanent accounts. I was concerned, however, about how much money I was making. I didn't think it was enough, considering the number of hours I had to put in to earn it: I netted about seventy thousand dollars in 1995. But I was busting my ass to do it. I was away from Lani all the time, out on the road, hustling. And believe me, that's what sales is: hustling. My volume commitment with Mr. Lee was now four pallets per month. But I was stretched out to the max. There was no way I could take on any more accounts. My routes were full. I didn't want to hire employees because with all of the theft my retailers experienced, I figured how much easier was it going to be for my employees to steal from me when they would be on the road with a van load of product with me unable to monitor them because I'd have to be on the road as well.

So I was beginning to see that my earning potential with this business was reaching its ceiling. How was I ever going to become rich on a lousy seventy thousand dollars a year? Things seemed bad to me, and then things took a decided turn for the worse.

In the spring of 1996, Mr. Lee had a massive heart attack while working inside his warehouse 212A. He collapsed to the cement floor, to his knees first, and then onto his back, legs folded beneath themselves, furiously gasping for a breath that would not come. It was a cold morning, and windy. As he writhed in agony on the floor, clutching his chest, his children and grandchildren, daughters and sons-in-law, all gathered around him and watched, helplessly. But, and I wasn't there personally but the entire incident had been relayed to me by Mr. Lee's second son, Gang Lee, just before Mr. Lee passed on, he looked up and, seeing his family all gathered around him, he smiled, and that's how he transitioned into the other world.

For his family members, however, it was unbearably sad. They were all very much affected for quite a long time: many years in fact. It was heartbreaking for me as well. I missed him very much. He was the man who had taught me about business and how to be successful. The only one not so affected by the tragedy was his eldest son, Ning. And now Ning was in charge of *Lee Industries* along with his wife, Why Lee. Ning thought his father had run the business too conservatively. He didn't think the wholesale price should be set by him, the importer, as Mr. Lee had done in order to create a stable work environment and keep many wholesalers in business at once. Ning didn't care if his wholesalers undercut one another, with the larger and more cash-supplied drop shippers lowering their prices, accumulating more and more customers, until finally bankrupting the little guys. That was just the cost of doing business: the Darwinian theory of capitalism.

Ning also didn't like the idea of only selling to a select group of wholesalers. He was toying with the idea of selling directly to the retailers himself, which would put all of the wholesalers out of business if he was successful. But there were significant logistical hurdles that prevented him from pursuing that goal. Number one, there were literally thousands of retailers his wholesalers serviced. He did not have nearly enough employees to fill that type of demand, and he never would because he, like his father before him, did not believe in hiring anyone outside of the family. So the prospect of the fifteen or so family members he had working for him being able to drop ship two thousand or more orders per day was preposterous.

Number two – and Ning himself had told me this derisively – he was getting a lot of flak from his relatives in Hong Kong, who were telling him not to disrupt the orderly and time-honored distributary chain that had been established by traders as far back as Marco Polo: manufacturer-importer-wholesaler-retailer. That is how the process worked behind the scenes, the price being bumped up along each section of the chain. It was all done quietly, like a big secret, so the consumer was unaware, when they picked up that bottle of shampoo at the local grocery store and saw the price of $3.99 on it and said to him or herself, 'Gee, that's a good price,' that the manufacturer had actually created that bottle for two pennies, and could have sold it directly to the consumer for five pennies, had it not been for the logistical impossibilities. That's what all of life boiled down to: logistics.

So Ning was holding off his plans of selling directly to the retailers. But because **Lee Industries** no longer set the wholesale price, my business had started to become impacted by the larger drop shippers, who had drastically lowered their prices and were mailing fliers to all the retailers letting them know of it. I still had business and always would, because of my personalized service. The storeowners didn't mind paying more for personalized service. It freed them up to handle other aspects of their business that required more attention, like monitoring employee and customer thefts. I also had been told by not a few of my retailers, that it was better to have stock available for the consumers than to have empty shelves, even if the margins were a bit lower. Empty shelves created bad will between the customers and the stores. But there was no doubt my customers were **definitely** buying less and less from me, and more and more from the few drop shippers who had survived the price wars.

From 1996 onward, my annual net dropped steadily, from my

previous year's high of seventy thousand dollars reaching a low of thirty thousand dollars by the end of 2000; poverty level for someone living in San Francisco. Lani and I wanted to have children, but we couldn't afford it. I also had to lower my volume commitment from four pallets to two pallets per month. That made Ning angry, but what could I do. I was angry myself because my goal in opening that business in the first place was to become rich. But I was never going to become rich the way things were going. I brought it up to Ning one day while visiting him at the warehouse. I told him my business was being destroyed because I just couldn't compete with the large drop shippers. It was then he who introduced to me the idea of dropping staple items, and selling novelty items exclusively.

The idea didn't strike me at first because his father had always mentored me to sell staple items, the things everyone needed, so I would always at least make some money. But then Ning got out a calculator and showed me how big the mark ups were on novelty items: 200% – 400% – sometimes 600% or more. I asked him why the mark-ups were so large and he told me it was the nature of novelty items in the adult industry. The larger drop shippers would not take a chance on selling them because they considered those items to be too penny-Anny, which meant the places to find such items were scarce. Without the competition, those who carried novelty items could sell them for whatever price they wanted. It was only after a novelty item proved itself as a seller in the market place that the larger wholesalers would then carry them as well. But how could a novelty item establish itself in the market place if no wholesaler would take a chance on selling it to the retailers? That's where I came in, Ning said, me and my personalized service.

So I did it. I took Ning's advice. It was a big gamble but my whole life up to that point had been one big gamble anyway. In January of 2001, I had completely retooled my business from selling staple items to selling novelty items. I had no competition from the big drop shippers and most of the times I was introducing to my retailers an entirely new item that they had never seen before; and they liked it! I became a big success, netting over one hundred fifty thousand dollars by the end of that year.

Lani was happy. I was happy. Ning Lee was happy because I had upped my volume commitment back to 4 pallets per month. That's when Lani and I started thinking about buying a house. But we couldn't afford one in San Francisco because even a beat-up piece of crap, one-level ranch-style house in the Sunset District cost over a million dollars. We decided to move out of the city, and since I had a lot of accounts up north – in Richmond, Sacramento, Reading, and west in Reno and Sparks – we decided Sacramento was the place to be, since it was more centrally located for my business. Also, Sacramento was where the homebuilders were going crazy manufacturing hundreds of new homes up there each year at reasonable prices.

So on a hot day in early January of 2002, exactly one year after the retooling of my business, we packed all of our belongings into a moving van, including my stock at the 7th Street storage locker, and said goodbye to San Francisco. We then drove the two hours northeast to Sacramento, the state's capital. There, we moved into a rather large and relatively new apartment complex called **Gold Miners Manor**. It was on Gun Fight Avenue. It was a nice place with a community swimming pool, large common area with barbeque grills and picnic tables, and a walking path through the woods. We were happy there. We *did* want to buy a house eventually. But we wanted to get to know the city first, see what the neighborhoods were like, and see which area of the city was right for us and our future children.

Things weren't all roses for us though. I was totally stressed out by my retooled business because the novelty items were selling so fast. I was on the road all the time and it was causing me health problems. I couldn't sleep nights without the use of several prescription drugs. I had the nagging sensation that sudden death – a stroke or a heart attack – was right around the corner. The entire situation made Lani concerned for me and also furious at times. During the week, I would often wake up early in the morning while she was still sleeping, hit the road in my van and not get home again until late at night, when she was back in bed, sound asleep. She missed me. She'd cry sometimes. She said she didn't care about the money as much as I did. She wanted a family life. I was just not in a position as of yet to provide that to her. Not at that time. My business had to come first. We were never going

173

to become rich if I didn't hustle each and every day of the week. I took weekends off – most of the time. The problem was, because I was home and she had access to me on the weekends, that's when we argued; sometimes bad arguments, too, with her slamming out the door on me and taking off to the mall on her own where she went on huge spending sprees, coming home with four thousand or five thousand dollars' worth of new clothes, purses and shoes.

I didn't care about the spending. We had plenty of cash. I wasted thousands of dollars all the time myself on nothing but a good time out with my Sacramento friends, couples we had met at the apartment complex and had gotten to know. What upset me about her taking off was this: it was her who was complaining all the time that we weren't spending enough time together. So it seemed crazy to me that when we did have some time to spend together, she'd use the opportunity to start an argument with me, then get enraged and storm out of the apartment and spend the next five, six, seven hours by herself shopping at the mall.

I didn't know what to do sometimes. I wanted her to be happy. I wanted *us* to be happy together. But I had been working so hard for so many years to reach this point in my business. The goal was simple: to become rich. It was right around the corner now, waiting for me. Novelty items were going to make all of our dreams come true. It took me a long time to figure it out. I had wasted over ten years on selling staple items. So I had a lot of catching up to do now. I couldn't let health problems or family problems stop me. She would thank me when were millionaires. Of that I had no doubt. It was just making it over the rough waters until our boat finally came in.

Chapter Fifteen

I was finally off the Bay Bridge and on the wide lanes of the Embarcadero roadway, heading for Broadway Street and *La Castor Velu*. The clock on the dashboard read 3:15pm.

The city was cold. I reached down and turned on the heat. It whooshed out of the vents and felt good on my arms and face. Through the passenger side window, past the cardboard box on the bucket passenger seat, I could see Pier 2 and the Ferry Building; the reflection of my white van in its wide glass entry-doors; and the ornate, black sign above the doors that read: *The Gloucester House*.

There wasn't much traffic but there were a lot of pedestrians walking around outside: men and women holding hands; children; someone had a dog on a red leash; pairs of joggers in sweatpants, wearing Walkman's with microphones in their ears.

When I passed the empty slip of Pier 9, it reminded me of that terrible argument that Lani and I had almost six years earlier, when I thought I was going to lose her.

It was on a Saturday in early October 2002, 9 months after we had moved into our new apartment at the *Gold Miners Manor* complex in Sacramento. Lani's parents were on a fifteen-day cruise out of Honolulu, on a ship named *Singing Orca Seas*. The ship was crossing the Pacific and then making various stops at ports along the west coast of the U.S., the last stop being in San Diego, before it headed back across the Pacific for Honolulu again. It was called the *Pacific Triangle Cruise*.

Coincidentally enough, the ship was docking in San Francisco that Saturday, at Pier 9, arriving at 10am and then departing again at 5pm. Lani and I would have seven hours to spend with them, and she missed them terribly. She had flown back to Hawaii three years earlier, in 1999, to visit them for a week, but hadn't seen them since. I couldn't go with her on that trip because that was when my business was in shambles, with Ning Lee letting all his wholesalers have a price war. So I hadn't seen her parents since our wedding in Hawaii back in 1995. We did talk to them regularly on the phone: nearly every weekend. But Lani was really looking forward to that Saturday and us taking her folks all over San Francisco, to the touristy places: the Flood Building and the retail district downtown, the cable cars, Fisherman's Wharf, the taffy factory and See's Candies.

But there was a problem that Saturday. I had gone to Santa Cruz the day before, on Friday, and I hadn't finished the route, the one and only time that had ever happened to me. I got caught up in some un-expected traffic. The town of Los Gatos was having its annual Pumpkin Festival and Route 17 was solid with traffic for miles and miles. I had to go through Los Gatos in order to get to Santa Cruz. So I had missed stocking two of my big accounts in Santa Cruz. I used my cell phone late Friday afternoon to call both of the owners at those places and asked them if they would stay open late for me but neither one could. Each had plans to go out for the evening. So I promised them I'd stop by the following day, Saturday, to take care of them.

When I had finally arrived home to the apartment that Friday evening, I told Lani what had happened. I knew we had this date with her parents. It had all been scheduled two months in advance. But what could I do? I promised my two customers that I would be there on Saturday morning. She tried to talk me out of it but I told her not to worry. I told her I would leave for Santa Cruz early in the morning, get down there and finish up by noon time, make the one and a half hour drive back to San Francisco, call her on my cell phone when I was almost there, and we would all meet at ***The Gloucester House*** so we could have a late lunch or an early dinner together. That way I would at least be able to see them for a few hours and also be able to see them off when they re-boarded the ship. She could take her own car into the city that morning and meet them at Pier 9's slip at 10am, and it would give her lots of quality time to spend alone with her parents. Lani agreed to all that because it sounded like a good idea.

So I woke up early that Saturday morning, a bit before 6am, made myself a cup coffee, and walked through the narrow hallway that led to the single car garage on the northern side of ***The Quinn Estate***. That's where I kept my stock. I had industrial shelves in there that went all the way up to the ceiling, loaded up with boxes full of novelty sex toys. It wouldn't be for several more years, after I had become overwhelmed with excess pallets of stock that I kept buying from Ning Lee in order to maintain my low price point, that I would have to relocate my storage needs to the two car garage. Anyway, I had to load the van that morning because I had broken my rule of always loading up the night before. It didn't take long, though, and I was on the road by 7am.

The drive from Sacramento to Santa Cruz was usually about 2 hours and 45 minutes. I drove fast and got there by 9:30am. I went to ***Linda's Honey Jar*** first. I was there for only one hour. Linda needed to be restocked on eight of the novelty items I was now carrying. One advantage of novelty items over staple items, novelty items came in display boxes, 24 pieces to a box. Tear off the cellophane wrapper, flip over the front cover and bam! All 24 items were ready for purchase, and you only had to write the cost of the item down one time, on the white circle that was on the flip cover. With staple items, each separate piece had to be priced individually and then placed separately on the shelves or, in the case of magazines, loaded into the display racks. So novelty items saved time.

I would have been out of Linda's shop in under an hour had I not had a new item to demonstrate, one that Ning had just started importing from his family in Hong Kong. It was called the *penis cigarette lighter*. It was 5inches long so could easily be carried in one's pocket; it had a small chain with a split ring at the end, so it could be used as a keychain; it came in various colors – red, white, black, green, tan, blue;

a very versatile item.

So I showed it to Linda and she liked it, buying two boxes from me that day. She thanked me, I said no problem, and I was on my way to my second and final stop of the day: *Rosie's Unmentionables*. It was just a five-minute drive away on the university side of town.

When I stepped through the door at Rosie's place, the little bell above the door dinged and everyone in the store turned to look at me. There were four people all crowded around the front counter by the cash register. Rosie was there, voluptuous in her one-piece stretch garment, neon pink, the sides of her ample breasts sticking out of the V-neck. John and Amy, two of her employees, were there also. There was another woman there as well. I had never seen her before. But she was holding up a sexy bra in both hands as though demonstrating it for everyone in the store.

"Well hello there, Cree!" Rosie said. She said it like a song. She said everything like a song.

"Come over here and take a look at this stuff! This is my friend, Dr. Gale Fischer. She's the Dean of the Marine Biology department at the University of California here in Santa Cruz. She also designs and makes her own line of naughty lingerie."

Rosie let out a shy laugh and covered her mouth with her two hands as though she were embarrassed. I thought that was cute: here's Rosie, the owner of an adult retail shop in a college town, selling all kinds of sex toys, sex magazines and sex CDs, getting embarrassed by sexy lingerie.

I walked up to the counter, smiling.

I held out my hand.

"How are you, Dr. Fischer," I said.

"Fine," she said, gently shaking my hand, smiling back at me.

Her hair was black and in a tight bun. She was middle aged but good looking, and professionally attired, in an executive dress, nice stitching down both sides, purple, the hem several inches above the knee, but covering the entire rest of her body all the way up to her collar bone, the waist cinched curvedly with a black vinyl belt with wide silver buckle. She was wearing a delicate gold chain around her neck, with a gold dolphin pendant.

"You don't have to call me Dr. Fisher," she said. "You're not one of my students. Call me Gale."

"Okay," I said.

"This is the guy I was telling you about, Gale," Rosie said, reaching over and touching me on the arm. She was on the customer side of the counter, standing to the right of Gale, a stool between them, a large, brown grocery bag on top of the stool, filled with clothing. John and Amy were behind the counter, both leaning on it with their elbows, chins on top of their folded fingers.

"Look at these gorgeous garments she makes," Rosie said, reaching into the bag, lifting out bras and panties and holding them up so I could get a good glimpse.

"I call it my Sea Shell Collection," Gale said.

Rosie held a pair of red, see-thru panties right up to my face with small, felt seashells – periwinkles, scallops, conch, and clams – all around the elastic waistband. I could smell the newness of the sheer material. She then threw the panties back into the bag and pulled out its matching bra, with the same felt seashells all along both straps.

"They're lovely," I said.

I took a step forward, reached into the bag and started lifting out panties and bras, examining them, the quality, stretching them to see how durable they were.

"This particular collection comes in four colors," Gale said – "Coral reef red, atoll white, aqua green, and deep ocean blue."

I left the bag alone and took a step backwards.

"So you make these yourself?" I asked, looking at Gale.

"Yes," she said. "I have a whole manufacturing center in the basement of my home. Bins filled with bolts-of-cloth, many textures and colors, rolls of white felt that I dye myself because I like to create my own colors. I draw the designs on the big artist's note pad I have on my easel, then cut the material on my work table and stich it all together with my sewing machine, sometimes my hand held one if the work is delicate."

"Who do you sell to?" I asked. "Or do you place items on consignment?"

"I just started doing this recently," Gale said. "About three months back. It started off as a hobby. I didn't plan on selling them to stores. I was just going to have lingerie parties at my house once in a while on the weekends and sell them that way. I had my first party last weekend and invited Rosie because we've been friends for over five years now. Rosie's the one telling me I need to get these items into stores."

"The quality and beauty of her work blew me away," Rosie said, "and I immediately though of you, Cree. She's talented. She needs a distributor. But none of those drop shippers are going to give her a break because they only deal with the importers. Do you think your other stores will buy this stuff and retail it? I know I'm going to start carrying her stuff in my store."

I thought about it for a little while, looking back and forth between Rosie and Gale, both of them biting their lips and gazing back at me nervously. It was high quality stuff, there was no question about that, and it was sexy, too; and sexy was what my whole industry was all about.

"I can bring some samples around with me," I said. "I think it **might** just sell."

Both women squealed with delight and Rosie threw her arms around me and hugged me. She then let me go and Gale gave me a quick hug also. John and Amy pushed themselves off of the counter and began clapping.

"Alright, Cree!" they said in unison.

"You two need to talk," Rosie sang, adjusting her right breast in the neon pink stretch garment. "Get everything arranged, how you're going to get the lingerie to him and how he's going to pay you. All that stuff. But not until you fill up my empty shelves, Cree!"

It took me a little under two hours to restock Rosie's shelves. Gale stayed in the store the whole time, her and Rosie chatting excitedly about how I was going to get her lingerie into all of the stores I serviced, how Gale and I would become millionaires because of it, with both of them squealing excitedly over the prospect of it all. They also set up a display together that Rosie had John and Amy go pull out of storage from the back of the store. It was a big black-wire rack about 6ft tall and 5ft wide, which stood up like a tripod on the two metal poles chained to the back. Rosie and Gale used clothespins to display various matching sets of panties and bras onto the front of the rack, and then they set it up at the front of the store so customers could see it as soon as they walked through the door.

When I was finished, I walked over to both women, who were now standing at the rear end of the counter in the back of the store, whispering things to one another. John and Amy were at the front of the store, assisting customers.

I was holding Rosie's invoice in my hand.

"Before I total this up," I said, looking at Rosie, who was giving me a suspicious smirk like they had been talking about me, "I have one more item to show you. It's new."

I reached into my front pocket, pulled out the *penis cigarette lighter*, depressed the switch on the side and a long blue flame shot from the head.

"Ah-h-h-h-h-h-h!" they squealed in unison, obviously delighted.

"That is so cute!" Rosie sang.

"Can I try it?" Gale asked, holding her hand out.

I passed it to her.

She depressed the switch and the flame shot out.

John and Amy, finished ringing up their customers now, came over and laughed when they saw it.

"It's butane," I said, "refillable, and it's a key chain too."

"How do they come packaged?" Rosie asked.

"In a display box of 24 pieces," I said; "A very nice presentation for your counter top."

"How much per unit?"

"I charge you $3.00 apiece; you retail them for $5.99 apiece."

"No way!" Rosie sang. "I'm charging $8.99 apiece. These college kids around here will eat these things up! I'll take eight boxes, Cree!"

"You got it," I said. I knew those lighters were going to be a good seller. They only cost me 50cents apiece.

I brought Rosie's lighters into the store, set seven boxes on the low shelf behind the counter and opened one of the boxes, flipping over the front cover to create the display and using a magic marker to write the price – $8.99 each – onto the white circle provided. I then set the display on the counter between the two cash registers. All the colorful penises stuck straight up into the air because of the Styrofoam insert on the bottom of the box. It had a good look to it.

Rosie signed my invoice.

I tore off the top white copy and handed it to her, keeping the yellow copy for myself.

Rosie looked her copy over.

The total was $1,776.00 dollars.

"Good," she said. "You kept it down this time. Thanks."

Both Gale and I said goodbye to Rosie, with Gale hugging her, and then Gale and I headed out the door together. We agreed to have coffee and talk business at the café across the street.

La Café Etude had a green façade, a large plate-glass window, outdoor tables and chairs, and was sandwiched in by multiple other retailers on either side.

There were lots people walking along the sidewalk past the café, in both directions; students mainly, backpacks slung over their shoulders and cell phones in their hands.

We entered the café and ordered drinks: one grand mocha Frappuccino for her and a small house coffee for me. We then sat at one of the small tables outside in the mild autumn air.

"It's Saturday," I said, taking a sip of coffee from my paper cup. "How come there's so many students walking around today?"

"The frat houses are right around the corner from here," Gale said. "The university is just at the end of this boulevard."

She pointed down the street, in the direction of some tall brick buildings with lots of windows.

"Besides, lots of students do their papers and research work on Saturdays at the library on campus. Didn't you go to college, Cree?"

"Yeah –" I smiled. "I remember doing papers on Saturday."

She was cupping her frappuccino in both hands, steam rising from the top.

She took a sip of it then gave me an embarrassed look.

"What?" I asked.

"Nothing," she said, "Just thank you. I hope I'm not putting you out."

"In what way?" I asked.

"I don't know," she said. "Just the whole way Rosie and I ambushed you when you walked into her store earlier."

"It's no problem," I said. "It's just business."

"She called me last night and told me you'd be coming today. That's why I was at her store. I was waiting for you."

I smiled at her, took a sip of my coffee, and then set the paper cup down on the table.

"All that stuff you sell," she said, "where do you get it from?"

"I have a primary supplier. He's actually my only supplier. Ning Lee. He owns a place called Lee Industries in Richmond."

"Where does he get his stuff?"

She sipped her drink.

"His family makes most of it in Hong Kong and they ship it to him."

"He's not going to be upset at you for helping me, is he?"

"No," I said, shaking my head. "This is *my* business, not his. As a matter of fact, the more I think about it, the more I like this idea. I think your stuff is going to do well. A lot of the adult stores, especially the ones in small towns up north and in Nevada, sell lingerie because there's no other place in town selling that kind of stuff."

"Sounds great," she said. "Now how do we handle the money aspect? Are you going to buy the items off of me and then resell them at a higher price or do you have something else in mind?"

"I'll take the stuff on consignment," I said. "Whatever sells, we split the profit 50/50."

"But that's not fair to me," she said, "because I have all the production costs."

"I have all the distribution costs," I said.

"Okay," she agreed. "How do we set the prices?"

"I'll take care of that," I said. "I know what this kind of stuff should retail for. Although I'll tell you, your lingerie is of a very high quality and should retail for more than the crap I see in most stores. But we want to come in low at first, so they'll start buying from us. Then we can raise the prices later."

"Sounds great," she said. "I'm excited."

"Do you have items to give me today?" I asked. "That way I can start showing your stuff around this coming Monday."

"The only items I brought with me were in that brown bag, and those I promised to Rosie."

She looked at the clock on her cell phone.

"I have lots of completed panty and bra sets at my house," she said, looking back at me. "Do you have time to take a drive over there with me? It's only five minutes away. I live right around the corner from the university."

"Yeah," I said. "We can do that. Let's finish our coffee first."

She smiled and sipped her drink.

A group of about ten students, all carrying backpacks, walked past our table.

"Hi, Dr. Fischer," one of them called out. It was a young man, skinny with wild blond hair, wearing a green t-shirt that said **Dead Head** on it and blue shorts. He was walking backwards, in flip-flops, looking at us.

"I'm looking forward to the unveiling tonight," he said. He then turned around and continued walking with his group.

"That sounded interesting," I said.

"Not really," she said, exhaling loudly as though something were troubling her.

"What's the matter?"

"Well," she began, "it's not really that big a deal. It's just that the new term began last month. This is the time when the Board of Regents, the people who are actually in charge of the ten universities comprising the UC system, along with the president they appoint, personally visit the chancellors in charge of the individual campuses. They want to see how things are going; see if the chancellors require anything, funds for a new library or a statue of themselves."

She rolled her eyes and laughed.

"So what was that young man talking about when he said he was looking forward to the unveiling?" I asked.

She rolled her eyes again.

"It's silly, really," she said, gesticulating with her right hand while holding her Frappuccino in her left. "Each of the campuses is in competition with one another. They want to show the regents and the president how wonderful their particular university is, how culturally significant it is for the growth of the communities in which each resides."

"Okay," I said. "I understand a bit of healthy competition. What exactly does each campus do to show how wonderful they are?"

"Well," she said, "UCLA always pulls out their extensive collection of pre-Columbian ceramic vessels and sculptures from Peru, collected and catalogued by their own archeologists."

"Not bad," I said.

"Yes." She sipped her Frappuccino and went on. "UC Davis pulls out some of its more rare artworks, like their collection of prints by Francesco Bartolozzi drawn in the 1700's; or their Cezanne print, *Portrait of the Artist*... That one was drawn in 1873, I believe."

"Better," I said. "They sound valuable."

"Of course!" she said. "That's why they pull them out and dust them off – showing off for the regents."

"Well, I'm sure your campus has some pretty decent stuff."

"Yes," she said, "especially the biology department. We have a marvelous collection of completely articulated mammalian and avian skeletons."

"What?" I said incredulously. I almost laughed. "How can you guys compete with pre-Columbian ceramics and Cezanne prints with just mammal and bird bones?"

She gave me a mock-angry look, almost laughing herself.

"They are not just bones," she said, squishing her face up for comic relief.

She then got serious again.

"They are complete skeletons, with skulls, mounted fully erect; the most significant skeleton of all belonging to my department."

"And what type of skeleton is that?" I asked.

"The complete skeleton of an Orcinus Orca," she said.

"Orca," I repeated. "A killer whale, right?"

"Yes, 27ft long, completely articulated – well, it will be completely articulated after I finish snapping it together this afternoon. Just four more metal ball joints to go. There are thirty ball joint connections all together. I started it yesterday."

"That thing must be heavy! How does it stay all put together?"

"Woodworth Hall," she began, "an amphitheater style lecture room, is the only room large enough in the biology department to exhibit the skeleton. There are numerous wire slings in the ceiling there that operate on a remote control, dropping down with the push of a button and disappearing again in the same manner."

"Why are there wire slings in the ceiling?" I asked. "Sounds very Dr. Frankenstein-ish."

She laughed.

"I know it does," she continued, "But there are various classes taught at the university, especially upper division ones – Indigenous North American Predators, structural anatomy, marine mammal biology – that require the exhibition of large mammalian skeletons. They hang those skeletons from those wires."

"So that's how the killer whale skeleton stays together," I said. "You're hanging the parts on those wires."

"Yes, with the assistance of some of my students. That young man who called out to me today helped me yesterday."

"Who's helping you today?" I asked.

"No one," she said. "But the difficult part is done; the backbone vertebra, ribs and skull. Only the fins remain."

"So that's what he meant by the unveiling," I said.

"Yes," she said. "The regents and the president are in town today visiting the university. They always make their rendezvous on a weekend so they don't disrupt classes during the week. They make a courtesy stop to all of the heads of the various departments, and will be seeing me this afternoon."

"That's incredible," I said, "displaying an entire killer whale skeleton just to show off."

"That's right," she said, laughing.

"I don't really know anything about complete killer whale skeletons," I said, "but are they rare? I mean, how does your skeleton stack up against the things those other campuses are showing off?"

She looked at me in shock.

I shrugged.

"What?" I asked.

"This skeleton is priceless!"

"Really?" I sipped my coffee.

"Americans can't own marine mammal body parts," she said, "neither flesh nor bone. It was outlawed by the Marine Mammal Act in 1972."

"How come you can own this one?" I asked.

She reached over the table and gave me a playful slap on the wrist.

"I don't own this one," she said. "UCSC owns it."

"But if it's outlawed –" I began. She interrupted me.

"If someone or an entity acquired the parts prior to the law being enacted, and has proof of the date of acquisition documented, they may retain possession of the parts."

"I conclude that your biology department has documentation," I said.

She nodded.

"So that killer whale skeleton is irreplaceable," I said.

"Yes, it is," she confirmed. "If any part of it went missing, we couldn't replace it with the real thing. We'd have to substitute a model."

"Are model parts any good?" I asked.

"I've seen the model bones they make these days – they're okay, but it's not like having the real thing. The color's always off and the real bone has a certain texture to it –anyone in the academic community who is at all familiar with bones and anatomy can tell right off when it's a model."

"Well," I said, "I can see why you put that thing together every year for the regents. Now that you've explained it to me, it's actually quite impressive, your killer whale skeleton."

"Thank you," she said.

"Where does the thing stay the rest of the year?"

"In polished, walnut boxes," she said. "Rather large ones with shiny brass hinges. Each separate piece has its own box, with a spongy, formfitting mold it sits in. So there are thirty-one boxes all together."

"Wow!" I said. "That's a lot of boxes."

The wind started picking up. It was blowing papers down the boulevard like someone had dropped their writing assignment.

"What time this afternoon are you seeing the regents?" I asked.

finding parking around Pier 9 where the ship was anchored. By the time I arrived there, the ship had already departed. There was an old man in an Irish cap standing on the sidewalk looking out into the now empty slip.

"Did you see the ***Singing Orca Seas*** depart?" I asked.

He pointed to his left, out into the bay, where a large cruise ship was making its turn at Alcatraz Island, in the direction of the Golden Gate Bridge.

Lani was nowhere to be found.

Two hours later, when I arrived at our apartment in Sacramento, Lani was furious.

"Where were you!" she shouted. "My parents wanted to see you!"

She turned, stomped into the kitchen, opened the microwave door, pulled out a plate and then slammed the door hard.

She then stormed into the living room, sat on the sofa with the plate on her lap and began eating the sandwich she had made for herself.

I followed her into the living room and stood in front of her on the opposite side of the coffee table.

"I tried to get there on time," I said, my hands in front of me, gesticulating.

"You did a lousy job of it!"

She took a bite from her sandwich. She wouldn't even look at me.

"Look," I began.

"Shut up!" she shouted. "I don't want to talk to you!"

"Darling, please!"

"Don't darling me! I'm not your darling!"

"Darling, would you stop that," I said. I was trying to be logical and calm about the whole thing.

"My mother and father were looking forward to seeing you! They kept asking me all day, 'Where's Cree? Why doesn't he show up?' I said 'He'll be here! He'll be here!'"

"I'm sorry," I said. "Things happened."

"What happened?"

"I had to talk to this woman."

She slammed her plate onto the coffee table and stood up fast.

"What's wrong with you?"

"What woman?" she screeched.

"Nobody!" I said, shaking my head, trying to compose myself.

"What woman!"

"Her name is Dr. Gale Fischer. She's the Dean of the Marine Biology department at UC Santa Cruz. She's also a friend of Rosie's. You know – the woman who owns *Rosie's Unmentionables*. I talk about her all the time."

"What about her!" Lani screamed.

"Well, Gale also makes sexy lingerie and –"

"You bastard! You missed my mother and father for a woman who makes sexy lingerie?"

"It was business!" I said.

She squeezed her fists together and gave me the meanest looking face I had ever seen in my life.

"Darling, please!" I said.

She turned and stormed into our bedroom, slamming the door shut and locking it behind her.

I followed her and stood outside in the hallway, talking through the bedroom door.

"It was just business!" I yelled. "Rosie wanted me to help her! Wants me to help her sell her lingerie! She's talented, Rosie says! What could I do? And then the Pumpkin Festival Traffic! I tried! Honest to god I did!"

After about ten minutes of that and her not responding, I became angry.

I went into the kitchen, pulled out my cell phone and called Rye.

"Hello!" Rye's voice said.

"Rye, it's Cree."

"Hey, what's up, buddy?"

"This is bullshit man!"

"What is?"

"I've been busting my ass all day and Lani doesn't even give a shit!"

"Are you guys fighting again?"

"I have to get out of here – what are you doing tonight?"

"I'm in Fairfield right now. I have a set later on at the comedy club there. Come on down and see me. Take your mind off of things."

"Fairfield, huh? That's only twenty minutes from Sacramento."

"Are you coming?"

"How'd you get to Fairfield?"

"John drove me. He has a car now."

"Is he there with you?"

"Yeah! Linda and Betty, too. They're all here to see my set. I have a lot of new material. It's too bad you and Lani are fighting. She should come down here too. We haven't seen you guys in a while."

"What time is your set?"

"9 o'clock."

"It's 7:30 now. Do they serve liquor there?"

"Yeah!"

"I'm on my way."

"Great!"

I hung up the phone. I then walked over to the bedroom door again to give Lani one last chance.

"Darling, would you please come out?"

I waited for a few seconds but there was no response.

"Darling, please! I love you. I don't want to fight like this. I just told Rye I was going to Fairfield to see him do his new material at the comedy club there, but I don't want to go without you."

No response.

I wasn't angry anymore. I was nervous.

I didn't like when she was this upset at me. It frightened me. I didn't want her packing a bag and taking off on me to Hawaii, which is what I always thought of when we argued like that.

I stood there quietly for a minute, my ear close to the door.

I could hear movement inside now: heavy footsteps pacing here and there and a sliding of clothes hangers.

"Darling-g-g!" I pleaded through the door.

I heard a light *thud*!

I then heard drawers opening and closing and a shuffling of clothes.

I visualized her packing a suitcase.

My throat began constricting.

I couldn't catch my breath.

I was shaking.

My stomach cramped.

I felt like I might vomit.

And my childhood memories, like a pugilistic reptile, came slithering out of that black reservoir in the back of my mind, crawled right up to me and bit a great big chunk out of my heart.

I folded, and began to cry.

"Lani, would you please open the door," I said softly, wiping the tears from my eyes.

No verbal response but I could still hear movement.

"Please forgive me, darling."

I wiped my tears again.

"Linda, Betty and John are all at the club in Fairfield to see Rye's set. Let's you and I go meet them there. We don't see those guys that often now that we're here in Sacramento. It would be nice for all of us to get together again."

I heard footsteps approaching the door now.

The lock giggled.

The door opened.

Lani stood there in the opened doorway, the dark inside of the bedroom and the hallway light allowing me to see her naked body thru her sheer aqua nightgown.

"Darling, I'm sorry," I said. I wrapped my arms around her and we hugged tightly for a very long time.

I then took a step backward, held her shoulders and looked into her eyes. They were red. She had been crying also.

"Let's stop arguing all time," I said. " I love you."

"I love you too," she said, her sad eyes still moist with tears.

"Will you please come to the comedy club in Fairfield with me so we can be with our friends?"

She looked at me for several seconds, silently, and then said in a whisper:

"I just want to spend some time alone with you – I miss you."

We did not go to the comedy club in Fairfield that night. Theo was born nine months later.

Chapter Sixteen

I turned onto Broadway and drove several blocks past all the run down brick and cinderblock buildings, the multi-level parking garage, the greasy auto mechanics shop, the seedy diner, the convenience store with all the porno-mags in the window, the cigar shop, the liquor store, the arcade with its entryways wide open. I then turned left, into the alleyway between the ***Minotaur Triple-X Movie Theater*** and ***La Castor Velu***.

After parking the van on Pelli's parking pad in the back, I walked around the building to the brightly painted red bricks of the building's façade and entered the store through the front entrance.

"Bon Soir!" Pelli greeted me as I walked toward him. He was standing in the middle of the store, right beside the giant bin that held all the blowup dolls, looking back and forth between his two employees, who were behind the elevated glass counter by the cash register, and the three customers in the store, all middle aged men. One customer was in the CD aisle; one was in the back of the store looking at the porno-mags, the cellophane wrappers crumpling with each one he examined; the third was picking up and turning around in his hands the novelty items on the shelves at the front of the store.

"Cree, my friend."

He hugged me and then held me at arm's length by holding onto both of my arms. He was wearing a blue-white-red shirt tucked into a pair of black slacks. His shoes were highly polished.

"You have not been around for six months."

His accent made the word six sound like *seeks*.

"What's the sense in me being around?" I said. "You guys are all buying your novelty items off Ning Lee directly since he set his cousin up in the wholesale business. What's that cousin's name again?"

"Sycolin Lee," Pelli said.

"Is he still driving around in a van delivering personal service to you guys the way I had?"

"Oui." Pelli nodded. "Yes."

Both the impact of the Internet, and then the impact of the recession, had been affecting my business for two whole years, all of 2006 and all of 2007. It happened gradually, with me not really paying any attention to it at first. I kept my volume commitment with Ning, continuing to buy four pallets of stock each month for the whole of 2006, even though I was only selling three pallets worth per month by about the middle of that year. Ning was giving me good prices at that volume. I didn't want to lose that. I was absolutely positive that things were going to turn around and I had no problem keeping the excess stock in my garage at **The Quinn Estate**. It was no big deal to me. I'd just sell the stuff when things got better. But by August of 2007, I had no choice but to drop my commitment to three pallets per month, and I didn't even need that much because by that time, I was only moving one pallet per month. Unsold goods kept piling up, so much that I had to switch garages, moving everything into my two-car garage. By December of 2007, I had no choice but to stop buying product off of Ning entirely. I had sent that two hundred thousand dollars to Geier Campbell at T-Rex Fuels in January of that year, and I was just plain out of cash, not even able to pay our mortgages, business was so bad.

Ning was furious. I told him about all that stock in my garage and asked him if he would please allow me some time to sell it off.

"No!" he exclaimed. "No pallets, no wholesaler status! It's gone! You're not a wholesaler any longer!"

It was a bit dramatic on his part, I thought, but I didn't let it bother me too much. I was expecting the economy to turn around soon which would allow me to sell off my excess inventory. By then, I figured Ning would be cooled down and grant me my wholesale status back. But I was dead wrong. He had no intention of selling to me ever again.

Instead, he used the opportunity to implement his long dormant plan of selling to the retailers directly, by setting up his cousin in business, giving Sycolin a van, installing the wooden floor and shelves in the back – just like my van – and sending him around to all the businesses that I had once serviced, giving them the same personalized service that I had once delivered, and undercutting my prices by half! That was the real reason I had gone out of business: no one would buy from me any longer because my prices were double those of Sycolin's.

"I am sorry I had to stop buying from you," Pelli said. "It is the recession. I had to save money where I could so I had no choice but to buy from Sycolin."

"I understand," I said. "But I'm in real trouble and I need your help."

"Of course I will assist you," Pelli said, "as long as you do not ask to borrow money, because I have none to loan."

"I need two blowup dolls," I said.

"But why?"

He gave me a curious look.

I began tapping the edge of the blowup doll bin. I was getting nervous.

"Did your wife leave you?" he said.

"No, it has nothing to do with that."

"Then what, may I ask?"

I looked at him, not knowing what to say.

He looked back at me, head askance and arms folded. He began rubbing his trimmed, steely beard with his left hand.

"I have to do something," I said, "and the blowup dolls play a crucial role for me logistically."

He shrugged and then put the palms of his hands out in front of him, questioningly.

"What is this thing you must do that requires blowup dolls?"

A customer walked up to the bin, standing right beside us practically, and began examining the blowup dolls, picking up the boxes in which they were folded, looking them over through the front cellophane window, ostensibly trying to choose the color he liked the best.

I looked form Pelli to the customer to Pelli again.

"Come to my office," Pelli said. "It is more private there."

We walked into his office at the rear of the store and Pelli closed the door.

He sat down at the chair behind his desk and I sat down on the one chair in front of his desk.

"Are you alright?" he asked. "Because you look like there is something terribly wrong with you."

"My whole life has fallen apart," I said. "My business is gone. My four investment houses have been repossessed. I lost two hundred thousand dollars in a natural gas drilling fiasco that went belly-up at the beginning of this month because all four wells in the deal were dry. My wife and I had to declare bankruptcy in January. It was fully discharged last month, so we are officially out of debt, except for the two mortgages on our home. The First Sacramento Savings and Loan is about to repossess that house, leaving us with nothing, unless I can pay off the one hundred thousand dollar 2nd lien on it with the Bank of Northern California."

"Mon Dieu!" he said. "I am very sorry to hear this."

He began gesturing with his hands.

"But I told you already, Cree, I cannot loan you this money! I do not have it to loan!"

"I'm not here to ask for a loan! I'm here to ask for two blowup dolls!"

"Why?"

"The whale," I said.

"The whale?"

"Yes."

"You mean the one all over the news? The one that hit the Golden Gate Bridge?"

It sounded like he said the *Goal-don Ghaat Brrreegh!*

"Yes," I said. "I'm going to cut off its head. The skull is worth one hundred thousand dollars to me. I need those two blowup dolls as a distraction. I'm going to inflate them and hang one from either side of the bridge on the San Francisco side. I figure after about twenty minutes to half an hour of them hanging there, blowing in the wind, all the tourists on the bridge will be gathered around them because it will be a funny distraction, don't you think?"

"I think it is possible but –"

He shook his head and then went on:

"But, Cree, this is insane! You cannot do this! It is impossible to cut this thing's head off. It is too large!"

He shook his head again and looked at me like I was nuts.

"How is this skull worth one hundred thousand dollars to you?"

"I have a friend – I can't tell you her name – but she is the Dean of a marine biology department at a certain University of California campus. This campus was in possession of a complete killer whale skeleton, but not anymore. My friend started dating one of her students –"

He interrupted me.

"A teacher dating a student?" he asked. "Is this not illegal in this country?"

"This guy was a twenty-eight year old PhD student in marine studies," I said. "It's no big deal. Anyway, this guy was also the Captain of the rugby team on campus. Near the end of last year, they were going to be playing UC Berkeley's rugby team for the divisional title. This guy didn't like the campus mascot, which happens to be the banana slug."

"The banana slug?" he said curiously. "What is this?"

"It's a slug that eats bananas," I said. "Anyway, this guy gets my friend drunk one night three days before the big game, takes her keys from her purse, along with the master key that opens all the doors in the biology department, and he takes that killer whale skull from its case in the biology department's storage locker."

"For what reason would he do this thing?"

"He was going to take the skull to the divisional game and set it up on a pole on the visiting team's side of the field, hoping, if they won the game, that the skull would be considered good luck, making it a good chance the university would make the killer whale its new mascot."

"And is this what in fact did happen?"

"No," I said, "because *he* was drunk, too. He ended up leaving the skull on the front seat of his car the night he borrowed it and, the next morning, he finds the passenger side window smashed in and the skull gone."

"Mon Dieu! What will your friend do?"

"She has three months to come up with a new skull," I said. "No one knows it's missing except for her, her now ex-boyfriend and whoever it was that stole the thing. But three months from now the Board of Regents and the university president will be visiting the campus, and she'll have to put that skeleton together for their visit, and it will be without a skull, unless I get her this one."

"Why can she not just buy another skull?"

"It is illegal to own marine mammal bones in this country," I said, "unless you got them prior to 1972 and that must be documented. There is no store in this entire country where she can buy a real killer whale skull."

"Are there not fake skulls available?" he asked.

"She could buy a model," I said, "but all of the professors in the biology department there, who are thoroughly familiar with bones, would spot it right away."

"Are there no traffickers in this type of illegal contraband?"

"Yes, in Canada," I said. "But they are asking more money than she has."

He looked at me for a few seconds, rubbing his beard with his left hand, a thoughtful look on his face as though he were calculating everything that had been said. Until finally:

"I understand why you would like to do this thing, Cree. But you will not be successful. You cannot cut off a whale's head. The task is too monumental. Sometimes we must be resolved to our fate. You will lose your house. It is sad, but it is what will be. At least you will still have your family, your wife and your little son. What is his name again, I forget."

"Theo."

"Yes, little Theo," he said. "And family is the most important thing of all."

"That's the problem," I said.

"What is the problem?"

"I don't want to lose them."

"What makes you think you will? Your wife has stayed with you through everything you have already told me: loss of business, investment houses, money, bankruptcy."

I looked him in the eyes.

I could feel myself shaking.

I could feel my heart pounding in my chest.

He stopped rubbing his beard.

"You look very sad," he said, "even more than usual. What is it, my friend?"

"I'm afraid," I said. "More than ever before in my entire life. I can't live without my wife and son. I need that skull. Please, Pelli – give me two blowup dolls."

"Take them," he said with a brush of his hand. "But I fear for you, Cree. May God watch over you as you do this impossible thing."

He looked at the ceiling, made the sign of the cross and whispered in French:

"Protegez-le le seigneur."

Chapter Seventeen

I was driving furiously now down Broadway in the direction of the Golden Gate Bridge. Sidewalks, mailboxes, intersections, stores whizzed by me in a blur. Vehicles, pedestrians, dogs and cats stayed out of my way. Traffic lights be warned: signal in my favor.

I disappeared into the darkness of the Broadway Tunnel and reappeared into the light at the opposite end. The two blowup dolls, folded neatly in their individual boxes, were both inside the large cardboard box on the bucket passenger seat beside me.

My toolkit was complete.

My plan was complete.

The clock on the dashboard read 4pm.

I turned on the Radio for news.

The storm would be here early; possibly late this evening.

Now was the time!

The whale approaches.

I made a series of right and left turns, until I could finally see the towering red pylons of the bridge in front of me in the distance, its arched roadway delicately hanging from the two main cables and equidistant vertical cables like a lovely, geometric pendant meant for a giant's necklace. I was one lucky bastard, too. I can tell you that. All the cosmic tumblers were falling into place for me that day. I had driven like a maniac all the way there and would have been hauled off to jail had a cop seen me. But not that day. Only one word to describe it: destiny. That skull was mine!

I drove into the bridge parking lot on the San Francisco side. It was where anyone could park, provided a meter was available, who wished to walk across the bridge on one of the pedestrian walkways. There was one space left at the far end. I pulled into it. I did not turn off the engine or get out of the van to feed the meter with quarters. I didn't plan on staying there very long; just long enough to get those two dolls blown up and get about twenty feet of nylon rope around each one of their necks.

I pulled the two blowup doll boxes out of the cardboard box and threw them into the back of the van. I then moved back there myself between the two bucket seats. The wire-basket shelving units didn't give me much room, but the small corridor adjacent to the sliding side-door was all I needed. I examined the wooden floor for splinters. There were none.

I ripped open the box with the peach colored blowup doll in it first and fully unfolded it across the corridor on the floor. The battery-operated air pump was in the pouch on the back of the driver's side chair. I pulled it out and flipped the switch to on. The loud flow of expelling air filled the van.

I filled the peach colored doll with air. It slowly rose to human size like a giant pizza dough rising in a brick oven. When I was finished, I stood it up in the back of the van with its feet on the wooden floor and its airhead pushing against the van's ceiling. I then tore open the other box with the cocoa colored blowup doll in it, and filled her up with air as well. I stood her up next to the other one. They were pretty good looking for dolls, mostly smooth with their plastic-flesh, but with hair in all the right places. They did look funny, though, with their arms extended and their mouths opened wide like that.

I reached into the cardboard box on the passenger side chair and pulled out the 100ft coil of nylon rope and the foot-long steak knife. I measured with tugs of my hand two equal feeds of rope, about 20 feet long apiece, cutting them to size with the knife. I then made two hangmen's loops and placed one of the loops around Peachey's neck, pulling it tight; the other around Cocoa's neck, pulling hers tight as well. I then placed the knife and the remaining coil of rope back into the cardboard box, along with the air pump.

Leaving the dolls standing back there with the ropes around their necks, I sat back down in the driver's seat and pulled the van out of the parking lot, heading toward the tollbooths. Time to implement my plan. There was only one way to make this thing work efficiently, without getting caught. It was going to cost me two tolls, but that was the price of doing business with the whale.

There was a lot of traffic. Tens of thousands of people lived in Marin County and commuted to San Francisco for work. Friday afternoons, many of them left their jobs early to get a jumpstart on the weekend. I was caught in that traffic: the going home to party traffic. And people were anxious to begin the party, too. There were cars all around me, jerking forward, stopping short, honking their horns in anger and protest and fun.

The guy ahead of me, in the yellow mustang, flipped his middle finger to the guy ahead of him, in the BMW, who flipped his middle finger back, as if the gesture could get us anywhere.

I was in the center toll lane.

There was a woman in a black SUV to my left. She wasn't even watching the road as she drove. She was looking at her teeth in the rearview mirror. Her vehicle maintained a steady speed and bearing the whole time she wasn't looking. It was amazing how women could do that – drive carefully without looking. I saw women driving without looking all the time, combing their hair, applying makeup, spraying on perfume, flossing, looking out the driver's side window at the horizon. But they always maintained a steady, straight course. Yet they couldn't make a right hand turn onto the highway unless there was a whole football field of distance between them and the cars approaching. Depth perception – it's a bitch!

We crept along like herded insects.

When I finally reached the tollbooth, I rolled down my window and handed a ten-dollar bill to the tollbooth operator. She wouldn't take it. She pulled her body back as if repulsed by me. She was a big woman, too: middle-aged, cropped orange hair, wearing a ribbed tank top and a pair of sunglasses. Her arms were meaty and flappy like a pro-wrestler's arms.

"What are you, some type of psychopath?" she said to me.

"What are you talking about?" I asked. There was a round sticker on the outside of her booth that read Golden Gate Transit.

"I could see straight through your windshield as you rolled up here," she said. "I saw what you have in the back of that van."

"They're just blowup dolls," I said.

"Was that ropes around their necks?"

"Yeah."

"Whaddaya have, a fetish?"

"Yeah, lady," I said. "I have a fetish."

She took the ten dollar bill, gave me my change and I pulled onto the open span of the bridge while rolling up my window.

I put my blinker on, pulled over to the far right lane, and drove the speed limit, not wanting to be pulled over for a ticket now that I was so close. Cars were whizzing by me on my left. The bridge's roadway arched upward. Red cables were all around me. The black water of the bay was below me, its surface wrinkled like a silken sheet that's been disturbed. I passed beneath the southern pylon, the San Francisco side pylon. At the center of the bridge, I saw the familiar sign that read *Welcome to Marin County*. I passed beneath the northern pylon and, after reaching the first exit, put my blinker on and turned right, onto the paved roadway of the Marin County observation area. I rolled my window down then just to test the air. It smelled like rotten fish.

There were many tourists on the other side of the low wall at the observation area. Those weren't the people I needed to distract. They were facing the eastern side, inner bay side, of the bridge. They wouldn't be able to see me when I was in the water beneath the bridge because the span of the roadway would block my view. It was the people parked at the observation areas along the sea cliffs of the Marin Headlands, which faced the western, open ocean side of the bridge, who I needed to distract.

I turned my van around on the turnabout, drove back onto the highway and back onto the bridge, heading back to the San Francisco side. I know it sounded crazy, but I had to do it this way. It was the quickest and safest way of getting those dolls hung up.

Halfway across the bridge, after seeing the sign that read *Welcome to San Francisco*, I put on my emergency flashers and began to slow down. I didn't slow down quickly: I took my time about it. I didn't want to be rear-ended, which would ruin my plan, fast.

I looked at the cars behind me in my rearview mirror. They were slowing down too. I was in the right-hand lane. There was a long, segmented but interconnected cement barrier between the driving lane and the pedestrian sidewalk. It was only about three feet high.

About three quarters of the way across the bridge, on the San Francisco side now, I came to a complete stop. My emergency flashers were still on, blinking away like Christmas lights. The cars behind me started pulling into the left, center lane, moving around me.

I shifted the van into parking gear.

I kept the engine running.

I slipped into the rear of the van between the two bucket seats.

I slid open the side-door, metallic rollers banging to a stop!

I grabbed Peachey's neck with my right hand and collected up the twenty feet of rope in my left.

There was much light outside, but it was starting to become overcast.

The storm was coming early.

I stepped onto the roadway through the van's opened side-door, used my left hand holding the rope to catapult myself over the cement barrier, Peachey held high in the air, ran across the sidewalk, pedestrians walking by –

"Hey!"

"Watch it!"

"Sorry!"

Lovers holding hands –

Parents –

Children –

"What's that guy doing?"

"Is this a joke? '

"What's he holding mommy?"

"Nothing! He's crazy!"

I tied the end of the rope to the hand railing and flung Peachey over the side of the bridge. I then looked over the railing, downward, the water far below, and watched as she swung steadily, like the bob of a clock, in the mild breeze that was steadily gathering.

People stopped walking and looked over the railing at Peachey, just as I expected.

I ran back across the sidewalk, hopped over the barrier, entered the van through the side-door, closed it – *Bam!* – sat down in the driver's seat, turned off the emergency flashers and shifted the van into drive. I was now on my way again.

I had no choice but to exit the bridge, turn around in the parking lot where I had originally inflated Peachey and Cocoa, and enter the tollbooths again.

I paid the $5.00 toll a second time, stayed in the far right lane, put on my emergency flashes almost right away, still on the San Francisco side but on the east side of the bridge now, stopped the van, slid open the side-door again, hopped out of the van with Cocoa's neck in my right hand, the rope in my left, hopped over the barrier, ran across the sidewalk through the stream of pedestrians – similar questions and comments and suggestions of insanity – tied the rope to the hand railing and now flung Cocoa over the side of the bridge, and then back to the van. It was done.

With my girls creating a distraction for me, I now pulled into the fast lane, drove across the bride again to the Marin County side and exited, with a left-hand turn this time, driving up the two lane road that wound upward onto the side of the sea cliffs of the Marin Headlands. At the first observation deck, where there was a dirt parking lot, I parked the van, grabbed the large cardboard box off of the passenger side seat, set it on the ground in the tall weeds, and then got the inflatable boat and the two plastic paddles out of the back of the van. The cardboard box was big enough to hold the inflatable boat which was not yet inflated but was all folded up neatly like the two blowup dolls had originally been. There were five other cars parked there, but I couldn't see anyone around. People went up to those cliffs all the time to not only sightsee and marvel at the view of the Golden Gate Bridge, but to walk around in the prairie lands up there or hide in the tall grasses, couples making love outdoors.

I made sure the blue bath towel and my change of clothing was covering the meat cleaver and the knife, then stuffed the folded up rubber boat into the cardboard box. It didn't fit in all the way. Half of it was still flapping outside, but it was good enough. And the box wasn't that heavy. I picked it up off of the tall weeds, balanced it in my right arm as I knelt down to pick up the two plastic paddles with my left, then headed downward through the scrub brush, along a narrow, winding trail that led to the water below.

It was warm outside.

It smelled like rotten fish everywhere.

The wind was blowing but not hard.

There was plenty of sunlight left.

A small patch of sky was beginning to turn grey, but that was far to the east.

The red span of the bridge was in front of me.

On the San Francisco side, I could see Peachey, hanging over the edge of the span, a tiny, pale dot swaying back and forth like the dot on the words of a song that one followed.

Green scrub brush covered the sides of the cliff like a summer hat.

Off to the left of me, there was no scrub brush at all, just a disorderly mass of crumbling dirt and stone.

The ocean lay below me like a vast, eerie face gazing back.

Halfway down the steep decline, my sneakers – carefully placed but hard steps nonetheless – sending clumps of dirt and small stones rolling down the hill toward the water, I turned a rocky outcrop, and there it was: my killer whale, black and white, just as Dr. Waverly Seymour had described it on the Mike and Ike radio show. It was on its left side, black back and floating dorsal fin facing me, white stomach hard against the cement base of the pylon, tail fins saying back and forth in the swirling currents, a round mass of seagulls pecking away at portions of its tail. It looked like it was floating, but I knew because of the recent avalanches that Dr. Seymour had described, that the water was just a couple of feet high where the upper half of the deceased animal's body was resting, giving merely the appearance of flotation. Its lack of movement, other than the tail fins, revealing its stranded condition.

It was difficult to walk because the dirt trail was becoming ever so narrower and the cardboard box was blocking my view, its bottom edge cutting into my shoulder and forearm, the plastic paddles in my left hand dragging through the tall weeds behind me.

I finally made it to the bottom of the cliff.

The ground was flatter by the water's edge.

I dropped the paddles then set the cardboard box down into the scrub brush.

I pulled the bulky rubber boat out of the box and rolled it out onto the relatively flat, sandy shore.

The smell was really bad now.

The breeze blew it right up my nose.

I pulled the gauze dust mask out of the box and stretched the elastic band around the back of my head, the mask now securely over my mouth and nose.

My breath felt warm and moist inside the mask.

To the creatures swimming in the ocean, I must have looked like a space alien about to perform an experiment.

I got the battery-powered air pump out of the box and began blowing up the boat.

I looked around as I did, trying to see if there was anyone close by.

There was no one.

I was all-alone.

My stomach hurt.

I was nervous.

The smell wasn't so bad now, but still hung in the air like the annoying buzz of gnats that was swarming in front of my face now.

The boat fully inflated rather quickly; it was nice and plump now: about six feet long and four feet wide, yellow sides, blue bottom; enough room for two grown men or one man and a whale's skull.

I placed the boat into the water.

I placed the paddles into the boat.

I placed the cardboard box into the boat.

I took off my sneakers and socks, set them into the boat, rolled the bottom of my jeans up to my knees, stepped into the water – it was cold – and pushed the boat several feet away from the shore.

My toes sunk into the loose silt.

Waves, about a foot high, splashed against my jeans, soaking me.

I was knee deep in water.

I climbed into the boat.

Water and silt from the bottom of my feet dripped into the bottom of the boat.

I threaded the paddles into the hard, round oar stations on either side of the boat, and began paddling for the whale. I was about a quarter of a mile away from it. There were long, low swells riding beneath me, causing the boat to rise and fall, rise and fall, like clockwork. The closer I got to the animal, the more I realized how much that dust mask was saving my life, because if it smelled that badly with it on, I couldn't imagine what it smelled like with it off.

I had been paddling with my back to the whale, peering over my shoulder to make sure I was headed in the right direction.

Halfway there, I turned the boat around so I could face the monster.

I paddled toward it now, watching it as I approached.

It seemed relatively small when I first began my paddling, dwarfed by the colossal span of the bridge, but both grew steadily larger, and larger, and ever larger, the closer I came.

The squawking of the seagulls was becoming annoying.

I was about 30ft away now, moving up – then down – up – then down in the ocean's swells.

The beast was a giant! All 28 feet and 9 tons of it in my face, stinging my nostrils with its putrid odor.

The bridge, too, was a monster, looming and titanic!

I became nauseous: the smell and swells were getting to me. I needed to just sit there in the boat and relax for a minute and hopefully start feeling better.

I had stopped paddling, but inertia carried me forward and the bottom of the boat ran over the floating dorsal fin and became stuck. I reached down to the water and touched the dorsal fin. It was smooth and wet and cold.

Suddenly, something broke the surface of water about twenty feet away from me.

"Holy shit!" I said out loud, gazing upon the giant dorsal fin of a Great White shark.

It wasn't heading toward me. It was heading for the whale's tail.

I saw the shark's head emerge from the water, giant gums and rows of teeth; it tore a basketball-sized chunk of flesh right out of the whale's tail.

The seagulls went berserk!

I had to be very careful out there. I was now in the water, in a rubber boat, with sharks.

I unthreaded one of the paddles and placed the flat end against the edge of the dorsal fin, shoving hard, freeing the boat from its stranded condition and sending me floating toward the whale's head. I then placed the paddle on the floor of the boat. I didn't require it any longer. At least not until the job was done. So I unthreaded the other one and placed it on the floor of the boat as well. I then stood up in the boat, careful not to capsize myself and turn myself into shark chow. My pant legs were still rolled up. I was feeling better. Maybe filled with adrenaline now, having seen the shark and also having to free myself from the dorsal fin stranding. The mask seemed to be working better, or maybe I was just acclimating to the odor.

The head was right there in front of me now, on its side, about four feet above the water. I placed my hands on it. The skin there felt hard, like an old piece of black rubber all dried out by the sun. At least I had done it. I had made it to the whale. Now all I had to do was cut off its head.

I carefully reached down into the cardboard box, fumbled through the change of clothing and the towel, and reeled out the meat cleaver. It was heavy. I also pulled out the wooden mallet. I didn't need it yet, but **would** after I cut away enough flesh and blubber to expose the neck vertebra.

I set the mallet down on the floor of the boat.

I then realized that hacking away at the beast was going to make the boat move all about. I needed to secure myself somehow, so I wasn't out there hacking for a few seconds, then paddling back in place, hacking for a few seconds, then paddling back into place – but how? I was out in the middle of the water with nothing around but a big whale and an even bigger bridge pylon. Not to mention dangerous sharks and annoying seagulls.

I then came up with an idea.

I carefully set the meat cleaver back into the box and pulled out the 60ft of nylon rope I had left over.

The seagulls squawked.

The breeze brushed my cheeks.

I moved up and down with the swells.

I used my hands to push against the whale's body, the momentum causing me to float back again toward the dorsal fin. Once there, I carefully knelt down onto the floor of the boat, took the long measure of the rope at one end and made a giant hangman's loop, tying it off. I took that loop with both hands, bent so low that my chest rested on the side of the boat, the water right there in front of my face, and I thrust the rope into the water, placing the loop around the upper part of the dorsal fin. I then yanked the rope tightly, lassoing the dorsal fin like a cowboy lassos a calf. That accomplished, I used my patting technique along the animal's body again to float myself back to the head. There, I carefully reeled the knife out of the cardboard box and used it to cut the rope down to what I estimated to be a 15ft length. I then stuck the knife into the left front pocket of my jeans, covering the handle with my shirt. I was going to need that knife to help shave off the flesh from the whale's head, like Gino did to the rotating meat at *The Last Stand*, the Greek restaurant down the street from my apartment.

I threaded the 15ft length of rope through the right oar station, and then made another, smaller hangman's loop at the end. I then carefully stood up and, reaching my arm over the top of the beast's head to its opened mouth, snagged that loop onto a rather large tooth in the back of the animal's mouth. And that was it. I had done it! I had tethered my boat to the whale, on a 15ft line of nylon rope running from the dorsal fin, through my boat's oar station, to the animal's mouth. I could now go to work.

I carefully reached into the box and pulled out the meat cleaver. I then used my eyes to calculate the exact spot where I should begin hacking: right around the blowhole. I needed to expose neck vertebra.

I then needed to trim away the skin and muscles and blubber so I could get the skull down to a size where it could be reasonably handled and transported. It couldn't be too heavy or it might capsize the boat.

The seagulls squawked.

The wind whipped my hair.

The swells brought me up – then down – up – then down.

Salt water sprayed into the boat and against my right cheek.

Standing there in the boat, facing the whale, I held the meat cleaver over my head in both hands and –

A sound –

A crackling –

A microphone in the wind –

"Put down the weapon!"

"What?"

I turned my head but not my body so I didn't go reeling into the water.

The meat cleaver was still over my head in both hands.

There were a multitude of small boats dotting the bay, moving this way and that. But seven boats were very close to me – five motorboats and two sail boats. They formed a cluster about 60 yards away, in the water beneath the span of the bridge. Their decks were cluttered with people, and they were all looking at me, some of them holding binoculars.

Boat traffic. It was the only thing I hadn't counted on. It never entered my mind when I had put my plan together.

"Put down the weapon!"

I still didn't realize what was going on.

I turned slowly, not wanting to capsize the boat, the meat cleaver still in my hands above my head.

One of the boats from the cluster was approaching me dead on. It was about 60ft long, white bow slicing the water in giant waves. When it got about 40 yards from me, it made a sharp left turn and stopped. That's when I saw the familiar red and blue stripes, the crossed anchors and shield, and the words ***U.S. Coast Guard*** written in black letters on the side. Standing on the deck, I could clearly make out four men in blue uniforms. Three of them were pointing rifles at me. One of them had a handheld microphone to his mouth.

"Holy shit!" I thought. I couldn't believe it!

A smaller Coast Guard patrol boat, about 20ft long and orange, snuck out from behind the bigger one and was nearing me fast.

"Put down the weapon or we will shoot!"

"No!" I thought, watching the scene play out before my very eyes, Coast Guard patrol boats and weapons pointed directly at me.

I lowered the meat cleaver to my side but continued holding it in my right hand. I needed it. I still needed that skull.

The orange patrol boat was approaching fast.

"F-ing no!" I said to myself. My mind was frantic! Chaotic! I may have snapped at that particular moment and become, at least briefly, insane.

"This can't be happening!" I was thinking. "I need that god-damned f-ing skull!"

Then a vision of my family appeared on the movie screen in my mind.

"Lani! Theo! I need to get back to them! I can't let these guys get me!"

I used the meat cleaver to cut the nylon rope, untethering myself from the whale. I was going to make a run for it because I knew the water was too shallow for them to get any closer. All I had to do was paddle myself as close to shore as possible beneath the bridge, until grounding myself on the avalanche debris, then I'd abandon my boat and make a scramble through the shallow water for the cliffs, a dirt path, my van and freedom!

I held the meat cleaver in the air and shook it wildly attempting to look menacing so they'd stay away from me.

Bang!

A shot was fired.

It whistled eerily far above my head.

I wasn't thinking straight. All I could think of were Lani and Theo.

I grabbed the whale's opened mouth and began pulling myself toward the shallower water.

Bang!
Plud!

That one entered the whale's head just inches away from my arm. I could see the large, bloodless hole and the grey brain matter seeping out.

"There goes my goddamned f-ing skull!" I said to myself. "Shattered now inside that dead whale's head!"

I held both hands in the air, still holding the meat cleaver, and turned, slowly, to face them.

It was all over.

I couldn't risk a bullet in the back.

My poor darling and baby – I couldn't die on them.

"This is your last warning! Drop the weapon!"

I carefully dropped the meat cleaver into the cardboard box. I then raised my shirt and pulled the knife out of my pocket, carefully dropping that into the box as well.

Waves that had been created by the larger boat when it had turned were striking the side of my boat now, splashing water over the side. I was now standing in about six inches of cold seawater.

The orange patrol boat was only about 25 feet away from me now, motionless, at the other end of the whale, by its floating tail fins. The seagulls were all aflutter in between us, squawking and dive-bombing for the fleshy, exposed tidbits along the whale's shark-ravaged tail. But I could see through the windows of the boat's wooden deckhouse. There were two Coasties inside: a woman at the steering wheel; the other, a man, who was pointing a handgun at me out the opened window.

"Sit down!" the one with the handgun commanded.

I sat down in the freezing cold water.

"Take that mask off!"

I removed the dust mask and dropped it into the cardboard box.

"We will not approach you any further," the one pointing the handgun at me said. He did not have a microphone. He was just yelling out the window.

"We cannot risk grounding our vessel. You will approach us, slowly."

My hands were shaking.

My teeth were chattering.

I threaded the paddles into the oarlocks.

It took me forever because I was freezing cold, soaking wet and practically hypothermic.

The sky was beginning to be overcast.

The wind had picked up.

The swells were decidedly larger and more threatening.

I looked up at the whale's head one last time, rigid and black with two holes in it now, one bullet hole and one lifeless, breathless blow-hole; the wretched stench from its own decomposition, nauseating.

"There goes my home and probably my wife and son," I thought. That skull was my last chance. I had to talk to Lani. I had to somehow call her. I had to make this right –

"You will begin paddling to us now, or I will fire upon your boat," the Coastie pointing the handgun at me said.

I began paddling. It was damned difficult, too, not only because I was freezing and shaking, but because of all that water inside my boat: it was heavy.

I got myself moving pretty good, and then accidentally paddled myself onto the whale's dorsal fin again. I was stranded.

I looked over at the two Coasties in the orange patrol boat and shrugged, thinking they realized what had happened.

A shot rang out and whistled inches over my head.

The seagulls vanished in a frenzy of flight.

I cringed when I heard it.

It scared the freaking hell out of me.

"That was a warning," the one pointing the handgun shouted. "The next shot will pierce your boat."

"I'm stranded on the dorsal fin!"

"Come again!"

"I'm stuck on the dorsal fin! I'm going to stand up and free myself with one of these paddles."

"Affirmative! Do not jump into the water and try to escape or I will shoot."

I unthreaded one of the paddles and slowly stood up. The water on the bottom of the boat splashed against the sides as I did, making standing very difficult.

I placed the flat end of the paddle against the side of the dorsal fin and pushed as hard as I could; again; and one more time.

With the help of a rising swell, the boat slid off the large fin and was floating again, moving parallel to the whale's tail.

The nylon rope was still tied around the top part of the dorsal fin, its length floating westerly now with the tide.

The cold wind whipped my face.

The swells brought me up high – down low – up high again.

It was difficult to stand.

The seagulls were back and they made a frightening cackle as though suddenly disturbed by an unsettling presence. It alarmed me as well and, before I could take my seat again and restart my paddling, I saw the eerie silhouette of a Great White shark glide beneath my boat, dwarfing it, just feet below the water. Its giant mouth, exposed gums and rows of saw-like teeth began gnawing wildly at the whale's tail, tearing out a beach ball sized chunk of flesh. Its thrashing periscope tail, now breaking the surface of the water, struck my boat hard with a *thud!* sending it sideways, toppling me over, sending me headlong into the water.

Splash!

A swell struck my face *slap!* as I sliced into the sea like a dive-bombing gannet.

Sinking, all muffled now and slow, swallowed by the frigid ocean, holding my breath, frozen in pain, a million needles stabbing simultaneously, salty minerals filling my orifices, mouth, nose and ears.

I struggled onto my back, arms and legs thrashing for the surface, surrounded by a trillion tiny bubbles and peering skyward through the milky brine, I see the turning shark heading straight for me, opened mouth just inches away, dripping shards of bloody blubber dangling from its giant teeth. Its streamlined, sandpaper head and jaw brushing right against my face as it passes, its pectoral fin striking me hard in the shoulder, sending me into an underwater spin!

"I'm dead!" my mind howls.

A hand from above grabs my shoulder.

"I'm saved!"

Chapter Eighteen

I was at the Coast Guard holding station on Treasure Island. Seaman Apprentice Ndidi Obama, who had been steering the orange patrol boat, saw the shark bump me into the water, and had the good sense, skill – and above all, compassion – to bring the boat close enough to me so that Seaman Ryan Murphy, the one who had been pointing the handgun at me the whole time, could reach down into the water and pull me up to safety. I was very grateful to the both of them for that. I did have a severe bruise on my left shoulder where the shark's pectoral fin had struck me.

I was sitting at a wooden table in a small, windowless room off of the command center. Captain Kofi Fredericks was seated across from me. He was wearing an officer's uniform, white with gold buttons, many decorative medals pinned to his chest, and I could see the insignia on both of his shoulders: two silver eagles. He had a look of concern in his dark, deeply-set eyes and crevassed forehead.

When Seamen Obama and Murphy had first brought me into the station, Captain Fredericks was angry at me and he demanded to know exactly why I was out there on the open ocean in nothing but a small, inflatable boat, and what exactly I meant to do with that meat cleaver. I told him: the whole story, Lani, Theo, Gale, the stolen whale skull, our home, our bankruptcy, repossessed investment houses, the lousy bank, Ning Lee, T-Rex Fuels – everything. It took me forever to tell, too, but he patiently listened to the entire narrative.

At the end, he told me he was sorry. He told me he had three relatives in California, two aunts and his wife's brother, who were going through the same thing, bankruptcy and repossession of their homes, and it was devastating to them and their families. He began treating me very nicely. He let me take a shower in the men's bathroom. He ordered Seaman Murphy to retrieve the cardboard box from the orange patrol boat so I could have my change of clean clothing which, fortunately for me, was still dry. He gave me a new pair of brown, Coastie boat shoes because my sneakers were still soaking wet. He let me go to the mess hall which was open for dinner, and I had a hot pastrami sandwich with Swiss cheese on light rye, and a cup of hot coffee.

"How was that sandwich?" Captain Fredericks asked. He was sitting back in his chair with his hands folded in his lap.

"It was good," I said. "I was starving."

I had my arms on the table, holding my cup of coffee in both hands.

"I have been around the sea for a long time," he said.

His manner was calm, soothing.

I blew away the steam from my cup of coffee and took a sip.

"30 years, Mr. Quinn. All that time in the Coast Guard. I joined when I was 25 years old. I grew up in Oakland, just across the bay from here."

He pointed in an easterly direction. He then lowered his hand and continued:

"Over half of that duty spent right here in the Bay Area. A few years at the San Francisco Air Station by the airport and now here as Commander of this holding facility. I did travel a lot earlier on in my career. I have been to air stations in Los Angeles, Corpus Christi, New Orleans and Porto Rico. I thought I had seen it all; heard it all."

He laughed, shook his head and continued:

"But this one takes the cake. I've never heard a story like this one before. You either have a lot of guts or you are certifiably crazy."

He smiled at me.

I attempted a laugh because I could see he was trying to be nice to me, but I couldn't stop thinking about Lani and Theo. I had just seen them that afternoon before I left the house to head for San Francisco; but the pain of missing them was exquisite at that moment.

"May I call my wife now?" I asked.

"Yes. Do you have a cell phone or do you need to borrow this one."

He pointed to a landline phone on the tabletop beside us.

"I have my cell," I said.

"It survived all that water that filled the bottom of your boat?"

"Yes. I tucked it into the pocket of my spare jeans in the cardboard box before paddling out to the whale."

Another officer entered the room from the command center. He immediately walked up to my side of the table and saluted Captain Fredericks. He was wearing a blue officer's uniform with double-silver-bar insignia on both shoulders. I looked at the nametag on his chest: Papadopoulos.

Captain Fredericks saluted back.

"What is it, Lieutenant?"

"Sir, Channel 10 News just got off the horn and have informed me that a news crew, along with reporter Pricilla Pan, is on their way over here right now and they are requesting an interview with Mr. Quinn."

"Thank you lieutenant."

They saluted once more and Lieutenant Papadopoulos exited the room for the command center.

Captain Fredericks looked at me.

I looked at him.

"Would you like to give an interview?" he asked.

"I don't know," I said.

"It might help your case," he said. "If it were up to me, I would let you go home right now. But it is not. The San Francisco County Sheriff's Department is sending a squad car here to pick you up. They plan on booking you into the County Jail tonight. Also – and I hate to have to be the one to inform you of this – they plan on throwing the book at you. The state's District Attorney in San Francisco *himself* told me that over the phone, not forty-five minutes ago when you were in the shower. Because they feel you might be a danger to yourself or others, he has already gotten a judge to deny you bail for the next three days, so they can keep you locked up all weekend. On Monday morning at 9am, you will be arraigned in the county Superior Court on several counts: trespassing, malicious mischief, concealed weapons possession and the violation of the Marine Mammal Protection Act. You need a good lawyer. When you are on the phone with your wife, let her know all this. Do not hide it from her. She needs to be in that courtroom Monday, along with your son, so the judge can see you have family ties to the community. So that way your wife might just be able to get you out on bail come Monday evening."

I was in shock.

I sat there frozen.

I couldn't believe what I was hearing.

"Concealed weapons charges and malicious mischief?" I said in disbelief.

I shook my head.

"What the hell is going on here?" I said. "I was just trying to save my home and my family."

I became sick to my stomach and dropped my face into my hands.

What was my Lani going to think?

"Just stay calm," Captain Fredericks said. "Some of those charges are trumped up. Did you ever actually touch the bridge?"

"No," I said, looking back up at him.

"Well then, is the DA actually going to claim you trespassed on Golden Gate Transit's property when you were only out on the open ocean?"

I shrugged and threw my hands into the air and shook my head. I had no idea what was going on or what I was going to do to get out of this mess.

He went on:

"Also, the concealed weapons charge is based on that knife you had hidden in your pocket. But he knows what your intentions were out there. I cannot see him making the claim you intended to hurt anybody with that knife."

"It wasn't hidden," I said. "I just needed it to help me with what I was doing."

"Well, the DA is calling it a hidden weapon anyway. That is how those snakes play the game, through sophistry and word manipulation."

He paused for a moment.

He looked me straight in the eyes, an expression of concern on his face.

"Mr. Quinn, I want you to know something. I, personally, would never have described to the DA the contents of your cardboard box. But it was Seaman Murphy who first took the call, and he told the DA's office everything."

"Shit," I said. "I'm screwed."

"You may very well be."

"What's the criminal mischief charge for?" I asked.

"There are apparently witnesses who saw you hang two blowup dolls off of the sides of the bridge. Did you do that?"

I lowered my eyes.

"Yes! God damn it!" I said. "Yes!"

"Well, San Francisco has you on that one," he said. "But as for violating the Marine Mammal Act, that is a federal law, and would require a federal prosecutor to bring you up on those charges. Also, I have been told by Seaman Obama that you did not actually desecrate the carcass in any way other than to tie a nylon rope around some of the animal's body parts. Is that also correct?"

"Yes."

"Well, it seems to me they have a mixed bag on you."

"Do you think I have a chance to beat it all?"

"I am not certain," he said, shaking his head. "It could go either way for you, depending on how much the state and federal prosecutors in this case cooperate with one another. The Coast Guard patrols these waters every day. We catch all kinds of people performing all kinds of illegal activity out on the water; most of them young men doing stupid things because they are poor, desperate and uneducated. I do not condone their activities, but I have seen many a young man's life destroyed, thrown into jail for years and years, on trumped up charges; all so the

DAs can make names for themselves and run for politics. And believe me, that is what *your* case is all about. Politics."

We looked across the table at one another.

I could tell he felt for me; his eyes were full of compassion, as though he had witnessed many tragic things in his life and he didn't want to see anymore.

"Call your wife," he said, pushing his chair back and standing up. "I need to head back to the command room. Are you going to do that interview with Pricilla Pan?"

He looked at me with hope in his eyes.

"Yes," I said.

"Good! Then even if that squad car gets here before the news crew gets here, I will not release you into their custody until after the interview."

He smiled at me and said:

"There are benefits to being station commander."

"Thank you, Captain Fredericks, for everything."

I stood up and we shook hands.

He nodded at me and left the room.

Before the door closed all the way, I heard him in the command center yelling at Seaman Murphy.

"Murphy! Get the hell over here and bring that damned cardboard box with you!"

I had to call Lani now.

I was afraid too.

I was nervous.

What would I say?

She was going to be angry.

I sat down at the table again and tried to calm myself down with deep breathing: deep breath in – deep breath out – deep breath in – deep breath out.

It wasn't working. I was going to be in jail all weekend long and was ready to vomit all over myself just thinking about it. I was trying to visualize what that experience might be like. I had never been in jail before. I had never gotten in trouble before, except for speeding tickets. But I had seen shows on TV and at the movies about guys in jail. I didn't want to get violated. So what would I have to do to keep that from happening? Was I going to have to beat the crap out of the biggest guy in there as soon as they closed the door on me? Just walk right up to the bulkiest, hairiest, most biker-looking guy in the place and **bang!** Right in the jaw. What if I missed and only grazed him? He'd be pretty pissed at me. That would cause me a whole new set of problems right there.

I figured the best thing to do was to not think about it. I had to give Lani a call before the news team arrived because after the interview, I was going into that squad car and wouldn't be able to call her then. She needed to know what was going on.

I pulled my cell phone out of my front pocket and flipped it open. I dialed her number.

Ring-g-g-g!

Ring-g-g-g!

Ring-g-g-g!

"Hello, this is Lani."

I was silent. I didn't know what to say.

"Hello –"

"Ah-h, hi darling, it's me."

I said it too softly. She didn't hear me.

"Who is this?"

I spoke up.

"It's me darling! It's Cree."

"Hi honey, where are you? You've been gone all afternoon and we should have gone out today looking for apartments. I'm upset with you because of that. I told you to stop dreaming. We're losing the house and there's nothing we can do about it."

"I have something I have to tell you," I said.

"What?"

I hesitated.

"What do you have to tell me, honey?" she said. "You didn't get another speeding ticket, did you? Because if you did, I'm going to be very angry at you."

I was silent.

My heart was pounding. Breathless. Ill.

"Honey," Lani said, "I'm cooking dinner. Maui pork with rice. Tell me what you have to say so I can get back to it. And you need to get home, now."

"I'm in trouble."

She said nothing for a few seconds, then:

"What do you mean?"

"You know my friend Gale Fischer, right?"

She said nothing because she didn't like Gale. She had never met Gale or spoken to her, but she didn't like her anyway.

"Darling, are you there?" I asked.

"Yeah!" she snapped. "What about that bitch? Did you get her pregnant? Are you cheating on me?"

"No, darling. It's nothing like that."

"Then what about her?"

"Her ex-boyfriend borrowed a killer whale skull from her and he had it stolen from him."

"What the hell does all that mean?"

There was a commotion going on in the command center now; many voices speaking loudly all at once. I believe I heard Pricilla Pan's voice as well.

"Darling," I said quickly, "I don't have time to explain it all to you so I'm just going to come right out and say it. Gale needs another killer whale skull and said she'd give me one hundred thousand dollars if I got her one. We needed that money to pay off our second lien with BNC."

"Did you do something crazy?"

"It all depends on what you mean by crazy."

"Would you tell me where you are right now, Cree, because I don't like the sound of your voice?"

"I'm at a Coast Guard station on Treasure Island in San Francisco."

"What!"

She was screaming now.

"I told you – I needed to get Gale another killer whale skull."

"That whale at the Golden Gate Bridge?"

"Yes."

"What'd you do?"

"When I left the house at noontime today, I had a meat cleaver and a knife and a few other things with me."

"And!"

"I drove to San Francisco. I did a few things. To make a long story short, I took that rubber boat of mine out into the water beneath the Golden Gate Bridge and I tried to cut the whale's head off. But then the Coast Guard came. I tried to get away but they started shooting at me."

Click –

Silence –

"Darling are you there?"

Silence –

She had hung up on me.

I called her back.

Ring-g-g!

Ring-g-g!

Ring-g-g!

Ring-g-g!

Ring-g-g!

My phone began buzzing.

She had called *me* back.

"Hi, darling."

"Don't call me darling! I'm not your darling! So what's going to happen now?"

"I'm doing an interview with Pricilla Pan for the Channel 10 News. I don't know when it's going to air but I'm hoping tonight at 10pm. Watch for it please."

"When are you coming home?"

I was silent for a few seconds, then told her the rest:

"They're keeping me in the San Francisco County Jail all weekend and I'm going to be arraigned in court on Monday at 9am on several charges. You need to be there, and Theo. Please. I love –"

Click –

The door opened.

I stood up and turned around so I could see who was coming into the room: one white haired man holding a giant video and audio camera on his shoulder, Captain Fredericks and Pricilla Pan.

She looked over at me.

"Hi, there, I'm Pricilla Pan."

She walked quickly towards me, smiling, stopping at the edge of the table where she set a plastic box down.

"I'm Cree Quinn. It's nice to meet you."

We shook hands.

She continued smiling.

She wasn't very tall, maybe 5ft, but cute, with a bob style haircut, red lipstick and light, freckly face. She was wearing a conservative businesswoman's skirt and jacket combo, grey plaid, with a white button shirt, black ribbed nylons and black high heels.

"Captain Fredericks told us you wanted to do an interview so you can get your side of the story out there. Is that right?"

"Yes," I said.

"Okay, that sounds great. Do you give us permission to tape record your voice and video tape your image."

"Yes."

I was a little nervous. I had never given an interview before.

Pricilla turned to Captain Fredericks.

"Is this the only room available?"

Captain Fredericks nodded.

"Okee dokee! This will do!"

She turned back to me.

"What do you think of the weather?"

"I've been in this place for an hour and a half now," I said. "No windows. Why, what's it doing out there?"

"Black clouds!" she said emphatically, spreading her hands in front of her. "The storm is early."

With that, I heard the tearing of the sky outside!

It startled me.

"There it is!" Pricilla said. "While Jack and I –" she looked over at the camera man – "were driving over here, the swells on the bay were enormous! I wouldn't want to be on a boat out there right now!"

She shook her head while opening the plastic box she had placed on the table, pulled out an applicator and began applying makeup.

I heard it again! – The cacophonous crackle of thunder and the ripping of heaven asunder. That's when I realized it – through the audio-contextual-messaging of that second lightning strike – had I still been out there on that boat hacking away distractedly at that whale's flesh, I might not have survived the evening.

"Jack, are you ready?" Pricilla asked.

"All's a go," Jack responded, holding the two handles at the bottom of the shoulder-balanced camera and looking into a rectangular box on top. He was to my right, close to the wall and the door that led into the command center, moving around, trying to get a good angle.

Without moving his eyes from the rectangle, he motioned with his hand for us to step to the left.

We moved together, as one, toward the middle of the room, eyes on the camera.

"That's it!" he said. "Now I have you two and the Coast Guard logo on the wall."

"Let's start off with the Captain," Pricilla said.

She turned to me, smiling.

"Is that okay?" she asked.

"Yes."

It went back to the table and sat on the edge, close to Pricilla's makeup case.

"Captain Fredericks," she said, "would you please stand where Cree was standing."

Captain Fredericks was standing at the opposite end of the room from the cameraman. His white uniform was in stark contrast to the grey wall. He moved toward the middle of the room and stood beside Pricilla.

They both looked toward the camera.

"Give the count, Jack," Pricilla said.

Jack held three fingers up, and then counted them down.

"Three, two, one –"

"This is Pricilla Pan here at the United States Coast Guard holding station on Treasure Island in San Francisco. I'm standing here with Captain Fredericks, the commander of this station."

She turned somewhat, standing at an angle to him. Captain Fredericks was about the same height as me, so Pricilla's head only came up to the medals on his chest. She had to look up as she spoke to him.

"Captain Fredericks, you are currently holding a man at this facility for something he did out on the bay beneath the Golden Gate Bridge earlier today. Is that correct?"

"That is correct," he said.

"Would you please describe the situation for us."

Captain Fredericks thought calmly for a moment, and then began speaking. His hands were folded behind his back.

"At approximately 5pm this afternoon, this facility received a radio communique from a civilian vessel, *The Shy Moon*, that indicated an individual was beneath the Golden Gate Bridge in a rubber boat, in close proximity to both the bridge's northern pylon and the whale carcass that has been stranded there these three days now. Because we have been working closely with Homeland Security in the Bay Area since 9-11, I am compelled to view such activity as suspicious, and responded by dispatching two of this facilities' patrol boats."

"What did the two patrol boats discover?" Pricilla asked.

"They discovered a gentleman out on the water, in an inflatable boat, in the vicinity as reported, with a meat cleaver. He had tethered himself to the whale with a rope."

"For what purpose?"

"I will let him tell you that."

"How did your patrols respond to the situation?"

"They took the gentleman into custody."

"Was he cooperative?"

"Yes."

"We have reports that shots were fired."

"Accidental discharges by rookie Seamen."

"You have ordered the crews of those patrols to say nothing more about the situation. Is that correct?"

"That is correct."

"Why?"

"This situation no longer concerns the Coast Guard. This is a civilian matter and will be handled by the San Francisco Sherriff's Department who are on their way sometime this evening, with a squad car, to pick the gentleman up and bring him to the county jail."

"Thank –"

Captain Fredericks interrupted her.

"There is just one more thing I want to say about this young man. He and his wife have recently suffered a terrible tragedy. This recession destroyed his business and they have lost everything they own. I am not condoning what he did today, but for reasons I will keep to myself, I find myself sympathetic to his cause."

"Thank you Captain Fredericks," Pricilla said.

He nodded, soberly, and moved toward the far wall again.

Pricilla turned toward me.

I stood up from the table and moved to the middle of the floor beside her.

"Sir, would you please tell us your name."

She was looking up at me, sympathetically.

"Cree Quinn," I said.

"Captain Fredericks said his patrols discovered you tethered to the whale's carcass and with a meat cleaver. Would you tell us why?"

"I was going to cut off its head."

"A whale's head is extremely large," she said. "Wasn't it an impossible task?"

"I had to try."

"For what purpose?"

"I needed the skull. Someone I know was going to pay me one hundred thousand dollars for it."

"Who?"

I lowered my head.

"I can't tell you."

"What were you going to use the money for?"

"The bank is going to repossess my home. It's the first home me and my wife, Lani, have ever lived in. We have a five-year-old son, Theo. The bank will refinance it and let us keep it if I can pay off the second mortgage, which is one hundred thousand dollars. I was just trying to save my home. It's all we have left. We lost everything else to bankruptcy after I went out of business at the beginning of the year. Just like Captain Fredericks said."

I still had my head lowered.

"Don't you think the move was a bit desperate?" she asked.

"Yes," I said, looking at her again. "But I was out of options."

"You could have been killed. Do you hear the storm out there?"

"Yes."

Even with the door closed, I could hear the rain slashing against the large windowpanes of the command center.

Pricilla gave me a sympathetic look and then turned and faced the camera.

"A desperate move by a man trying to save his home for his family – another victim of this recession. This is Pricilla Pan reporting from the Coast Guard facility on Treasure Island."

Chapter Nineteen

It was just like all the TV shows and movies people see. The squad car came with two sheriff's deputies. One drove the car and the other handcuffed me, loosely, read me my rights and said '*watch your head*' as he helped me into the back seat. They then drove me, through the pouring rain, wind and occasional lightning flashes, over the arched span of the Bay Bridge, through the square and rectangular geometry of the now storm-darkened city, beneath the highway over pass, passing as they did the cinderblock wall of the 7th Street Self Storage, and turned onto Bryant Street, finally pulling into the large, opened parking lot of the San Francisco Hall of Justice, the giant, ominous, multi-windowed building that housed the Superior Court and the county jails.

Before taking me out of the car, with rainwater coursing down every window, obscuring the outside view, both officers turned and looked at me while I was still sitting in the back seat.

"We heard what you did and why you had done it," the one who had handcuffed me said.

"It was one damned jackass stunt."

His dour face broke into a sudden smile, and he laughed.

"You have a lot of balls," he said. "We both wish we didn't have to do this to you. We think it's bullshit. We're just doing our jobs, okay?"

The driver gave me a quick nod, letting me know he was in agreement.

"Thanks, guys," I said.

We moved quickly through the pouring rain and entered the building in the rear, through a single red door by the trash dumpster.

"We usually bring suspects in through the double glass doors on the western side of building," the officer who had handcuffed me said. "We snuck you in this way because the media's waiting for you at those doors right now."

"You're kidding me," I said, as he was taking off my cuffs and placing them back into the leather case on his utility belt.

"No, I'm not," he said. "Everybody's out there, channels 4, 5, 7, cable outlets, newspaper reporters. There must be ten news cameras set up in the vestibule over there between the inner and outer doors. Everybody wants a piece of you."

They brought me, unhand-cuffed, to the *green room* to begin my processing.

As I was being processed, one of the processors, not an officer – a thin, rat-faced guy in a window so I could only see his head and chest – gave me a sneering look, made a clicking sound with his tongue and gums and shook his head, looking down at my check-in sheet.

"Concealed weapon," he said provokingly. "Malicious mischief. Marine Mammal Act violation –"

He looked up at me and snickered.

"That's a new one on me," he said, "Marine Mammal Act. I didn't know there was such a thing. You're going away for a long time, buddy."

The last step in the check-in process was passing by the duty station, a large square of counter top sitting between two opposing cell-blocks.

There were three officers inside the duty station, all dressed the same, in tan uniforms and holstered handguns. Two had silver badges. They were both seated with their backs to one another. One was surveilling several computer monitors, prisoners in street clothing all over the screens, which were the camera angles inside the Northern Detention Center. The other, in front of several computer monitors as well, did the same for the Southern Detention Center.

The third officer was standing up, peering at me with stern brown eyes. He was tall, several inches above my head; his short, tight curls were starting to grey on either side of his head; his huge, gnarled hands were resting on the counter of the duty station, looking like he could tear it into tiny splinters with his bare hands if he chose to. He had three gold stripes on both arms and a gold badge. That was Sergeant Pierce.

"I'll take him from here," Sergeant Pierce told the officer who had been escorting me the whole time throughout my processing.

"Yes, Sergeant."

The officer walked away.

Sergeant Pierce looked at me, not saying a word for several seconds.

"I'm supposed to put you in there," he finally said, pointing to the Southern Detention Center.

I turned to the right and looked beyond the grey bars of the wall and door, casting my gaze here and there throughout the Southern Detention Center. There were many large men in there, moving about slowly, as big men do because they have the least amount to fear and have the luxury of slow movement.

"Those are the accused felons," he said, "waiting for their arraignments on Monday."

He was looking at me dead on, his strict eyes never flagging, barely blinking. His demeanor was tough but in control, a man who was used to having his orders followed.

"But I'm not going to put you in there," he said. "I'm going to put you in there, with them."

He pointed to the Northern Detention Center.

I turned to my left and gazed beyond the grey bars of the wall and door, looking here and there inside the Northern Detention Center; much smaller guys in there. I exhaled with relief.

"Those are just the accused misdemeanors and traffic violators," he said. "No one will bother you in there and we'll be monitoring you out here. Okay?"

"Yes sir," I said.

"One more thing," he said, still gazing at me sternly, but fatherly as well.

"What you did is all over the news now, the radio and the TV. There are protesters outside this jail right now, standing in the rain, wearing rain jackets and holding umbrellas, about twenty of them. They're animal rights activists and they're calling for your head."

"Holy shit," I whispered.

"That's right," he said with a nod. "But between you and me, I disagree with them, Okay?"

"Thank you, sir."

He walked through the opening in the square duty station, gently placed his giant hand on my back and escorted me across the room to the Northern Detention Center.

"Just keep your cool in here this weekend," he said.

"I will," I said.

He raised his hand and one of the officers at the duty station pressed a button, causing the cell door to open electronically on giant, metal wheels.

I took two steps into the cell then stopped and looked around. It was a long, rectangular space with two long rows of bunk beds on either side of a wide aisle. The floor was cement and the ceiling was white drop panels and very high up, forty feet maybe. There were about twenty-five or thirty other men in the cell with me, of various ages but mostly young, all merely the accused and not convicted yet, having had the unfortunate luck to have committed their alleged crimes on a Friday afternoon, ostensibly lacking the resources to get bail, and now having to spend the entire weekend in the detention center until Monday morning's arraignments. They were all wearing regular street clothing. Most of them were lying on their metal framed bunks, some on the lower bunks, most on the higher ones, and just about everyone was watching this program that glared from the TV above my head, mounted to the wall high above the cellblock door by a triangular metal bracket.

Just about everyone ignored me, their necks craned upwards as they watched the TV show. The five biggest guys in the room, however, *were* looking at me. They were all seated together at this long, plastic picnic table in the center of the cell, playing cards. I then watched as all five of them cringed in terror, looking away from me quickly, going hastily back to their card game.

I turned and saw Sergeant Pierce, standing in the cellblock doorway, giant forearms folded menacingly, gazing in the direction of the five men with a look of wrath on his face.

"No one's going to bother you this weekend, Cree," he said. He took two steps backward, raised his hand and stood there watching as the cell door closed electronically; and he was right: nobody did bother me that weekend. Although some of the accused in the cell with me had already heard of the story of the crazy man who had gone out on the ocean that day, in nothing but a rubber boat, to cut off the head of the killer whale that was stranded at the base of the Golden Gate Bridge's northern pylon, no one knew it was me because the only news person to get an interview with me that day, and get my image on camera, was Pricilla Pan. But by 10pm that very Friday evening, the Channel 10 News happened to be on the TV in our cell, and there was my picture, my entire story, everything that I had done that day, and my complete interview with Pricilla Pan.

Everyone in the cell cheered.

Everyone in the cell became my friend.

Everyone wanted to shake my hand and tell me how sorry they were over what the recession had done to me and my family.

I was a star.

And then the most unthinkable and outright miraculous thing of all occurred: those few animal rights protesters who were calling for my head on a silver platter a' la John the Baptist on Friday evening – they were gone; replaced by thousands of new protesters from all over the state. They erected a tent city on the sidewalks and grassy areas outside the jail, and they marched in front of the San Francisco Hall of Justice building, all up and down Bryant Street, all day Saturday and all day Sunday, yelling and screaming at the tops of their lungs and shaking signs in the air; news media from all over the country and the world set up outside as well, interviewing the ones who were calm enough to make a statement:

"We demand the federal government and the state of California step in and do something about this recession!"

235

"See all these people? There are thousands of us. We've all lost our jobs and our homes."

"No more repossessions!"

"The greedy banks are the ones who thrust the knife into our hearts and now the state of California and the federal government sit back and watch them twist it!"

"When is it going to end?"

"How many more have to suffer?"

"California's District Attorney should investigate the banks and mortgage companies! Not prosecute a victim of the recession who was just trying to save his home for his family!"

"Are dead animals more important than human beings?"

"Hell no! We won't go!"

"Hell no! We won't go!"

"We demand they release Cree Quinn from jail!"

"Cree Quinn is our poster child!"

"Free Cree!"

"Free Cree!"

"Free Cree!"

And the whale was gone – washed out to sea Friday evening by the storm.

Chapter Twenty

There was another time when I was young and took a bus with Badley into the city. It was summertime and early, Boston's skyline softly glistening as dawn's new sun poured out its light. We crossed a street, out in the middle, for some incalculably small measure, time stopped, or so it seemed, as the giant blue windows of the new John Hancock Tower reflected my image into the windows of the old John Hancock tower, on the other side of the street, which reflected my image back, and then back and forth, back and forth infinitely. That instant that caught me by surprise, freezing my gait, stealing my time as I gazed upon my refracted self – what is that instant called? Is there a name for that portion of time that staggered? And if it were not time that came to a sudden but brief halt, but merely I who lost the moment, what is this moment of loss called?

There aren't enough words in the English language. Because thoughts and emotions, like a refracted image, are infinite. And this is why the words we do have fail so often.

"I hate you!" someone yells. When in fact, it is the opposite that is true.

When we open up ourselves to love, pure happiness resides at the peak of the sine wave. If that love goes sour, the trough of the sine wave is where we realize it's at an end and we must get out. Yet there are infinite points along the way between the peak and the trough, and it is there, hopeless romantics as most of us are, where we reside, as etherized patients strapped to hospital beds, high on the morphine of tender tidbits tossed by loved ones, burned by the medieval hot irons of their angry tirades. And if hurt, we are eager to hurt back, creating those verbal emotional correlatives we believe are our only chance at making our loved one feel the depth of pain that they have created within us.

"You bitch!"

"You bastard!"

"Go to hell!"

"I'm leaving you!"

"Fuck you!"

Neuroscientists try to make us believe that words come from the left side of our brain. Verbal ability is the left-brain's forte, they say. But I tell you words come from two places, both struggling to dominate the human species. They come from the brain and they come from the nart. I say nart because in the past it was believed that emotions arose from the heart. But we now know that the heart is an organ that both oxygenates and regulates blood flow. So if it is not the heart from whence emotions arise, then where? What organ? What part of the brain? I call it the nart for not being the heart, but close to it.

It is this nart – our emotional organ – that struggles with the left-brain for control of us! And when we speak, half of our words are from the brain and half are from the nart. This is why we never really say what we mean. This is why the words come out so wrong so often. This is why we argue and complain and yell and scream and fight, all day long and all night long – the uncooperative nature of the brain and the nart.

So we often must content ourselves with pictures, images conjured up within the fiery caldrons of our minds, creating the visual emotional correlatives we desire. We are all of us a canvas at birth, a canvas painted upon by our parents, and our teachers, and our friends, and then ourselves. It is we who attempt to complete our own pictures when we get older. It is ourselves who take that brush in hand and we furiously paint and paint upon the edges of that canvas that is our own human life, trying desperately to complete ourselves before death. But it rarely ever happens, and we are all, ultimately, doomed to be unfinished works when we perish from this earth.

After it was all said and done; after all the camaraderie that existed in that cellblock those three days and nights – Friday, Saturday, Sunday – after all the news casts and crowding around my bed and the friendly pats on the back and the conversation about the whale and the protesters and my case, at bedtime, when it was lights-out, and the place was a frighteningly pitch black, my thoughts returned instantaneously to the one and only thing I truly cared about in this whole world: my family. And there, splayed across the giant movie screen in my mind were the heart-wrenching images of my Lani and my Theo, Lani packing a bag in the bedroom closet, preparing for departure.

Instantly the silent tears overwhelmed me, overflowing my eye sockets, streaming down my temples and soaking the pillow beneath my head, and then began that silent, plaintive pleading that had been ritualized by those imperforated memories swimming in that black reservoir tucked not so far away anymore in the back of my haunted mind:

"Oh God please don't take my Lani."
"Please don't take my Theo."
"Give me another chance, Lord."
"I'll do it differently this time."
"Oh God I'm begging you!"
"I'll do anything."
"Anything at all, Lord."
"Dear God please don't take my family from me."

Chapter Twenty-One

It was Monday morning, just before 6am's breakfast call. I could hear the inane whispers and idiotic chuckling of the prison cafeteria workers, the tiny wheels of the metal food carts they pushed around making a cacophony of sound as they headed toward the felon's side of the jail. I was awake in my upper bunk, beneath the blanket, fully dressed. My legs were folded together like the blade of a pocketknife, forming a tent out of the center of my thin, green blanket. I was nervous, swaying my knees from side to side beneath the blanket in an attempt to alleviate some of the painful cramping in my stomach. It was arraignment day. I was due in court at 9am. I had barely slept all night.

I hadn't brushed my teeth or put on deodorant for three days now. My last shower was at the Coast Guard holding station last Friday evening. And I had been wearing the same pair of wrinkled blue jeans, dark blue t-shirt, white sports socks and brown boat shoes ever since they locked me up. I stunk. There weren't any mirrors in the prison bathroom, in case one of us might use a smashing blow of the elbow to gain a broken shard of glass, ending it all with a slash to the wrist, or ending it all for someone else. So I only had a vague idea of what I looked like, but I felt like a steaming pile of crap with a long, jagged stick up my ass.

The night before, while washing my hands in one of the bath-room sinks, I had seen my distorted reflection in the chrome faucet and, bending closely, saw that my hair was sticking out wildly in all directions. That and the three days whisker growth on my face made me look demented, like Ted Kaczynski, the Uni-Bomber, after they had caught him in the woods, or that lunatic factory worker in Illinois who, having been laid off, returned to his former place of employment with a rifle and shot up the place. This was going to be a tough day for me. I just knew it.

I had reveled in the protesters, watching them every chance I could on the TV above the cell door. Their chants of "Free Cree!" "Free Cree!" filled my heart with joy and the type of relief that people always feel when they know that others are on their side. My cellmates enjoyed watching the protesters on TV as well. They felt it was *The People* sticking it to the *Man!* And they seemed to enjoy their time in the cell with me, crowding around me all weekend long, in between newscasts, while I sat on my upper bunk or at the plastic picnic table eating, begging me to retell the tale of how I braved the frigid and perilous waters of the open ocean and the bay, intrepidly attempting an impossible task for an honorable goal: the wellbeing of my family. They gave me a nickname: they called me *Whale Man*, and they said it with respect.

The problem was, I didn't know how it was all going to play with the federal and state prosecutors, or the judge. Maybe if I had kept my mouth shut and didn't give that interview, they would have gone easy on me, seeing as how I have no record and have never before been in trouble with the law. Maybe that interview and the protesters have enraged them. What if Captain Fredericks was wrong and they hadn't actually planned on throwing the book at me until *after* I had given that interview?

"Trespassing," I said to myself, gazing at the white ceiling tiles far above my head, and I recounted the other charges as well:

"Malicious mischief –"

"Concealed weapons –"

"Violation of the Marine Mammal Act –"

With or without the protesters, I was screwed, and I knew it.

I heard a sound in the distance.

It broke my thoughts.

I unfolded my arms beneath the blanket and turned my head.

Looking toward the front of the cellblock, through the two rows of bunk beds lining either side of the aisle – the accused sleeping and snoring everywhere – I could see two officers standing at the cellblock door, looking in through the grey bars.

"Quinn!" one of them shouted.

It was Officers Brass and Knuckles. At least that was the nickname we had given them. They had utterly ignored me, and most of the other accused as well, my entire weekend at the jail. They were the muscle at the county lockup, the ones who were sent in to do the dirty work of shoving the accused around and getting into their faces, loudly, if the accused attempted to assert their rights of humanity. No accused was human in the prison; at least that's what the entire system – other than Sergeant Pierce – was designed to make everyone believe.

"Quinn!"

For some reason, I wasn't responding, and I just lay there, as if it were all a dream. It was 6am. My arraignment wasn't until 9am. Why were these two bozos looking for me now?

I realized then that some of the other prisoners were awake. They lifted their heads from their pillows and turned toward the officers.

"Quinn!"

That one was particularly loud and it echoed through the cell-block chamber.

Some of my friends, the accused, turned to look at me.

"You'd better go see what they want, Whale Man," one of them said.

Throwing off my blanket and swinging my legs over the side, I jumped from the top of the bunk to the floor below.

Thud!

I then walked toward the officers, the rubber bottoms of my boat shoes scrapping the cement floor.

More prisoners were waking now.

There was a sudden orchestra of yawning, groaning, tongue and cheek clicking and stretching.

"What's goin' on?" a deep voice asked.

"I don't know," came a reply.

"What's Brass and Knuckles doin' here?"

When I was about three feet from the cell door, officer Brass put his left hand out ordering me to stop.

I did.

He then put his right hand in the air, signaling the officers at the duty station to electronically unlock the door.

Click!

The barred door rolled open on the metal wheels.

"Come on!" Knuckles demanded angrily. He was the taller of the two, standing there beside Officer Brass with his fists clenched and a mean look on his face as though he were about to unload a punch to my jaw.

"Alright, Whale Man!" one of the accused behind me yelled.

I was still standing inside the cellblock, three feet from the opened door.

I turned around.

All of the accused were awake and standing up now, crowding the aisle between the two rows of bunk beds.

They were all looking at me, nodding and smiling.

"Good luck today, Whale Man!" someone yelled.

"Thanks, Cree!"

"Mother f-ing star, bro!"

"Good luck!"

Then a tentative clapping – slow at first – one person, then another joining in, and another, and another, until before you knew it, the entire cellblock was clapping and cheering and pounding air with their fists!

It was loud!

It was marvelous

I couldn't believe it.

I was stunned, motionless, and emotional by the unexpected manifestation of affection being shown by the accused.

"Whale Man givin' shit to da man!" someone yelled.

"Whale Man gonna overcome!"

"Free Cree!"

"Free Cree!"

I heard a metal cacophony on the floor.

I turned back toward the officers.

Four prison cafeteria workers had pulled their metal food carts to the front of the cellblock door.

The accused kept cheering for me.

"Settle down!" Officer Brass shouted.

The accused ignored him.

"Alright, you can all miss breakfast then!" Officer Knuckles said, waving the food carts away.

Sergeant Pierce walked over from behind the duty station.

"Stay right where you are," he said to the food servers.

The cart pushers remained motionless.

"These people are going to eat breakfast now," he said.

He stood in the opened cellblock door, giant forearms folded, gold badge glinting in the austere light, and peered menacingly about the cell.

Not a sound now, except for the occasional shuffling of feet.

"Good morning, Cree," he said to me.

"Good morning Sergeant Pierce," I said back.

"Good luck to you today."

"Thank you, sir."

Sergeant Pierce then walked back to the duty station.

"Come on," Officer Knuckles said, waving me forward with his right hand.

It wasn't demanding or condescending anymore.

Oh, what a good role model can do!

I walked through the opened door, out of the cellblock.

"Follow us," Officer Brass said, and all three of us, Officer Brass first, me in the middle, Officer Knuckles making up the rear, began walking past the duty station and down the hallway to the right of the Southern Detention Center. Behind me, I could hear one of the cart pushers talking to the accused.

"Time for breakfast, ladies!"

We were moving quickly down the long corridor.

"How come I'm not getting breakfast?" I asked.

"You got something special coming," Officer Knuckles said behind me.

"We turned left down another long corridor, stopping at two metal doors with a sign on one of them that read: *CONFERENCE ROOM 2.*

Officer Brass opened one of the doors.

A flash of white light flooded the hallway.

After adjusting my eyes, I looked into the room. It had dull, beige walls, adorned with numerous photos of stodgy legal types in old suits and hats, some oil paintings of boring woodland settings complete with trees, ponds and waterfalls, all hung in gold-leaf or ebony frames. Wide wooden floor boards, stained a glowing chestnut, framed the edges of the room, but much of the floor was covered by an expansive oriental rug, black oval design, edged by an elaborate lattice of intersecting red and beige lines, gold tassels on either end. Several tall, oak bookcases stood against the back wall, their shelves overburdened with official, leather-bound black and brown books, gold or white lettering on their spines. There were antique-looking, wooden end tables in several places, well lit lamps and telephones and fax machines resting on top of them with a tangle of phone lines running along the baseboards. In the middle of the room, centered on the Oriental rug, was a massive oval shaped conference table, dark stained and polished, surrounded by a multitude of leather-padded chairs. There were three men, all dressed alike – dark blue suits, red ties, white collared shirts – all seated side by side at the conference table, facing me. The two on either end glared at me, ominously, as I entered the room.

"Officers," the old man seated in the middle said, "please wait inside. We'll require your assistance soon, one way or the other, depending on the outcome of this meeting."

Officer Knuckles closed the door and leaned against it.

Officer Brass leaned against the wall to his right.

"Sit down please, Mr. Quinn," the old man continued. He had a skirt of white hair on the sides of his head, the top was bald and shiny, and he was wearing thick black glasses.

He motioned his hand toward a chair opposite him.

I pulled the wheeled chair out from beneath the conference table and sat down, with all three men still looking at me from across the table.

"How do you feel, Mr. Quinn?" the old man asked, using his index finger to push his glasses further up his nose.

"I'm nervous," I said. "And I'm hungry. They won't give me breakfast. My arraignment's not until 9am. Why am I here?"

The old man gave me an acknowledging half-smile and nodded.

"All in time, Mr. Quinn," he said. "All in time. I'm Mr. Richards, the Warden of this facility. To my left is Mr. Woolf."

I turned to Mr. Woolf. He had burning, bloodshot eyes and his half opened mouth revealed a rather large set of teeth. He never closed his mouth, either, as though he were ready to say something at all times. His unkempt salt-and-pepper hair was frizzy, and he had puffy sideburns.

"Mr. Woolf is the state's District Attorney," Warden Richards continued.

He motioned his hand to the right.

"And this is Mr. Erkens."

I turned to Mr. Erkens. Although seated, he looked tall, his torso rising in his chair several inches above the other two. A bit too much of his shirtsleeves stuck out from the arms of his suit jacket, I thought. He was slender, middle aged, with neatly combed black hair and piercing blue eyes as though he knew your every secret.

"Mr. Erkens is with the Department of Justice," Warden Richards said. "He's the top federal prosecutor here in San Francisco."

I looked back and forth between the three, anxiously, wondering what the hell was going on. Were they going to declare me guilty without a trial and hang me right there in the room? Is that why the warden told Officers Brass and Knuckles to hang around? Were they to be the ones to dispose of my dead body, disappearing into an invisible vastness like the whale?

Warden Richards pushed his glasses higher up his nose, then folded his arms and leaned back in his chair.

"Since I no longer have anything to do with your case," he said, "I'll leave this to these two gentlemen."

Mr. Erkens, the federal prosecutor, pushed his chair back, rose to his feet, stuck his hands in his pants pockets and looked down at me.

"You're an instigator," he said. "Do you know that?"

"I don't know what you're talking about," I said.

"Oh, yes you do," he said, smiling sarcastically at me.

He began pacing the room, back and forth between the conference table and the antique end table at the far end of the room.

"We know you've been watching the news," Mr. Woolf jumped in. "Think you're pretty cute, huh, giving that interview to Pricilla Pan? Got the whole state of California sympathetic to you."

"Why did you let him give that damned interview?" Mr. Erkens said loudly.

"I had nothing to do with it," the warden said calmly. "He gave that interview at Treasure Island, while in the custody of the Coast Guard."

"God damn it!" Mr. Erkens snapped. "We have a full blown situation on our hands here with these protesters."

He stopped pacing and turned to the warden and Mr. Woolf.

"This recession isn't over!" he said. "If they're protesting like this in California now, what's it going to be like across the country in a year from now, when millions have lost their jobs and homes?"

"It's this jackass's fault!" Mr. Woolf said, pointing at me.

"I was just trying to save my home," I said.

"You were just trying to save your home," Mr. Woolf sneered sarcastically. "And now the whole state is raging mad!"

He turned to the warden and Mr. Erkens.

"This guy has them all riled up," he said, still pointing at me.

"These people have lost their jobs and their homes," the warden said. "That's why they're angry."

"But Mr. Quinn here is their lightning rod," Mr. Erkens said. "These people never would have come together in the first place had it not been for this damned whale incident."

"And the news media is really playing up this whole protest thing," Mr. Woolf said. "Broadcasting it all over the world. We look like Greece, for crying out loud!"

"I know we do," Mr. Erkens said. "And the President –"

He paused and began pacing again, hands in his pockets, head low to the floor.

"The President?" Mr. Woolf queried, somewhat annoyed. "The President of what?"

Mr. Erkens stopped his pacing, turned to Mr. Woolf and said:

"The President of the United States! Who the hell else would I be talking about?"

"God damn it, Erkens!" Mr. Woolf shouted. "I told you Friday over the phone, I want the Federal government's involvement in this case to be at a minimum!"

He pointed at me and continued.

"He broke the laws of California, and it is my responsibility to prosecute him. And I don't care for any Federal interference."

"The Federal government has overriding jurisdiction here," Mr. Erkens said.

"This is why I hate cooperating with you Federal prosecutors!" Mr. Woolf said. "You guys always trample state's rights!"

"Let's keep our composures, gentlemen," Mr. Richards said. He then turned to Mr. Erkens.

"Exactly what is the President's involvement with this case?" he asked.

Mr. Erkens placed his hands on the back of his chair and began:

"What I'm about to tell you all must never leave this room."

He turned from the Warden, to Mr. Woolf, to me, to Officers Brass and Knuckles, back to the Warden, and continued.

"The President's Chief of Staff called me personally from Washington D.C. over the weekend to discuss these protesters. These people are demanding that the Federal government step in and do something about the recession. Now, although the current administration has instituted several policies that have proven to be quite beneficial to both the banks and the insurance companies, and are about to introduce some half measures to make it look as though they're attempting to alleviate the suffering of the American people, there's really nothing they can do for the average citizen. There's just not enough money to go around. And besides, these things are cyclical: they come when they come and they go when they go. But although there's nothing they can do about it, they don't want it to *appear* as though there's nothing they can do about it. And that's their problem with these protesters. The networks are broadcasting them all over the world and it's making the current administration look impotent."

"Is that the actual word the Chief of Staff used?" Mr. Richards asked.

"Yes. Impotent. And if this protest doesn't stop, they think it's going to affect their party this coming election."

"What a bunch of god damned governmental double speak!" Mr. Woolf quipped.

"Well, regardless," Mr. Erkens retorted. "They want me to do something about it."

"Like what?"

"Stop the protest!"

"There they go again!" Mr. Woolf snapped. "The Federal government pinching the ass of California's affairs! Well let me tell you this, Erkens! And you can tell this to the Chief of Staff too! There's nothing the Federal government can do about those protesters! There's nothing even I can do about it as the state's District Attorney! Unless they start getting violent, which none of them have shown an inkling to do. The Constitution gives the people the right of free assembly!"

"No kidding?" Mr. Erkens said sarcastically. "I must have missed that one in Constitutional Law 101!"

"Erkens, you jackass!" Mr. Woolf snapped.

"Let's stop turning on one another," the warden said. "You gentlemen are just here to weigh your options."

"Well, I'll tell you this," Mr. Woolf said. "The federal government intruding into this state's business is not an option."

"I have been asked to do something about this situation," Mr. Erkens insisted.

"You're not getting it, Erkens!" Mr. Woolf began again. "This is California! I don't like this protest either but there's nothing the Federal government can do about our citizens exercising their rights!"

"But there *is* something we can do," Mr. Erkens said, pointing at me. "This one is their poster child. Let's make him disappear."

"What the hell!" I exclaimed. "What do mean make me disappear?"

I turned around to see what Officers Brass and Knuckles were doing behind my back.

Nothing, just leaning there.

I turned back.

"I don't mean it that way," Mr. Erkens said. "I mean get you off the airways! Get your face off the news channels!"

"How are we going to do that?" Mr. Woolf asked angrily.

"The federal government is dropping all charges against him."

"What!"

"You heard me. The President doesn't want to see or hear any more news broadcasts of protesters chanting *'Free Cree!'* If we take away their rallying cry, the President believes this whole thing will start to settle down and the protesters will begin dispersing. If we prosecute him, the trial will take months, maybe years, and he'll be on the news every single god damned day with his sad whale story fishing to catch everybody's hearts!"

Mr. Woolf pushed his chair back and stood up. Leaning across the table, red eyes glaring at me, white knuckles pressed hard into the shiny wood, I saw a little bit of spittle in the left corner of his mouth.

My heart was pounding, ready to break through my chest. I didn't know what the hell this Woolf character was going to do. It looked like he might pounce across the tabletop and rip me apart with his teeth.

"What do you say, Woolf," Mr. Erkens said. "Are you going to give the President what he wants and drop the state charges against him?"

"Shit!" he howled. "It looks like I have too! I can't charge him with trespassing because he never actually touched the bridge. And I can't charge him with possession of a concealed weapon because the knife he supposedly had in his pocket mysteriously disappeared while at the Coast Guard station."

I couldn't believe it, and uncontrollably I felt myself cracking a gigantic smile. Good ole Captain Fredericks. You had to admire the man. He had principles.

"Oh, you think this is funny?" Mr. Woolf snapped.

"I don't," I said.

I was trying my best to stop smiling.

"I **could** still charge you with malicious mischief. That was a pretty cute stunt you pulled, hanging those two blowup dolls off of the sides of the bridge like that."

I was definitely not smiling now.

"Give the President what he wants, Woolf," Mr. Erkens said, "and he'll remember you if you ever decide to run for public office."

There was a long, anxious silence.

I looked from Mr. Woolf, who was still glaring down at me, to Mr. Erkens, who was standing there at the other end of the table with his hands back in his pockets, looking over at Mr. Woolf, to the warden, who was looking at me with a sympathetic countenance.

"Damn it!" Mr. Woolf finally said. "Fine! All state charges are dropped."

"Yes-s-s-s!" I cheered.

"Get the hell out of here!" Mr. Woolf shouted, pointing towards the door.

The warden winked at me.

"Officers," he said. "Please take Mr. Quinn to the *green room*, have him sign the departing documents, give him back his personal property and escort him pleasantly to the door. He's free to go."

And just like that, it was over. I was elated – but not for long.

Lani had hung the phone up on me that Friday.

I hadn't spoken to her for three days now.

I knew she was angry.

But how angry?

Would she and Theo be there when I got home?

I had signed my departing documents and my cell phone and keys were returned to me. The cell phone's battery was dead. All of my other property was in the cardboard box at the Coast Guard holding station. I thought about driving there that morning to thank Captain Fredericks. I had a long walk first, though. My van was still parked on the cliffs at the Marin Headlands. It was going to take me at least two hours to get there. I'd have to walk all the way through downtown, the Marina section of the city and all the way over the Golden Gate Bridge.

"Good luck, Mr. Quinn," Officer Brass said as he held opened one of the inner glass doors that led to the vestibule of the western exit.

"Thanks," I said.

I stepped into the vestibule, and that's when I realized what was going on. Through the glass of the outer door, I could see all the news cameras and reporters outside.

I stepped outside.

The glass door closed behind me.

I stood there on the Hall of Justice's Steps.

Several reporters, out on the sidewalk, turned to look at me.

They were headed my way, calling my name.

It was a cold July day, but bright and clear. The storm had made the air smell amazingly fresh. Or maybe it was just that feeling of freedom.

There were colorful tents set up all over the place.

I was swarmed by the media, worse than the seagulls.

Reporters and cameras and microphones were all around me.

"Mr. Quinn, it was just reported by the federal prosecutor's office and the DA's office here in San Francisco, that all charges against you have been dropped. Would you care to comment?"

"Mr. Quinn, how were you treated in jail?"

"Mr. Quinn, what do you think about all these protesters?"

"Mr. Quinn, were you almost hit by those accidental gunshots Friday?"

"Mr. Quinn, who was going to give you that one hundred thousand dollars for the killer whale's skull?"

"Mr. Quinn, are you aware that the whale is gone now?"

I put both hands in the air and everyone stopped talking.

There was a rush of cool air on my face.

The large clock on the tower in the parking lot read 7:30am.

"I was treated very well in jail," I said loudly, so everyone could hear me. "I was not almost hit by the accidental gunfire Friday and was, in fact, treated most generously by Captain Fredericks, the holding station's commander. I would like to personally thank Captain Fredericks and Sergeant Pierce, who is in charge of the men's cellblocks here at the county jail. I cannot comment on who was going to pay me for that skull. I do know that the whale is gone. There was a TV in my cellblock. As for the charges being dropped, I will make no comment on that other than to say I am grateful to be going home. And I know it's early and a lot of the protesters are still sleeping in their tents, but I would like to personally thank each and every one of them. I wish I could stay here until they all woke up and shake all of their hands but, as you can see, I haven't bathed or brushed my teeth or fixed up my hair for a while and I haven't eaten breakfast, and I have a very long walk back to my van in Marin County. So I really must be going now. Please tell the protesters for me how much I appreciate everything they did for me. And I'd like to thank the media as well, especially Pricilla Pan. Thank you everyone for your support. Thank you!"

"Mr. Quinn, where are your wife and son?"

Lani and Theo – I had to get back to them as soon as possible.

Oh God, please don't let me lose my wife and son.

I moved quickly around the crowd of reporters and made it to the bottom of the stone staircase.

"Your wife and son, Mr. Quinn. Where are they?"

I moved quickly along the sidewalk, passing the tents and the cars in the parking lot.

The reporters were behind me, following me.

"Where are your wife and son?"

"Does your wife know the charges have been dropped?"

"Did your wife know Friday you were going to be attempting to cut a whale's head off?"

Before making it out to the larger sidewalk on Bryant Street, I was startled by something, a familiar image and, turning to look, there was Lani, standing in the parking lot beside her car, holding Theo's hand. She was wearing a conservative grey skirt and jacket, with a white blouse.

"I got here early because I didn't want to be late for your arraignment," she said.

The tears fell from my eyes like running water.

I ran to them and we hugged; all three of us standing there and hugging each other beside the car, where Lani had just parked it. It was the very last space in the Hall of Justice parking lot.

I kissed her cheeks, over and over again.

I kissed Theo's cheeks, over and over again.

It felt so good to see them.

Nothing has ever felt so good to me my entire life.

The reporters were all bunched near the front of Lani's car, holding their cameras and microphones out to us, raining down questions nonstop.

We ignored them.

"Exactly how much trouble are you in?" Lani asked. "We don't have much money saved up now but maybe we should get you a better lawyer than a court appointed one."

"I'm in no trouble," I said, wiping the tears from my eyes with the back of my hand. "I don't need a lawyer. All the charges have been dropped. I'm free. Let's go get my van and go home."

"Mrs. Quinn!" the reporters yelled.

"Mrs. Quinn! Did you know your husband was going to cut off a whale's head?"

"Mrs. Quinn...!"

"Mrs. Quinn...!"

I placed Theo in his car seat in the back of the car and then buckled myself up in the front passenger seat.

Lani sat in the driver's seat.

She started the engine and pulled us out of the parking lot, the reporters still shouting out questions as we drove away.

Chapter Twenty-Two

It was December and the holiday season. Five months had passed since my incident with the whale. Lani, Theo and I were walking together along Coconut Avenue in Honolulu, me in the middle, holding hands with both of them. We were moving casually, swinging our arms together, heading toward Lani's mother and father's house on Hibiscus Drive, the home in which Lani had been raised. They were having a holiday party that evening and all of her brothers and their families would be there.

It was evening, the sun was down, but the lights of the single-family homes and condo complexes all up and down the avenue bathed the area in a calming yellow glow.

I wore white shorts and a white shirt with red lotus flower design.

Lani wore an elegant sliver and diamond patterned evening dress, low cut to show off her smooth, tan legs.

Soft breezes coming off of the Pacific swirled around the southern end of the dormant volcano, pleasantly bathing our exposed faces, arms and legs, and causing the palm trees lining the avenue to sway.

Not too far up ahead, we could see the sprawling greenery of the Diamond Head State Monument. In particular, there were three tall palm trees, forming one gigantic, interconnected palm umbrella, all lined up in a row near the entrance of the park. The tree on the left was wrapped up in colorful, blinking lights like a Christmas tree. The one in the middle had blinking white lights in the shape of a menorah. The one on the right had blinking yellow lights in the shape of a star and crescent.

"Isn't that beautiful," I said.

"It sure is," Lani agreed.

She looked at me for a moment, smiled, and then turned away, taking in the familiar scenery which I could see was affecting a tremendous contentedness within her.

I couldn't look away from her smile. It was captivating. I began drawing the line of her lips with my eyes; her chin; her eyes; her long, black, silky curls all free now, moving about as she gently tossed her head here and there so she could look about.

I picked up Theo, hugged him and gave him a great big kiss on his puffy left cheek.

"Who's your daddy?" I asked him, holding him in my right arm.

He answered swiftly, sweetly, the way he always answered when I asked him that question:

"Daddy's my daddy."

I set him down gently on the sidewalk and he ran ahead of us in his red shorts and gold tee-shirt, arms extended outward as though he were flying, playing superhero no doubt as mommy and daddy walked behind keeping an eye on him.

"Not too far!" Lani called out to him.

"I won't!" he called back, stopping and bending over now to examine a small green lizard that was straddling the sidewalk.

"Not too close," Lani said. "Be gentle."

She was holding the twisted-rope handle of a large, white paper bag in her left hand. ***Happy Holidays*** was written on both sides of the bag in multi-colored letters. Inside the bag was a pot full of Pork Adobo she had cooked in our apartment earlier, and two bottles of Cabernet Sauvignon: our contribution to her parent's holiday party that evening.

"Do you want me to carry that bag?" I asked. "It must be getting heavy."

"Sure," she said, handing it to me.

We had moved from Sacramento to Honolulu in August, into a beautiful two-bedroom apartment on Kalakaua Avenue. The back exit of the complex led right out onto the beach. It was fantastic living there! We went swimming in the playful ocean currents, diving into the high curling waves, walking along the beaches close to the water, our toes sinking into the gritty littoral sands, anytime we wanted to, day or night.

Lani was working with her seven brothers at *Leilani Malone's* downtown. She was a server when she worked the breakfast and lunch shifts, and the hostess when she worked the evening shift. She never even attempted to look for another job. Working with her family was all she wanted to do. Her parents, in their 70's but in good health, still worked at the restaurant as well, but traveled extensively also, especially to Australia and Alaska. Mr. Malone loved visiting the rough Outback on one of those alligator tours, and going on that Inner Passage Cruise, seeing the whales breach the open ocean waters, spewing their mist plumes high into the air, visiting all those quaint cities: Ketchikan, Sitka, Haines, Skagway, and the larger cities of Juneau and Vancouver, British Columbia.

In September, I responded to an ad I had found on the Internet. It was in the help wanted section on Craig's List. There was a guy in the city of Kailua, northeast of Honolulu, who lived on a farm off of Kapaa Quarry road. He had come up with a new type of coffee bean. He called them *Hawaiian Sun* coffee beans. He wouldn't give me specifics on its invention, other than to say that it was a hybrid made by two separate plants, one being a unique coffee bean plant that grew on Hawaii, the other being a coffee bean plant that grew somewhere else in the world. He had spliced them together and their genetics forged something miraculous: something much better than the originals, separately, could ever have dreamed of being alone.

I had visited him on his farm in late September. His name was Kala Mahi' ai. We walked together outside in the 80 degree heat through his vast field of *Hawaiian Sun* coffee plants. The plants were leafy, stick-like and tall, with thick pods of coffee beans, golden colored, all over the place. The plants formed their own jungle canopy, growing over our heads, but more over mine than his because he was several inches taller than me. He was a giant man in both stature and presence, and a genius, I think, talking to me as we moved through the canopy about the principles of biology, chemistry, genetics and horticultural splicing techniques. He wore a large Hawaiian shirt, red with pineapple design, and a pair of brown shorts with baggy side pockets. His long, thick, black hair was in a ponytail, held together by multiple rubber bands.

With his big hands, he quickly harvested a handful of the golden beans, carried them back to his house, roasted them in a swirling cast iron cauldron he had burning continuously, ground the blackened, aroma-filled nuggets into a mound of coffee silt in a battery powered coffee grinder, and then brewed it into a hot drink for me, pouring it into a ceramic mug and passing it to me.

It dazzled my taste buds!

Undoubtedly it was the most delicious cup of coffee I had ever tasted.

We discussed my extensive business experience and then he asked me if I wanted to go to work for him.

I said yes.

The job was only part time for the moment, 20 hours per week, on whatever day and hour combination I chose, with the potential of more hours being added when and if sales picked up. But I told him I'd like to keep it as a part time job, since Theo would be going to school soon, and I would be the one who got him up in the mornings, made him breakfast and a school lunch, got him out to the school bus on time and needed to be there to pick him up at the bus stop when he arrived home again.

Kala agreed to that.

He then told me what he wanted me to do.

He envisioned me fulfilling both a sales and marketing position: first, placing ads in local Honolulu, San Francisco, Seattle and Los Angeles food magazines, advertising the new beans; second, working the phones by responding to the voicemail messages requesting orders for the product, re-contacting those who had left the orders and shipping them their product only after proper payment had been made.

Kala didn't know anything about advertising.

Fortunately, due to my eight years as an economics major, I did.

I developed this ad for him: it was a photograph of a steaming cup of hot coffee, with a few of the raw beans beside the mug revealing their unique golden coloring, with these words, in large gold letters, above the mug:

Introducing the New Hawaiian Sun Coffee Bean
Let Coffee Rise over Your Horizons
Like a Morning Star

Kala loved it!

He instantly dubbed me his V.P. in charge of advertising, and he said he would pay me well with both a salary and commission. If the sales really started coming in big, he said I could switch to all commission if I liked and he'd give me an even bigger split.

I had placed the first ads in food magazines in mid-October, and two weeks later, the orders for **Hawaiian Sun** coffee beans started pouring in.

So, between my new job and Lani's salary and tips at **Leilani Malone's**, we made more than enough money to support our new, less luxurious but much less stressful, lifestyle on the island. In fact, we had a large sum of money in our savings account. Prior to leaving Sacramento, I had sold all of the stock I had in my two-car garage to Pelli. He lowballed me, offering me forty thousand dollars for items that I had paid over one hundred thousand dollars for. But I didn't care. I was happy to take the cash. I was out of the adult industry for good now and was just happy to be getting rid of all that stuff and it did feel good having all that money in our savings account. And our savings account was growing, slowly, each month. We just needed to let our credit scores build back up again and then we were going to use that money as a down payment on a new home. We were building up our credit scores with secured credit cards from the Honolulu First Chartered Bank, HFCB. That's where we had our checking and savings account.

As a matter of fact, things were so good for us and life was so much less stressful for me now, in those five months between July and December, between the whale incident and this holiday season in Honolulu, I was off of all of my medications. No more pill cocktail in order to get to sleep at night: I slept like a baby now without it.

We were still walking casually in the warm night air.

Lani and I were holding hands.

Theo was still ahead of us, running here and there and playing with the sidewalk lizards.

We turned onto Hibiscus Drive and could now see, several houses ahead of us, the white stucco walls, steep black roof and neatly cut lawn of the home in which Lani was raised.

"We're almost there, honey," she said, turning to me.

Her face was all lit up in a joyous smile. I could only imagine, upon seeing that house, the wonderful memories stirring within her.

I gently squeezed her hand.

I was so glad she had a good childhood. It was what I was living for now: to make sure Theo had a good childhood.

"Are Rye and Betty still planning on coming to visit us next spring?" she asked.

"Yes," I said. "That's what Rye's been telling me."

Rye phoned me just about every other weekend, in the mornings – which were my late afternoons – and we spoke for hours. He and Betty had moved to New York two years earlier and had a traditional Jewish wedding. He had been talking about moving back for years. He missed his family, and Betty preferred New York over San Francisco, too: just a one-hour train ride away from her family in Connecticut. Rye had even been able to get some paying gigs at places like **Stoolies' Funny House** and **Whacko's Comedy Cave** in Manhattan.

"Should we call John and Lisa and see if they would like to come to Hawaii and visit us sometime?" Lani asked.

"We could do that," I said.

Four years earlier, John and Lisa had moved to Lisa's hometown, 45 minutes outside of Green Bay, Wisconsin. It was a small farming community. I forget the name of the place but we still had their phone number and I called him occasionally to shoot the breeze and catch up on their goings on. They worked at Lisa's family's dairy farm now. They also had two children, a boy and a girl, Gabriel and Angelica.

"Who else do we know who we can invite to Hawaii?" Lani asked.

"No one," I said. "But there is something I'd like to tell you."

"What?"

"It's about Gale. Promise me you won't get mad."

"I won't get mad. I'm not angry with her anymore."

"Last September she sent me a text message. She said the guy who broke into her ex-boyfriend's car and stole the skull – he took it to a pawnshop in Santa Cruz and tried to get some money for it. The shop owner, going to the back of the store, pretending he was going to research on the Internet how much a skull like that was worth, actually called the cops on the guy and they came down and arrested him and then called the university because they didn't know what to do with a whale skull. The secretary who answered the phone didn't know what to do about it either, so she transferred the call to the biology department and, as luck would have it, Gale was the one who took the call. So she goes down to the Santa Cruz police department with the paperwork on the skull, documenting the school had owned it prior to 1972, and she gets it back, just in time to put the whole killer whale skeleton back together again for the visiting regents and the UC President. And nobody was the wiser."

"That's a nice ending," Lani said, smiling at me.

We were approaching her parent's house now.

"Wait for mommy and daddy," Lani called out.

Theo had already scurried up his grandparent's staircase. Holding one of the iron hand railings, he turned to us and began giggling, moving his little finger back and forth, pretending he was going to depress the doorbell's glowing white button to announce our arrival.

Kids are always doing cute stuff like that.

Lani and I stepped onto the staircase.

I was holding the bag with the food and the wine in my right hand.

Theo was in the front, finger up to the doorbell, still giggling.

Lani and I were side by side at the top of the steps holding hands.

"Okay, sweetheart," Lani said while smiling down at Theo. "You can ring it now."

Buzz-z-z-z...

Theo laughed and placed his hands over his mouth.

The door opened soon and there was Lani's mother and father on the sofa in the middle of the brightly lit living room, all of her brothers, sisters-in-law and an army of nieces and nephews of various ages and sizes, standing around them, crowding the room. They were all chatting away in various groups, happy and smiling, beers and mixed drinks in the adults' hands, sodas and juice boxes in the children's hands. There were three silver platters filled with appetizers – various cheeses, crackers, sliced meats, pates and olives – sitting on the coffee table and the two end tables on either side of the sofa. Myriad bottles of red and white wine of varying vintages, along with various dishes of traditional Hawaiian food, on large plates or in plastic containers, filled every available space of the dining room table. The aroma of home cooked food wafted out onto the porch where we were standing, filling us with the comingling emotions of love and contentedness that only homemade food can bring; and there were presents everywhere! On the floor beneath the Christmas tree, on the seats of the dining room table, on the floor along the baseboards by the sofa and chairs; all wrapped in colorful paper, trimmed with ribbons and bows.

As soon as the door opened, all of them turned to us simultaneously and shouted joyously, in a loud, harmonious greeting:

"*Yeah-h-h-h-h-h!*"

And that's where I want to leave it – with us standing on that porch, looking through that opened doorway into that warm and wondrous home, with all of those relatives freely expressing their love for us; their excitement over seeing us.

That was our life now.

I had been wrong for many years, believing that Lani and I were a business, a conglomeration. That was not what we were: we were a family. The clues were all around me, right before my very eyes, but I was blind and couldn't see it! It wasn't until my experience with the whale and my subsequent weekend of incarceration – where I had tortured myself every evening at lights-out with the thought that I was going to lose both Lani and Theo – that caused me to finally generate those inner eyes so that I could now *truly* see! And it was Vidur, owner of the ***Acorn Restaurant and Café*** at the Sacramento National Wildlife Refuge, who had ultimately proven to be right, when he had told me in that Ranger Station, after I had been bitten by the rattlesnake, that I would not know what I was looking for until after I had found it.

Well, I had found it.

About the Author

K.C. Woodworth is a Lynn, Massachusetts born author. Despite beginning his life in the notorious Curwin Circle housing projects, Mr. Woodworth is now a successful real estate agent in Leesburg, Virginia.

The seed, which sprouted into the tree that is the author, was first planted around the time Mr. Woodworth was five years old. After experiencing the sting of disappointment with an unentertaining children's show, Mr. Woodworth was determined to create something so entertaining that he would forget the sensation of ennui ever occurred.

Under the tutelage of Ernest Hemingway's novel *The Sun Also Rises*, Mr. Woodworth began his self-education in the ways of prose.

Mr. Woodworth would be remiss should he forget to thank his loving wife, Patricia, and his wonderful son, Matthew, for all of their support.

CPSIA information can be obtained at www.ICGtesting.com
Printed in the USA
BVOW05s1727300714

361072BV00002B/35/P

9 781628 381832